Secret Staircase Holiday Mysteries

a collection of cozy short stories

Connie Shelton
J.M. Poole
Mary Seifert
Rick Adelmann

and introducing
Jennifer J. Morgan

Secret Staircase Books

Table of Contents

Halloween, Hound, & Housesitting
A Katie and Maverick Mystery Short Story

By Mary Seifert

~ ~ ~

I should've known something was up when Mildred Larkin so readily agreed to my offer to housesit. We'd never met, but I answered her ad, and in our phone conversation, she said I came highly recommended. Though I'd only lived in Columbia, Minnesota for three months, it was a great place. I wouldn't get rich teaching high school math, but the compensation for the weekend would go a long way now that my dad had moved in with me.

"I promise to keep an eye on Harry," my landlady, Ida Clemashevski, said. "It'll do you both a world of good to have some time to yourselves." She hurriedly pitched the clothes I'd carefully laid out on my bed into a musty old duffel bag, like she couldn't wait to get rid of me.

I held up two hangers, debating whether I should pack the green or purple sweater. "I haven't received Ms. Larkin's promised instructions yet."

"You'll get them. She's been Devlin Hopkins' administrator and has conducted the house opening for the last thirty-five years." She grabbed the purple sweater, stripped it from its hanger, rolled it into a ball, and crammed it into the duffle. "She's quite capable of managing the property and readies it every October in anticipation of the event."

"Not that I'm complaining, but why is Mr. Hopkins willing to spend a small fortune for someone to babysit his house? He's even letting me bring Maverick." At the sound of his name, my dog's head popped up in a Sphinx pose. I removed the sweater and a pair of pants Ida had rumpled and shoved into the bag, refolded, and replaced them.

"Devlin was born on October 31 and has celebrated his birthday in that house every year. That is, until his unexpected heart attack last week. His doctor won't let him out of the hospital yet, and Devlin's firm about continuing the tradition."

"He doesn't have any family?" I shoved my hairbrush into the remaining space.

"His stepsister, Heather, avoids Columbia when she can, calling it the cultural Siberia of the Midwest." Ida sighed. "At one time, Devlin was the most sought-after bachelor—handsome, rich, smart, funny—"

"It sounds like you had a crush on him."

"Just from afar. I was happily married, I'll have you know." She crossed her arms over her ample bosom. "Devlin found an intelligent and beautiful woman who appreciated his penchant for Halloween. Parker Halliday remodeled the old monstrosity, filled it with mysterious trickery and practical jokes, and had just hired an assistant to help run the house. Everyone hoped Devlin would propose at his annual Halloween party, but at the unmasking at midnight, she was nowhere to be found." She shrugged. "I don't think he ever fully recovered, and he never married."

"Doesn't anyone live there?"

Her newly colored red curls bounced back and forth, her chin jutted out, and her fists landed on her generous hips. "No one's lived in the house since Parker left, but Devlin won't sell her masterpiece, even if he only visits in the fall. Maybe that'll change now."

I looked at my watch. "I need to meet Ms. Larkin in twenty-seven minutes and she was adamant about the time. Do you have any advice for me?"

Ida winked. "Have fun."

I slid into my yellow rain slicker and loaded the duffel into my van. Then I retrieved supplies for Maverick. "Are you sure it's okay for me to be gone all weekend, Dad?"

Harry Wilk sat at our kitchen table, penciling in answers to the crossword puzzle.

"You're only a phone call away and our busybody landlady …" Ida snorted loud enough for the entire block to hear.

"Da-ad."

"Sorry, Ida, I didn't notice you were there, or I might've said something I wouldn't regret." I liked his laugh. It's a good thing they enjoyed each other, or I'd be afraid to leave them alone.

"Be good, you two." I snapped on Maverick's leash, and we hopped into my van.

Ida assured me I wouldn't miss the largest parcel of property on the north end of Lake Monongalia. I reread the address and pulled up to a tall metal gate, flaunting a calligraphic H, and waited for it to open. When it didn't, I searched the entry. A smooth rectangle embedded in the stone wall looked like it might be a good place to start.

"Stay, Maverick." He blinked and never raised his head

from his paws. "Good boy."

The rain dribbled off my hood and onto my nose as I stood in front of the panel and furrowed my brow, reading the message scrolling across the screen above a standard keyboard. "Type the magic phrase. Entry denied in 4:13," "4:12," "4:11." I usually loved puzzles, but my brain froze as the time continued to wind down. I had just over four minutes to figure out how to gain access. I typed in my name and nothing happened. I followed with 'Devlin Hopkins,' this address, the date, 'Mildred Larkin,' and 'Parker Halliday.' The countdown continued. I wiped my face and tried 'open sesame' and 'abracadabra.' I chewed on my lower lip and thought I had it. I keyed in 'Halloween.' Nothing. With fifty-three seconds remaining, I used Dad's magic word. The iron gate squealed and opened as if cranked by hand.

I slid into my driver's seat with a grin on my face. I couldn't wait to tell Dad. "'Please' *is* the magic word." Maverick blinked, unimpressed.

The long drive meandered under sad naked trees, through a yard buried in leaves. We rolled past a man wearing black rain gear, juggling an armload of lawn embellishments in the shapes of stone-like grave markers and craggy hands. I waved but he eyed my van and then stooped, continuing to erect the creepy temporary cemetery. I circled under the porte-cochere and parked, staring up at the huge, dark-gray, two-and-a-half-story Gothic structure.

I shuddered beneath a pair of bizarre gargoyles, defending the gabled entry.

"Maverick, you're coming with me." Taking advantage of his reputation as a resource-guarding dog, me being the well-guarded resource, we bounded from the van, up a long ramp, zigzagging between large orange pumpkins festooned with artificial greenery. I searched for a doorbell but settled on the massive pewter knocker with the ghoulish face set in the middle of the wooden door.

I rocked on my heels until the door opened. "Hi, I'm Katie ... you're not Ms. Larkin."

The man lifted his chin. "And I expected Heather." I extended my hand, and he shook it, but only after he scrutinized my van and raised an eyebrow. "I'm Niles Turner. Mildred has given me the task of opening Hopkins House this year. You're the housesitter?" He was a short, stout man with a head of bright yellow hair which might or might not have been natural. The weathered look of his pinched face showed extra years of wear. His topaz eyes blinked behind dark-rimmed glasses and appraised Maverick. "And a dog!" His lips curled.

Maverick ignored the displeasure and wagged his tail.

Niles withdrew from Maverick's friendly overture and scowled. "We need someone on site for the weekend."

Niles stepped forward, knocked into a pumpkin, and sent it rolling down the ramp, colliding with three others in its wake. The shells shattered and a trail of slimy orange pulp, long fibrous strands, and yellow seeds cascaded onto the pavement. He rubbernecked over my shoulder, looking for the groundskeeper who had disappeared. "Where is that pony-tailed no account when you need him?" Niles muttered. "I wish he'd find a job he's better suited for."

He called loudly, "Emil, you'd better take care of this mess."

Then Niles shook himself erect and lugged the heavy double doors apart. We entered a wide marble foyer at the foot of a sweeping staircase. Niles slowly approached the large round table at its center. "Mildred has scheduled everything that's expected of you." He picked up the stack of printed pages and his eyebrows rose. "You do plan to stay tonight."

Maverick looked up. I nodded.

"Then you'll have time to check out the house. It's an architectural marvel, full of conundrums, like the gate entry code."

"I got lucky with that."

"Yes, you did," he snorted. "For more than thirty years, Mr. Hopkins hosted a gathering the Saturday before Halloween. Then he distributed goodie bags to the little darlings who dared to venture up the drive and he closed the house on November 1. This year he hired you to do it all."

My jaw dropped. "Ah…host a gathering?" Maverick's ears perked up.

Niles waved his hand, irritated with my unease. "All the work is done. The party planner will be here at five tomorrow. The caterer will arrive late Saturday afternoon."

My jaw didn't move.

"You're welcome to invite a few friends of your own." He added something that sounded an awful lot like, "If you have any." He shook his head. "A vacant house at Halloween is a magnet for vandalism. As you know, Mr. Hopkins is unable to attend himself. The guests are aware of his infirmity and will be here in a show of solidarity."

"I understood I'd be taking care of an empty house and handing out Halloween candy." I frowned. "I didn't bring anything to wear to a party." My mouth dried up. Hosting a Halloween gathering for strangers was outside my wheelhouse.

"It's a costume party. You can wear ..." He waved his hand. "... anything. I hope it's not going to be a problem." His left eyebrow rose.

I could use the money and the dollar signs replaced the niggling anxiety. My mouth closed. "No, no problem."

Niles grunted, and regarded me through the bottom half of his glasses. He jerked one sheet from the bottom of the stack of papers and offered it to me, snatching it away when I reached for it. "No expense spared at Hopkins House. Go ahead. Look around." He shoved the page in my face—a blueprint of the house. "Explore. Parker Halliday was way ahead of her time. I'm afraid if Hopkins' condition doesn't improve, however, he won't return and this will be the last celebration." We both took a thoughtful breath and then Niles handed me the rest of the pages and dropped a keyring on top. "I'll leave you to it. See you Saturday."

My jaw fell again as the front doors thudded closed behind him.

What had I gotten myself into?

I took a deep breath. "Let's go, Maverick."

Maverick wiggled and sniffed every square inch of the tile floor as we made our way under an arch into a brightly lit and spacious drawing room. Small groupings of chairs, divans, and tables provided seating for dozens. A lovely painting of a handsome woman hung over the gas fireplace. She wore a black, diaphanous dress and tied her dark hair back in a tight chignon. An oversized key, engraved with the name, 'Parker,' hung on a long gold chain around her neck.

"The riddle-maker, I presume."

I admired the portrait. The serious set of her blood-red lips in her pale face didn't match the mischief in her twinkling blue eyes as she gazed at the light beams piercing a crystal ball in her left hand. A dazzling emerald ring sparkled on her right hand as she pointed black-tipped nails at the strange playing cards fanned out on a tabletop.

Following Maverick's lead, we sauntered into a sunroom. From what little I could see of the scenery, I wished someone had thought to clean its floor-to-ceiling windows. Dusk had fallen, and the cloudy patterns on the glass stretched into elongated faces, gaping in silent screams, so we hurried into the next room, a library.

I reverently ran my fingertips over the bindings of some of the books lining the walls shelved and alphabetically by author, marveling at the number of volumes. Sliding a library ladder to one side exposed a bay window. Nestled in the niche stood a treasure chest with four rectangular indentations in the cover. I tested it. It wouldn't open.

Maverick and I sidled through an overstuffed pantry and stopped at the kitchen entrance. Ida would have examined all the accoutrements filling the room before whipping up one of her extravagant gourmet delights. The space could accommodate a large contingent of chefs and servers, but to me the pristine room resembled a chemistry lab with multiple experiments percolating. Three long black cords snaked between steaming cookers and connected unidentified appliances to an over-used outlet extender. A wire rack displayed flavored drink pods and a variety of mysterious additives next to a coffee machine with too many buttons. Tall carafes of unnamed herb-infused oils lined up like specimens along the light-colored granite backsplash. A glass jar stood on the scale in the corner. Yet the aroma wafting from the oven made my stomach growl and Maverick prance back and forth, slobbering on the floor.

I read from Larkin's pages. "Meals are included if you produce the correct combination." *Combination of what?*

My name was printed in large type at the top of a recipe card taped to the oven door. I peeled it off the glass and peeked through the little window. A deep brown mass bubbled in a black cast iron pot next to a long golden baguette. I tugged the handle. It wouldn't open and neither would the refrigerator. I hadn't asked enough questions and regretted Niles' hasty departure. A note on the corner appliance garage read, "If all else fails …" I pushed up the door and located a toaster, a sleeve of bagels, and a jar of peanut butter. *Just great.* I folded the recipe card and slid it into my back pocket.

A misaligned tap didn't fit the spotless kitchen, so I slid the faucet perpendicular to the edge of the counter and a cupboard door popped open. Another recipe card fluttered to the countertop. Before I tucked it back inside the door behind the canned fruit, I noticed my name printed at the top of this card too and pocketed it.

I inhaled and sighed. "Maverick, let's see about the rest of this strange house."

We walked through a well-stocked liquor closet and past a dark-cherry wood cabinet with a polished marble top, into a dining room with an oval table elegantly set for fifteen. The tall, dark, sculpted mahogany walls gave it a warm feeling but the cobwebs that fluttered near the ceiling had me checking for creepy crawlies.

The house plan noted two sets of stairs to the 'Guest Suite.' I'd seen one. The more I knew about the huge house the better. "Let's take the one labelled servants' steps."

I shouldered my duffle and followed the plan to a wood panel door. It opened to a wall—a dead end. I backtracked and climbed the main staircase to my room.

I bumped the door jamb with the duffle and the room lit magically, showcasing a king-sized bed covered with a thick quilted white satin coverlet, fluffy pillows stacked against an ornate headboard, and a blue-velvet chaise lounge. After I hung my wrinkled clothes in the empty armoire, I took a running leap and flopped on the comfy bed. Maverick joined me, licking my face until I convulsed in giggles. My phone tumbled from my hand and slid between the mattress and the headboard, out of reach.

"Maverick." I raised an eyebrow he ignored. I crawled to the floor and noticed a deep blue wall vent with odd spacing next to the bed. Upon closer examination, I detected an opening at the top of the grate, about the size of a note card. With the oddities the house hosted, I pulled one recipe from my pocket, unfolded it, and slid it into the slot. The letters on the card aligned with the spaces, but before I could read it, my phone rang. I reached as far as I could under the bed, but it rested beyond my fingertips. It rang again. I scurried around to the other side, but my phone was blocked by a small wooden box. I wrapped my fingers around the rectangle, turned it lengthwise, adding a few inches to my arm, and shoved. The ringing phone skittered across the floor out the other side, and the shoebox sized container rattled behind it.

I picked up the phone and connected with dead air, but grinned. The missed call came from Pete Erickson, one of my new friends and the emergency room doctor who had stitched up my head when I stumbled against a warning sign after Maverick found a body in the slough near our walking path. I punched in his number and let it ring until voicemail kicked in. I ended the call and returned to the message in the vent.

"Seven, two, three." I cocked my head but examining it from a new angle made no more sense.

I slid the second card behind the vent and read, "Turn oven off. Mix one teaspoon oregano, one tablespoon basil, and one teaspoon thyme with enough oil for serum to weigh three ounces."

I had a thought and we set out to raid the kitchen, where I fed Maverick. Then, channeling a past professor, I turned off the oven, reset the scale, and measured the dry ingredients. I poured the oil with a delicate hand, and when the scale hit three, the oven and the refrigerator doors popped open.

I rooted through the cupboards and drawers for dishes and silverware. I didn't have any choice but to use the fragile china with the back mark that read Royal Doulton, and I hated to sully the gleaming Gorham silverware, but I was famished.

I set the small table and filled a bowl with a savory stew, inhaling the enticing aroma. Tender pieces of beef swam in a thick broth next to perfectly diced sweet potatoes and caramelized onions. I tore off a large chunk of warm bread and slathered it with butter. My mistake was turning my back on Maverick. He licked the butter dish clean. But the feast was fabulous, and I finished off two servings of pumpkin flan.

After I put the last dish away, I inspected the small box I'd carried from the guest suite, turning it from side to side and up on its end, examining the padlock. It reminded me of the cryptex Charles once sent to tell me he loved me.

The memory of him brought tears to my eyes. I missed him. He died two years ago, protecting me, and they never found the shooter.

I swiped the tip of my nose. After a cleansing breath, I picked up the lock. The dial rotated smoothly from seven to two then three. The disks aligned, the pins slid into place, and the shackle popped, but I paused and justified opening the box by recalling Niles' terse word, "explore."

The cedar lined box held a deck of cards and a crystal ball, but the notebook was far more interesting.

The cryptogram on the first page fed my puzzle-guzzling habit. I cracked the easy encryption and smiled. The code identified the author as Parker, and she invited the reader to investigate and enjoy the peculiarities of the house. The next few pages revealed mysteries and clues to unlock doors, remove the barrier to the servants' stairs, and turn on a host of devices—igniting the fireplace, activating the sound system, and operating lights. Maverick raised his head at my chuckle when Parker included the keyword and I decoded her Vigenère ciphertext. It read, "The windows in the sunroom aren't dirty; they're permanently frosted in grimaces. Clean, clear replacements can be found in the cellar."

I decrypted the simple missives until jolted to a stop by a series of baffling number pairs written beneath a ten-letter word. If she used a Grandpré cipher, the word 'jeopardize' could provide the key. I flipped back through the pages, noting ten random words scrawled in the margins. I was in business.

The deciphered message read like a diary. But the excitement in her pages turned somber. I read, "Heather has been given the task of letting me down easy; I'm to leave as soon as my work is done. Devlin never meant to hurt me, she said, but he loves another. He's unavailable, finalizing an important business deal, but I'll leave one last message."

I frowned and replaced the notebook, not wanting to intrude further on Parker's personal deliberations. Poor Parker. She left, thinking Devlin didn't love her. Curiously, Ida indicated the opposite was true. I pocketed my phone and carried the box to the drawing room, intent on lighting the fireplace to chase away fall's impending chilliness.

The sun had set and, in the dark room, I noticed two dime-sized white circles on the floor in front of me. At first, they looked like the shiny reflection of cellophane, but when Maverick stepped near them, they disappeared. "Here, Mav." He waggled to my side and the dots returned. I passed my hand over the spots and interrupted fine light beams, originating from tiny holes in a wall. I yanked my phone out of my pocket and aimed the light at Parker's portrait, noting the similarity.

I reached into the box and retrieved the crystal ball. I held it in my left hand and aligned the light streams the same way Parker had. They converged on a tiny imperfection in the wood on the floor. I grazed the doorframe and the lights flicked on. Neat trick for a second time. I stepped carefully and scoured the floor for the aberration in the wood. Maverick found it first, plopped next to it, and panted with anticipation.

Realizing the mechanics of Parker's previous puzzles, I knelt next to the irregular formation, and my phone rang. Pete's name lit the screen.

"Hi, Pete!"

"Ida said you're staying at the Hopkins House for the weekend."

"Have you ever been here? It's crazy."

He laughed. "Dad said that place is full of surprises. He's attended Devlin's bash every year he wasn't working, and he'll be there Saturday too. He always appreciates Dr. Watland's attempts to replicate Parker Halliday's tricks."

"It'll be good to see your dad." Pete's dad recently had a heart attack and was on leave from his job as chief of police. "Who's Dr. Watland?"

"He was hired to figure out the mechanics of the house and dad says he's still trying."

It sounded like Pete would like to see the house for himself. "Would you and ..." Even though I had thought Pete might become more than a friend, he and Susie were a package now. "Susie like to attend the Halloween party too?" I pressed the bumpy knot in the wood on the floor and heard a grinding.

"Absolutely. Do you have any of the particulars?"

"It's a costume party, Saturday. I'll let you ..." I trailed off, eyeing the retracting wall. I picked up a fireplace poker and approached, primed if someone jumped out at me. I stepped to the opening. "Pete, a wall disappeared."

"Katie?"

I tapped the frame around the hole, hoping for illumination but nothing happened. I activated the flashlight on my phone and put Pete on speaker. My fingers crawled along the cool damp stone wall and my voice raised in pitch as I brushed unidentified gossamer threads from my face.

"There's a secret staircase, Pete," I whispered. I descended, watching for scurrying furry things, following Maverick, and dipped my head to peer into the shadowy space. "This is so—"

The tread gave way beneath my foot and I catapulted forward, screaming until I hit the floor.

I peeled my right eye open, then my left eye, shoved Maverick's persistent, slobbery kisses from my face, and groaned.

A determined little voice demanded attention. "Katie!"

I brushed dust and debris from my eyes and lips and reached for my phone. In a strangled voice, I said, "Pete?"

"What happened? Are you hurt?"

I propped myself up on one arm and wriggled into a sitting position. "I'm okay." I directed the narrow phone light beam around the room. "The step gave way and…" I blinked, slammed my eyes closed, cringing, then peeked through one squinted eye. "Pete, there's someone else here."

"Do they need help?"

"They're … beyond help." Black holes stared at me from a bleached skull. "It's a skeleton."

"I'll be right there. Don't move."

I no longer needed Maverick's first aid and he focused his emergency treatment on the bones, sniffing. "Here, Maverick." He didn't return immediately, so I clapped to get his attention and the overhead lights came on. He bounded over the rubble and lapped my face. I wiggled my hand under his collar, bowed my head to meet his, and gazed into his eyes, then gawked around the room. A panel of knobs and buttons, keypads and screens, microphones and joysticks filled one wall and looked like a NASA control center.

My first attempt at standing was met with a bout of vertigo. I waited, and sooner than I expected, footfalls thundered from above.

"Pete?" I croaked.

"Katie?"

"Over there." A voice sounded resigned.

Strong beams crisscrossed on the stairs. "Careful. Note the seventh step," another voice said. "The rest look sound."

A procession of shoes and pantlegs crept over the gaping hole and tapped down the remainder of the stairs led by Pete who came straight for me.

Temporary Police Chief Ronnie Christianson hitched his pants over the expanse of his gut when his foot hit the final tread.

Susie Kelton, Pete's nurse, colleague in the telemedicine fellowship and partner, followed, lugging a soft-sided black bag, her chestnut ponytail swishing in time with her hips. "Really? Again?" She exaggerated the words as if making a joke, made in poor taste, in my humble opinion. "You're lucky this victim is bones or your presence might be suspect."

A blonde with spikey hair wearing a dark gray suit looked around with trepidation. She stepped lightly and her eyes grew rounder as she took in the scene.

Officer Daniel Rodgers brought up the rear. His eager face and shining eyes contradicted his professional demeanor, his measured pace, and the set of his jaw.

Pete knelt in front of me, and my breath caught in my throat when I looked into his chocolate-brown eyes. Eyes were my downfall, and these were off limits. I swallowed hard. He cupped my chin in his gentle, slender fingers and tipped my head from left to right. I wanted to reach up and tuck the loose strand of curly black hair behind his ear until he interrupted my thoughts. "Anything hurt?" I recoiled at the penlight he flashed in my eyes.

"Not much." It went without saying things hurt, but

not as much as they could have. He helped me stand and propped me against the wall. Maverick stepped next to me, wagging his tail.

Pete turned to the bones and knelt beside Susie. She read the labels on vials she'd drawn from the coroner's bag and tapped on an electronic tablet as he examined the remains and took samples.

"Is it her?" a crisp, female voice called from the top of the stairs.

"Don't come down here, Heather. It's dangerous," said Christianson with a charm I'd never been privy to. "I'll be up in two shakes of a cat's tail." Maverick cocked his head and his tail stopped wagging. Christianson said, more quietly, "What do you think? Is it her?"

"We won't know until we compare dental records but the skeleton came from a Caucasian female, above average height … there is significant trauma to the back of the skull."

"Could it have come from a fall?"

"We'll see."

"Well?" said the imperious voice from above.

"I'll go sit with her, Ronnie," said the woman in the suit. "Before she gets in a real snit."

"Take Rodgers with you. And Mildred?"

She sighed audibly.

"Don't. Say. Anything."

The young man guided her around the damaged step and they disappeared at the top. I wondered what placating words they murmured as their shuffling footsteps moved overhead.

The camera in Susie's hands clicked. She took close ups of the skeleton and wider shots around the room.

"Katie, can you and your dog make it upstairs?" Christianson asked. "I'll speak with you shortly."

I clutched the handrail and prepared to drag myself to the top but stopped when Susie gasped. Her usually perfectly painted face paled and she sat back on her heels. Her eyes turned dark and her pupils contracted. Pete touched her arm and she said, "That's my family crest on the ring."

"I can call in—"

"No." She inhaled. "No. I just need a second. I've only seen one other ring like this and it belongs to my dad." The camera started clicking again. "Just surprised is all."

"Katie." Christianson wagged his finger, indicating I should continue up.

The fireplace had been lit and I joined the two women seated beneath Parker's portrait. The heavy curtains held the heat in the room. I wiped my sweaty hand before I offered it. "I'm Katie."

The woman in the gray suit shook it. "Mildred Larkin, but you can call me Millie. Did Niles take good care of you?"

Before I could answer, the other woman said sardonically, "What's she doing here?"

Maverick barked. The woman flinched and leaned back.

"Sit," I cued.

"This is Katie Wilk and her dog ..." Millie said.

"Maverick."

"Katie, this is Heather Hopkins." Ah, the stepsister I'd heard about. "Devlin had me hire a house sitter for the weekend so the festivities can go ahead as planned. His doctor won't release him—"

"What doctor? What are you talking about?" Heather said in a huff and sat forward.

Millie took Heather's hand. "Devlin had a heart attack last week—"

"Heart attack?" Heather snatched her hand back. "He's too young to have a heart attack. Why didn't anyone call me? I would've come immediately."

"He's in good hands. His physician doesn't want him to leave the hospital, and I know how much you hate this holiday, so I hired Katie."

"I have to see him." Heather stood. "Is he doing well?"

"He's well enough to run the Halloween party from his hospital bed." Millie checked her watch. "It's late. You can visit him tomorrow." Millie looked away for a moment. "You weren't scheduled to return until the first of November."

"I received a text message saying I should come home. I didn't recognize the number and Devlin didn't answer his phone, so I came. *Someone* attempted to keep me in the loop." She raised a perfectly shaped eyebrow, intimating that perhaps Millie was derelict in her duty in that regard. Heather's classic navy-blue dress looked expensive, and her shoes had the tell-tale red sole of Christian Louboutins. She dug in the pricey bag at her feet and extracted a MAC compact. She checked her reflection and dabbed at her patrician nose. Although she wore her money well, her carefully coiffed hair needed a touch up. Heather was not a natural blond.

Before I could tell them about Parker's notebook, Heather shot me a derisive smile. In a voice that hinted I must've planned to find the skeleton and completely ruin her return she said, "I suppose you let your curiosity get the better of you and you were poking all over this house."

"I gave Niles instructions to have her explore. She has the background we need to annotate every detail for a potential buyer. Dr. Watland's done well, but never accessed the control panel." My brow furrowed. I caught her eye and Millie blushed. "Devlin was looking for someone to unwrap the last of the house's curiosities and Ida suggested, with your degree in cryptanalysis, you might be able to decipher a few of the puzzles. And you did. This house is a rarity. Heather's brother—"

"*Step*brother." Heather wiped the fireplace mantel and checked her fingers for dust.

"Heather's stepbrother agreed. We need to understand all of the house's idiosyncrasies before we can move forward."

"I found a notebook," I said. "It contains Parker's house instructions in code. I've been able to translate much of it and I think it will help with questions you might have."

"That's wonderful." I expected Millie to sound more excited, but a lot had happened in a short time.

Heather examined a glistening gem on her left hand. "It must be difficult, Mildred. You'll finally be free when Devlin doesn't need you anymore." Millie sat back and blinked rapidly. "I can't wait until we cut loose this horror. It's been an albatross around our necks for over thirty years."

Oh, to have such an albatross.

Millie composed herself. "I'm sorry the notebook led you to the grisly bones, but maybe we can finally put her to rest."

"Do you know who it is?"

Millie gazed at the portrait. "Parker, of course. Who

else could it be?"

Three EMT's entered the drawing room, toting a stretcher. Millie directed them to the opening in the wall, but the postage stamp-sized space couldn't possibly accommodate so many bodies until Pete squeezed out like the melted filling of an ice cream sandwich. "We'll keep you informed," he said and headed for the door.

"Good evening, ladies. Katie," said a snippy Susie.

We sat in uncomfortable silence until Christianson exited from the wall, calling orders to the EMTs. He puffed out his chest, sucked in his stomach, and approached Heather first. "I'll get statements if I need them. Here's my card should anything come up." He handed one to each of us then directed the EMTs through the drawing room, carrying a thin black vinyl bag on a stretcher.

Millie rose. "You'll still stay, won't you, Katie?" I took too long to answer and she added, "I'll double the fee."

"I'll stay." I said it begrudgingly.

"You can't stay here tonight, Katie. Go home," Christianson said.

"Okay. I'll pack up—"

"I'm afraid you'll need to leave everything as is."

"May I get my van keys?"

"Officer Rodgers will escort you to your room."

Under Rodgers' watchful eyes, I tunneled my arms into my raincoat and pocketed my keys, regretfully leaving my favorite sweater, my most comfortable shoes, and Maverick's preferred stuffed rabbit.

I met Millie and Heather in the foyer.

"Do you have a ride, Heather?" Millie asked. Heather grumbled and shook her head. "I'll take you home. Do you need anything, Katie?"

I shrugged. Who knew?

"Devlin has connections. I'm sure you'll be able to get back in tomorrow. I'll lock up," Millie said and we headed to the front door. "The alarm code is one, zero, three, one. We didn't think you'd need it, but I'll set it on my way out."

Trying to make sense of the evening's disturbing events kept my addled brain occupied on my drive home. I turned onto Maple Street and the only house clearly visible at this hour belonged to my landlady. I cringed, noticing the windows Ida had chosen to light as a welcoming beacon took the form of the ghastly face of a titanic-sized, grimacing Jack-O-Lantern.

I unlocked the door to my apartment and Maverick rushed the unexpected figure seated in my kitchen. He wagged his tail and nudged for a scratch. With her free hand, Ida pushed a steaming cup of fragrant herbal tea across the table. "Dr. Erickson called. Sit," she said. "I heard about the bones. Tell me."

When I finished, Ida sat back in her chair, nibbled a spice cookie, and sipped from her cup. "I hope they don't belong to Parker." Ida shook her head. "It would crush Devlin. He's one of my oldest and dearest friends and I can't have this tragedy hamper his recovery. Finding out she's really gone might kill him in his weakened condition. You must figure out what happened in that house. What do you need?"

I had a sneaking suspicion I knew what Ida wanted, but answered, "I need a costume."

"There are loads at Hopkins House, but, meanwhile, you have to figure this out."

My amateur sleuthing had paid off before. I sipped my tea, formulating a new notion. "Ms. Larkin sounded certain the bones belonged to Parker Halliday."

"I suppose they could." She looked at her hands. "No one's heard from her for thirty-five years. Millie probably thinks if Parker's death is certified, Devlin will finally give up on the hope that she's still alive. Then Millie could convince him to marry her. I think she's been in love with Devlin for her entire life."

I exhaled slowly. "What about Heather Hopkins?"

"She turns her nose up at everything and everyone in Columbia. I don't know her well, but she's very protective of Devlin and, with Millie's help, takes good care of him. I'm not sure how well she got along with Parker because she spent most of her time and effort cultivating connections in the Twin Cities."

"Does she have someone special?"

"She's had a number of suitors over the years, but sooner or later they showed their true colors and it always came down to money. She shares equally in the substantial Hopkins estate but she's done very well in her own right as a financial consultant. She'd be quite a catch."

I took another sip of tea. "There was a ring on the skeleton and Susie said it bore her family's crest." I started to fade.

"Susie Kelton?" Ida searched her memory. "Her grandmother worked at Hopkins House. She disappeared years ago."

"What was her grandmother like?"

"Lenore was a lovely woman, and Susie is her spitting image. You don't think the bones belong to her, do you?"

"Anything's possible at this point." I yawned. "What can you tell me about the groundskeeper?"

"Katie, it's late. You're tired. I'm tired. You need sleep

if you're going to match wits with your students in the morning. We'll talk more tomorrow. When will you return to the Hopkins House?"

"When I get the go ahead from Officer Christianson. Rodgers said Pete needs to confirm the cause of death before they want me ..." I yawned again. "... anywhere near that house."

"Goodnight, Katie," Ida said, depositing the cups in the sink. "Go to bed."

She disappeared through our adjoining door.

* * *

The next thing I knew, someone shoved my shoulder. After the third thrust, I lifted my head from the tabletop, opened my eyes wide, and came face to face with Maverick's tongue. I swiped the slime from my cheek and let him into the yard as the first rays of a flamingo-pink dawn frosted the clouds. After a quick shower, I changed for school.

I taught on autopilot and the day zipped by, only later discovering my shortchanged students didn't mind; I'd forgotten to assign homework.

To improve my chance at being hired at Columbia High School, I offered to serve as an activity advisor. But when my science club students congregated in my room at the end of the day, I smacked my forehead with the heel of my hand, belatedly remembering our scheduled meeting. I shrugged off my fatigue and pulled out an in-case, backup plan—a walking robot STEM kit. They didn't even ask for assistance and went straight to work. It might've been a bit elementary—they completed the project in under forty-five minutes—but as they worked, they grilled me.

"How'd you find *this* body? You do know the police

department cringes every time you call," said Lorelei, raising her eyebrows.

"And Dr. Erickson doesn't want you to interfere," said Galen.

"Who told you that?"

He shifted his eyes to his girlfriend, Carlee.

"My dad," she said. My heart sank. I considered her dad, Chantan Bluestone, CJ, a friend and confidant, and he provided excellent veterinary care for Maverick in addition to search-and-rescue training. She brightened. "But he also said you have significant insight and you come up with remarkable solutions."

"Have you run into Dr. Watland?" said Brock. "He's an odd duck but a real genius. My dad said, back in the day, Dr. Watland used to design animated art from junk. A few years ago, some of the guys took a dare to see how far they could sneak onto the Hopkins House grounds. He must have cameras set up, because his robots cornered the guys in an outbuilding. He called the cops and those guys performed hours of community service for that escapade."

"What's Dr. Watland's first name?"

"Emil," Galen said. "Dr. Emil Watland."

Dr. Watland and Parker Halliday fashioned unique experiences from something else altogether. If he had assisted her, perhaps they worked well together or maybe he was jealous and wanted to take over the engineering marvel. He could've played a role in her disappearance. As I attempted to weave the appropriate threads together, my phone pinged with an urgent message. Before I could respond, it buzzed in my hand.

"Uh, hi?" I said, noting Mildred Larkin's name on the screen.

"Millie here. You can get back in the house this evening

and the party planner would like to meet with you at seven. Everything is back on even after …" she hesitated, "Devlin invited eight guests for tomorrow evening. You met Heather. Ida's bringing a guest." One corner of my mouth turned up. I should have suspected. "Chief Erickson and Niles are attending. Devlin's videographer is coming to film the highlights and provide live streaming for him." Then I heard a defeated hum.

"Millie?"

"The eighth guest is Emil Watland, our groundskeeper." She took a deep breath. "Do invite some of your friends. The more, the merrier they say. I'll arrive at four thirty and assist with any last-minute preparations. If anyone needs a costume, there are plenty to choose from in storage. Cocktails begin at half past six and dinner will be served an hour later. There are board games and card games available in the drawing room and dessert will be announced when it's ready. That's it," she sighed. "Devlin used to hold a dinner and dance with many guests in attendance, but when Parker left, the celebration began to shrink. Now it's an intimate dinner party. I'll see you tomorrow."

She hung up and my phone buzzed again.

"Hello." My chipper greeting met Pete's ultra-serious tone.

"Katie, you'll be allowed to return to the Hopkins House after six, but I wanted you to know the bones belong to Susie's grandmother, Lenore Kelton, which means Parker may be alive. Lenore was killed by a blow to the back of the head and went missing the same time as Parker. It was murder, and the weapon has not been found. The murderer or murderers have not been named." Pete took a breath. "Maybe you shouldn't go back to the house."

"I was hired for the weekend and the party's tomorrow night." I didn't admit I could use the money. "You and your dad will be in attendance. I'll be perfectly safe."

"You won't be alone *then*, but what about tonight?"

"I'll ask I if she'd like to sleep over."

"Katie, I know Susie sometimes rubs people the wrong way but she's a little fragile right now."

That I had to see.

"Will you help me watch out for her?"

My eyebrows rose. "Sure."

"She has questions for Heather and Mildred. They've been on every invitation list since Devlin began hosting his Halloween shindig and her grandmother worked Parker's last party. Although Heather has tended to avoid attending since then because she said it generates sad memories, she may have been among the last to see Susie's grandmother."

"Sure. I'll invite Drew, I, and CJ too. They'll help." He clicked off. I added the names to the list of recipients with the specifics Millie had given and hit send. I called back immediately.

"I can't wait for the party but why is Susie on the list?"

"She's coming with Pete," I said with a very slight reprimand. "You heard about the bones I found at Hopkins House."

"*You* found them? Oh, Katie! What am I going to do with you?"

"Hopefully stay at the Hopkins House with me tonight?" I said in a squeaky voice.

"Of course. I want to see this place for myself and you can give me the grand tour. But did you have to invite Susie?"

"The bones belong to Susie's grandmother."

"Ooooohhh!" she said. Understanding sank in slowly.

Then she said enthusiastically, "I'll bring the wine."

* * *

I let myself in at 6:05. In the ensuing quiet, I heard the faint tapping of raindrops on the window. I sat for a minute with Maverick curled around my ankles and examined Parker's portrait. Then I shook my head. I could've sworn the eyes in the painting moved, just like in the old scary black-and-white films. I hauled myself out of the chair and headed to the large front window. I pulled aside the heavy curtain at the same time a bolt of lightning exploded across the sky.

And I screamed.

A face under a hoodie stared back at me through the dripping window, looking like it screamed too, then it turned and bolted down the driveway. Maverick barked twice and sat. I fumbled, pressing numbers on my phone as I heaved the curtain back into position.

"Christianson," he barked.

"This is Katie Wilk at the Hopkins House. I think someone just tried to break in," I said, trying to catch my breath.

"Have they gone?"

"I think so."

"Stay put. I'll send Rodgers."

"Thanks." My small voice didn't carry far and I disconnected.

I inched a corner of the drapery fabric to one side and peered into the dark, empty yard. The leaves glistened from the rain. A chilly breeze circled my neck and I pulled the curtain a bit more to the side. Rain splattered through a twelve-inch opening in the adjoining window. I forced the slightly warped frame into its groove at the bottom and set the lock. After I checked the remaining windows and doors on the first floor, I returned to the drawing room and slumped to the floor. The storm boomed. I hugged Maverick.

Lights strobed through a narrow gap around the drapes, flashing blue and white from a police car as it roared up the drive at the same time my ringtone sounded. "Hello?"

"This is Rodgers. Can you let us in?"

"I'm on my way." I flew to the door as fast as I could, with Maverick weaving in and out of my legs. I pulled back the deadbolt and threw open the door.

"Please, come in." I stuck my head out and searched the yard before closing the door behind him.

"Can you tell me what happened?"

"I was sitting in front of the fire, thinking about the peculiarities of this house and listening to the rain pattering on the front window. Rain can be soothing so I peeked outside." My face scrunched at the memory. "There was a face in the window. I think we both screamed and the next time I looked, he was gone. At least I think it was a he."

"Was this person trying to break in?"

I replayed the scene in my mind, and told him about the partly open window. "What else would someone be doing outside of a window in the evening drenched by the rain?"

Rodgers nodded. "I'll make certain all of the windows and doors are locked, upstairs as well. You never know to what lengths a perpetrator might go to gain access. It was probably someone interested in last evening's goings-on."

"Or they didn't realize I'd been allowed back in the

house."

"Either way, we can't be too careful," Rodgers said. He added with an apologetic face, "We are required to do a thorough search."

Another officer entered, secured the front door, and walked toward the kitchen. Rodgers took the stairs. "Katie," he called from the landing at the top. "Do you know how to access the third floor?"

I climbed the steps to the guest suite and retrieved the blueprint Niles had given me. I accompanied Rodgers up a second servants' stairs annotated on the map, which emptied into a large storage area. Rodgers whistled as he slid the hangers aside and inspected the area behind the racks of costumes lining two walls. He circled the room and I continued to examine the variety of attire—witches' dresses, furry animal and hard-shell food shapes, superhero tights and capes, princess gowns, shoes, and crowns, and masks and props of all colors and constructions.

Rodgers called from the far end of the room, "Katie, look at this."

Identical mirrors hung parallel, across from each other, and reflected smaller and smaller images of the two of us. He laughed and brushed against a crumbling plaster wall. "I haven't found anything else. You?"

I shook my head.

Fifteen minutes later, Rodgers and I discussed safety over a cup of herbal tea. "The only window unlocked was the one in the drawing room where you saw the face," he said. "It hadn't been tampered with from the outside. Maybe when they opened the house, they aired it out and someone forgot about it, but you're locked up tight now. We'll patrol the area on our rounds. And ..." Maverick licked his hand. "You have an awesome roommate. Do you need anything else?"

"I'll be fine." I hoped. "And I Mackey is staying with me tonight too."

"You have our number on speed dial?"

I nodded.

He stood. "Then I'll bid you good night." I walked him to the front door where we met the party planner. Rodgers waited until the short meeting concluded, and escorted the planner out the front door. I threw the deadbolt behind them.

I paced until I knocked on the front door.

"Show me everything," she said and held up a bottle. "But first, wine."

I locked the front door, set the alarm, and duly fortified, I and I carried our elegant wine glasses through the hole in the wall. We picked our way around the damage done to the step, gripping the bannister and descending—with care. Yellow caution tape cordoned off the hole left when they'd dismantled the step and taken the plank as evidence. More tape bordered the chalk outline of the silhouette of a body drawn on the floor. The overhead lights blazed, exposing everything else in the room, glinting off the wall panel.

Engraved plates identified some of the controls. I flicked a blue switch labelled, 'sound,' and heard wind rustling. I turned the dial below it and the volume increased and changed its timbre from whistling to howling. A red toggle caused a moaning and crying. I pushed a button and we heard creaking floorboards under weighted footfalls. Heavy breathing filled the air when I flipped the yellow switch.

I used my sleeve to polish a plate engraved with the word, 'sight.' The curling, pink, embossed plastic labels identified eight small screens monitoring the main areas of the house. I pressed one of the buttons beneath the projection of the kitchen and a light turned on under a cupboard. Rotating the joystick beneath the library screen caused a row of books to fly off the shelf. I pressed a large button, and the drawing room came into view through what appeared to be, determined by the angle and line of sight, the eyes in Parker's portrait. With its puzzles and electronic gadgetry, this house was a cryptanalyst's dream.

Satisfied with the pleasant temperature of the house and not willing to unleash strange scents into the air I'd agreed to breathe for two more days, I didn't alter the settings labelled, 'feeling' and 'smell.'

"Parker assembled a fabulous house of riddles and tricks. I wonder what happened to her."

"No one's heard from her?" I took a large sip of wine before we visited the kitchen to partake of the charcuterie. Then we tried on and appropriated costumes from the third-floor storage.

I opened a second suite. "Thanks for coming, I."

"No problem. Thanks for the invitation. Holler if you need anything." She winked. "On second thought, forget I'm here."

The bed in my suite looked most inviting. I crawled under the smooth, cool sheets, and Maverick nestled next to me. I nodded off immediately, but woke often and rose early after a fitful night's sleep. I got up way too happy and I sent her packing.

* * *

At exactly four thirty Saturday, Mildred Larkin sashayed through the front door, wearing sandals and a shimmering gold lamé sheath with an elaborately braided black wig, a circular headpiece, and the tell-tale black kohl eye makeup of Cleopatra. She said in a haughty voice, "Report."

"The caterer kicked me out of the kitchen after her helpers polished the silver and plated the hors d'oeuvres. They're the ones wearing black shirts and pants, white vests, and bowties. Beverages are listed in the leather-bound folios on the bar and the bartender concocted a specialty drink for tonight—a Pumpkin Martini. The videographer's cameras are fully operational." I finally took a breath. "She's enabled the connection to live stream from the dining room, the drawing room, and the library for Devlin to view."

Millie nodded. "Everything is ready but you. Go get dressed." She gave shooing waves with her hands.

Only I could pull off wearing a belly dancer costume, but when Drew showed up in harem pants and a satin vest showing off his sculpted abs, he didn't look too shabby either. I'd selected a tight black mermaid dress and slinked across the floor like Morticia Addams. CJ didn't fool anyone in his tuxedo, black cape, and fangs. But Pete and Susie disappointed me. He wore a white lab coat over black pants and a button-down shirt, hoping he crossed over to mad scientist mode with the addition of a wig of wild Einstein-hair. Susie looked fetching in her coordinating antiseptic white nurse's dress and starched cap. Ugh. Ida and her guest, my dad, wore fifties garb; she in a pink poodle skirt, white frilly blouse, and chiffon scarf, chewing bubble gum; he wore blue jeans, a black leather jacket, and white tee-shirt, his hair slicked back with a little dab of Brylcreem. Heather breezed in wearing a shimmering bronze-colored sequined flapper dress featuring an art deco print and long fringe. Tufts of her platinum wig curled around a feathered headband. She twirled a long, knotted pearl necklace in front of her. Niles wore green tights, a belted tunic, and a green cap reminding me of Robin Hood or the Jolly Green Giant.

Lance Erickson flapped his red cape over his sky-blue tights and cornered me. "You're not investigating, are you?"

I forced a laugh. "No sir, Superman Chief, sir."

He struck a Superman pose. "Good."

Emil Watland was the wild card. Dressed as the Phantom of the Opera, he was the textbook guest—funny, engaging, and, given the tender looks he gave Millie, madly in love. "Parker told me about the notebook, but I never saw it. I'm glad you finally found it. She created quite a house."

The delicious surf and turf dinner went off without a hitch and we retired—that sounded so refined—to the drawing room where Susie cornered Heather. They conversed over two of the smooth signature cocktails, their serious exchange ending in a one-sided hug—Heather's arms were pinned to her sides. Millie rescued Heather and allowed Susie to grill her about her grandmother who had been employed as a server for the party the last time she and Parker had been seen.

Susie downed two more cocktails, and her voice carried across the room. "I never got to meet her, but my dad said she was great," Susie's voice cracked. "Law enforcement told my grandpa that some women just aren't cut out to be wives, and they gave up looking." Her voice quavered.

"To think she'd been here the entire time. Someone ought to pay."

"At least now you can have some closure," Millie said.

Susie bolted upright as if she'd been slapped. "Closure? There's a murderer running loose and I'd bet money on Parker Halliday."

Pete spirited her away before she could say more. "Thanks everyone. We've had a wonderful time," he said, but his smile didn't quite reach his eyes. I hoped she was good enough for him. He ushered Susie out the door and the revelry dialed down a notch. Shortly after dessert, the subdued guests called it a night. I bade everyone a safe trip home and a Happy Halloween.

"Nice party," my dad said, offering his elbow to Ida. "See you tomorrow, kiddo."

"Thanks for the tour," I said, ogling Drew. They locked hands and swung their arms as they strolled down the incline through the pumpkin path.

CJ accompanied Maverick and me on a quick, but necessary, jaunt around the misting grounds. We waved at Emil as he lit the spooky Halloween display and this time he returned the wave.

"What a nice evening. Thanks for inviting me," CJ said.

"I'm glad you liked it, but it would be even better if we knew who killed Mrs. Kelton."

"Katie, I think it best if you leave the investigating to the professionals."

I'd heard that before, but it couldn't do any harm if I just thought about the possibilities, could it? "You told Carlee I had significant insight with remarkable solutions."

CJ rustled Maverick's ears and fished his keys out of his pocket. "Goodnight, Katie." He slid into his vehicle and pointed to the front door. I waved with gusto, then stepped inside, and set the alarm.

The cleanup crew had left the house sparkling; I checked each room before turning out the lights, and headed to the guest suite, overwhelmed by exhaustion.

The next thing I knew, I dragged my heavy eyelids open and stared at the mocking red numerals on the bedstand clock, wondering why I had awakened. It read one minute after one and I cringed, knowing morning would come all too soon. I counted and breathed with as much regularity as I could, in with the good air and out with the bad. I felt my chest rise and fall as I drifted back toward welcoming slumber. Then Maverick barked, and my eyes flashed open.

"Now what?" I tossed the bedclothes to one side and drew on baggy Cougar sweats, hoping our high school mascot would bring me strength. I yanked on the cords of the window blinds. I didn't see anything. The house needed a quick check.

On my pass through the foyer, Maverick came to attention at the front door. "Come, Maverick." He looked over his shoulder and I could almost hear him say, *Wait for it.* I intended to haul him with me when the heavy knocker sounded. I jumped back and upset a decorative bouquet of flowers on the table. "Who is it?" I righted the vase, swishing water droplets onto the floor.

The knock reverberated again.

I switched on the porch light and peered through the glass next to the door.

The voice from a wheelchair said, "I just want to ask about Devlin."

I punched in the code and opened the door. Parker Halliday looked much like she did in her portrait, now silver-haired, a bit thinner, a few wrinkles perhaps, but with the same twinkling eyes.

"I'm sorry to bother you. I came as soon as I heard. Is he going to be all right?"

"I believe so."

"Not a day goes by when I don't think of him. I still miss him terribly and when I heard he'd had a heart attack, I had to come."

"Where are my manners? I'm Katie Wilk. I'm housesitting. Please come in."

"I'm—" She rolled through the entry.

"I know who you are. You're the genius behind the tricks in this house. I'm so pleased to meet you." I stuck out my hand at the same time Susie's words came back to haunt me. Could Parker be a murderer? She's present, again, after all these years, two days after I found Lenore's skeleton. I forced my lips to smile while my thoughts swirled.

Tears spilled down her cheeks.

"May I get you something to drink?"

She shook her head. "While I worked on this house, I thought Devlin and I had something special. As the house renovation neared completion, I was told Devlin never loved me. He was just being kind. I decided if my feelings weren't reciprocated, then my ego wouldn't allow me to stay. I left a letter with my friend Lenore, detailing my itinerary and contact information, should he care to join me. It was a test but he never came." She sniffed. "When I finally worked up the courage to confront him, I was hit by a car and left for dead. I ended up in this chair and didn't have it in me to subject him to such a burden. But I still care for him. And I heard about them finding Lenore."

Maverick rushed into the drawing room and barked.

We trailed him. The wall had retracted. Parker followed me to the opening and clapped. The lights came on.

"I'll check." I feigned an upbeat tone. Maverick hurtled toward the opening, but I nabbed his collar and he jerked to a halt. I dropped onto the top step and ran my hand down the length of my dog to calm him. Rubbing his silky ears settled my racing heart too. "Out, Maverick." He took four steps back.

I crept down.

Niles Turner's glassy eyes stared up at me. He rested at the bottom of the stairs, outlined by the chalk border, his body contorted in a way no body should be.

I glanced up at Parker.

"What's happened?" she asked.

Maverick barked furiously, then yelped. Parker's chair rolled forward, teetered, and clattered down the steps, crashing to the floor. My heart lurched to my throat. I was horrified.

I crawled to her side. Her eyes were closed. "Parker?" Her neck pulsed beneath my fingers. I massaged her hand.

The wall at the top of the stairs whooshed closed.

Maverick's muffled barking continued.

An alarm wailed. I smelled smoke. I raced to the monitors. My attention was drawn from the legs and shoes of a dark figure darting across the foyer to Maverick pacing near the wall and the flames crawling up the drawing room curtains. I reached for my phone and remembered I left it in its charger in the guest suite. I pushed all the buttons on the panels, hoping one might draw back the wall or Parker would wake and know another way out.

"Maverick, get help," I yelled. He hesitated, unsure. "Get help." I said forcefully, and he disappeared from the screen. He'd be safe.

I wrapped Parker's arm over my shoulder and started our slow ascent, dragging her unconscious, feather-light body around the caution tape. "Help's coming," I lied.

Succumbing to the smoke billowing through a crack at the foot of the wall, I collapsed at the top of the stairs.

"This is it. My Alamo," I said. My cheeks felt damp. The tears came unbidden. "I love you, Dad." I coughed. I had one tender thought: Charles would be waiting for me. I cradled Parker, closed my eyes, and leaned back.

All at once, the wall disappeared and we sprawled through the opening. Wary of being let out of the smoky room and into the blazing inferno, I searched for whoever released us, and my heart skipped a beat. Orange and yellow lights danced on Maverick's shoulders and on top of his head like a halo, flames reflected off of his shiny black coat. He sat primly near the couch, with his paw squarely planted on the abnormality in the floor, looking pleased.

"Maverick." I didn't recognize my own raspy voice, but still he came. He grabbed one sleeve and helped me drag Parker across the tile toward the front door.

* * *

I woke to Pete shining that penlight in my eyes again. Someone should take it away from him. I knocked his hand away and shook my head.

"Where's Parker?"

"She's okay. She doesn't remember anything except being towed across the floor by a wolf."

"Maverick." I almost laughed, but coughed instead.

"Rodgers had a heck of a time getting him to let the

EMTs take the two of you. What happened?"

"Someone pushed Parker down the stairs, closed that wall, and started the fire, but how did we get here?"

"Emil Watland knew the code and pulled you to safety. The alarm company hadn't had a single call in thirty-five years and almost didn't respond. Good thing they have a fire policy: ask questions later. The firefighters saved most of Hopkins House," Pete said. "Tell me about Niles Turner."

"He's dead."

"I know. Rodgers found him after they put out the fire. But what was Niles doing in the house?"

"I don't know," I said, but then random ideas took shape in my fuzzy mind. "Niles could have found out about the bones and, with a morbid sense of curiosity, went to check it out, or maybe he somehow caused Lenore's death and went to clean up any evidence of his crime?"

Pete hummed, unconvinced.

"Maybe he broke in to steal something. The house is filled with valuable and beautiful treasures."

"There are rumors that he'd enlisted the services of a fence. He may have been trying to unload items he'd already taken from the house."

"But it looked like he died the same way Lenore died. Decades apart."

I hopped off the exam table.

"Where do you think you're going?"

"With or without you? Parker's still in danger." We walked. I talked. When he finished listening, he made some calls, and I put on another costume.

* * *

I sat in the dark sterile hospital room, hunched in a wheelchair, play-acting feebleness, and scratched under the uncomfortable wig, observing the figure lying still on the bed in front of me when the door opened. It didn't make a sound, but the dim light from the hall lit the mound at the foot of the bed and then went dark.

I tucked my chin and squeezed out, "Hello, Heather." I worried I might have overdone acting frail. I coughed into my cardigan.

"How did you know it was me?"

"I saw your shoes in one of the control panel monitors, running through the foyer after the fire started."

"Why did you come back? Everything was perfect. Devlin loves me, you know. Only me."

"I believed that once. When he didn't respond to the note I left, I presumed you were right, and I had no place in his life. But you never let Lenore deliver my message, did you?"

"You had her dress like you so she could take your place and give you time to get away. Behind the masks, no one knew the difference, but she couldn't contain her happiness for you. She had to share your letter with me. She thought it was so romantic. I tried to sound enthusiastic as I read the note, happy for you, but I seethed inside. I knew about your wall trick, let her in on *our* little secret, and told her I'd send Devlin. I hit her and pushed her down the stairs. I hadn't intended to kill her, but when she didn't get up, I took advantage of the circumstances, burned the letter, and closed the room."

I said sadly, "What did you think would happen?"

"I thought he'd come around, but he wasted his

entire life, pining for you. No matter. I'm his partner in everything else." She sighed. "I'll just have to settle for the family fortune."

I peeked over my left shoulder. The edge of a white lab coat floated nearer.

"This time it shouldn't hurt."

"This time?" Shocked, I said, "You ran P—I mean, me down?"

"You just wouldn't die." She snorted. "You'll feel a little prick and drift off to sleep and that will be the end of it."

"Did you kill Niles too?"

She barked a laugh. "What a fool! Niles sent the anonymous text that brought me here, but I caught him breaking into the house, *your* house. He promised he'd provide for me in the manner to which I'd become accustomed. He even tried to kiss me and when I refused, he said he'd keep my secret if I married him. I thought he'd figured out I'd killed Lenore, but ..." she laughed contemptuously. "... by the time I determined he'd only found out I'd embezzled some of my clients' funds, which, by the way, Devlin promised to repay, it was too late."

"You killed Niles and Lenore." Where was Pete? "For no reason?"

Heather edged closer. I didn't have much time. Her hand was on the back of my chair.

"They were in my way, as are you now." She grabbed for me, and caught the wig as I squirmed out of reach. "What is this? Where's Parker?" She raged and shook the silver hair. She took a menacing step toward me.

Pete and Officer Rodgers crashed into the room. Rodgers drew his gun. "Put the syringe down."

"Noooooo," Heather screamed, lifting the hand

holding the needle and rushing me. Pete seized her wrist and wrestled the syringe free. Heather fell to the floor, sobbing.

Rodgers cuffed her and led her out of the room, almost colliding with the wheelchair Susie steered through the door.

The man, who'd been lying still in the hospital bed, rolled over, smiling. "Is it over?"

"Devlin?" Parker whispered.

"My darling." He took her hand and kissed the tips of her fingers. "I never gave up hoping. Will you marry me now?"

"I've waited my entire life to hear those words. But this chair …" She pounded the armrests. "… and I are inseparable. I can't bring much to our united table." She lowered her chin, holding back tears.

"Poor Heather. But it's always been you. Please, marry me, Parker."

She paused a moment, then lifted her head. Happy tears poured down her cheeks and her blue eyes twinkled. She said, "Yes." He sat up and leaned forward, planting a kiss on her welcoming lips.

"We'll hand out Halloween candy tomorrow and see the Justice of the Peace soon, and you're all invited. I love you, Parker. You've made me the happiest man on earth."

He turned to me. "I think it's about time for her wedding gift. Ms. Wilk, could you and Dr. Pete get it for me?"

* * *

Pete held the magnetic Tarot cards and I placed them

in the depressions on the cover of the chest in the same order as in Parker's portrait. When I straightened the final card, the lock clicked, and I carefully raised the lid.

A pair of white cotton gloves lay atop a large pile of books. I shimmied the gloves over my hands and eagerly picked up a first edition of Edgar Allen Poe's *Tamerlane and Other Poems*. Under that were a signed first edition of King's *Salem's Lot*, a copy of the first printing of the first illustrated edition of Shelley's *Frankenstein*, and a signed edition of Bram Stoker's *Dracula*.

I gazed at Pete, and my stomach fluttered.

What more could one want in a wedding gift!

* * *

Bonus Recipe

PUMPKIN MARTINI

1 oz Vanilla Vodka

1 oz Pumpkin liqueur

1 oz Irish cream liqueur

1 pinch of ground cinnamon

1 pinch of ground nutmeg

Pour over ice. Shake. Garnish with a spritz of whipped cream and a cinnamon stick. Serve.

* * *

About the Author

Mary Seifert has always loved a good mystery, a brain teaser, or a challenge. As a former mathematics teacher, she ties numbers and logic to the mayhem game. The Katie & Maverick mysteries allow her to share those stories, as well as puzzles, riddles, and a few taste-tested recipes.

When she's not writing, she's making wonderful memories with family, exchanging thoughtful ideas with friends, walking her dog whose only speed is faster, dabbling in needlecrafts, and pretending to cook. You can also find her sneaking bites of chocolate and sipping wine, both of which sometimes occur *while* writing. Mary is a member of Mysteries Writers of America, Sisters in Crime, American Cryptogram Association, Dog Writers of America, and PEO.

**Get a collection of free recipes from Mary
—visit her website to find out how!**

Visit Mary's website: MarySeifertAuthor.com/
Facebook: facebook.com/MarySeifertAuthor
Twitter: twitter.com/mary_seifert
Instagram: instagram.com/maryseifert/
Follow Mary on BookBub and Goodreads too!

Books by Mary Seifert

Maverick, Movies, & Murder
Rescues, Rogues, & Renegade
Tinsel, Trials, & Traitors
Santa, Snowflakes, & Strychnine

Praise for the Katie & Maverick Mysteries:

"I thoroughly enjoyed this debut book by Mary Seifert! This well written and thoughtful story kept me engaged with fun characters, interesting information and mind and math puzzles. Looking forward to book two!"

—James, 5-star review

"Fun read! The author has an authentic voice and has done her research. The plot covers many topics: dogs, history, the inner workings of hospitals, family dynamics, and more. I especially enjoyed the puzzles and little-known historical facts that were part of the story. *Maverick, Movies & Murder* kept my interest and left me wanting more. Highly recommend!" —Beth, online 5-star review

"...very much looking forward to her next!!! I can't get enough of Ms. Seifert's books!!" – proudarmymom, 5 stars

"...plenty of unanticipated twists and turns. It kept [me] up reading to see what was going to happen next!"

– RHN, 5 stars online

Case of the Secret Staircase
A Corgi Case Files Short Story

By J.M. Poole

~ ~ ~

1

W hat are we doing here? And tell me again why you wanted me to bring Sherlock and Watson? I … wow. Someone really enjoys decorating for Halloween, don't they?"

I should probably backtrack a bit and tell you what's going on. For those who may not know me, allow me to introduce myself. My name is Zack Anderson. I'm happily married to my beautiful wife, Jillian, and together, we live in a small town in southwest Oregon by the name of Pomme Valley. PV, as we tend to call it, is situated less than ten minutes from Medford, and we're about thirty minutes from Grants Pass, which lies northwest of us.

I also own two corgis, who go by Sherlock and Watson. They have got to be, hands down, the smartest four-legged critters I think I have ever encountered. Those two dogs— believe it or not—are actual working dogs for the Pomme Valley PD, with me as their handler. On paper, we're consultants, but everyone knows those two dogs are the only thing the police department cares about. They are, in fact, PVPD's secret weapons. The only title I hold is Filler of Food Bowls.

The four of us had just walked up the steps, onto the front porch, and seeing how the main entrance had both double doors propped open, stepped inside PV's favorite historic building. Inside, we encountered a short, narrow hallway with a single door on either side. The right side, I knew, had the old den, and the left? Jillian said it was something that was originally called the reception room. As for now, it was simply a closet.

My wife purchased this place recently as a business investment. The only way she had been allowed to buy one of the town's historic properties was with the promise that she was not going to sell the house anytime soon. Instead, the only stipulation the mayor of PV had given was that it be given a complete overhaul. Since Jillian's plans were to convert the building into an old-fashioned bed and breakfast, she had agreed on the spot.

Renovations had been interesting. Turns out, this building had a few secrets of its own. The first, we discovered, was that this home had once belonged to Dame Hilda Highland. Apparently, Highland House had been built with the sole purpose of keeping things hidden. In this case, keeping stashes of illegal alcohol away from prying eyes during Prohibition, and as such, a number of secret rooms and passageways had been discovered. The second was that Dame Highland had used all the various nooks and crannies at her disposal to hide her more valuable jewelry.

And, of course, I would be remiss if I forgot to mention the people of PV thought the building was haunted.

Entering the former living room, which had been turned into a lobby, my eyes were automatically drawn to the right, which was where the dining room was located. The long, rustic oak dinner table, which had room for twelve, had been shoved up against the wall. What captured my attention, though, was what was *on* the table and, for that matter, practically every square inch of space in and around the room.

The table had been draped with two different cloths; light blue on the left, and a deep purple on the right. The two different colored linens had some type of white lace pattern on it, but I couldn't tell what it was due to the enormous amount of … *stuff* on it. Bright orange marigolds were everywhere, and if I'm not mistaken, paper flowers of just about every hue you can think of were scattered along the surface. The next thing I saw was a large, black candle—currently lit—that was situated at the back of the table and was set on some type of raised platform. Black candles aren't really that spectacular, but when it was shaped like a skull, with a huge grinning smile, it was bound to get a second look.

As I slowly inspected the table, I saw several more of the skull candles, only they were a few inches shorter than the large one. Directly in the middle of the table, arranged in an altar, were photographs, not of one person, but of many. Also present was a collection of plates and baskets. What was on them? Food, of course. I was looking at loaves of bread, baskets of fruit, a plate of enchiladas, and so on. My stomach threatened to rumble if I lingered too long over the display. The walls had additional pictures, more paper flowers, and brightly colored fabrics as backdrops. I could also see several plush animals placed here and there, only they didn't look like any type of child's toy I had ever seen before.

Stepping back from the table, the first thing I thought I

was looking at was an homage to someone who had recently passed away. Only, thanks to the numerous photographs, I knew that wasn't the case. This certainly wasn't any funeral reception I had ever been to. Since when were there jet-black skull candles *and* brightly-colored flowers in the same friggin' room? I was clearly missing something.

"*¡Feliz Día de Los Muertos!* Mrs. Anderson! Mr. Anderson! Thank you so much for coming!"

We turned to see Lisa I, a Hispanic woman in her early thirties. Highland House's manager was wearing a white, frilly blouse, a floor-length gray skirt with ruffles on the edges, and a red sash around her waist. Her long, black hair had been braided into twin pigtails, and she wore a floral tiara on the top of her head, which consisted of a series of flowers that resembled a rainbow when viewed side-by-side. What stopped me in my tracks was her face. No, don't get me wrong, Lisa is very attractive. What took my breath away was the simple fact that her face was painted bone-white, her left eye socket area had been painted black, and her lips were also black. She produced a silver tray and held it out to us.

"Calaveras?"

"Cala-*what*?" I wanted to know.

"Calaveras," Jillian repeated, smiling. "And of course, I'll have one. Zachary? Will you try one? They're edible. I mean, most calaveras are not, seeing how they're used for decorations, but these? Something tells me that you'll like them. I just hope they taste half as good as they smell."

"Mmm, tastes just like a cookie," I said, after taking my first bite. "I don't care what they are. They get two thumbs up in my book."

"That's because they *are* cookies, Mr. Anderson," Lisa

clarified. "Kimmi made them last night." In case I didn't mention it, Kimmi is Lisa's girlfriend. She's Hawaiian, and basically uprooted her entire life to move out here when Lisa took the job as manager of the Highland House B&B. "If you'd like to see some actual calaveras, then you're in luck. Kimmi made some of those, too. I helped decorate, of course. And here, I made these myself, for your two wonderful dogs."

Lisa squatted to present two decorated doggie biscuits. Sherlock and Watson promptly sat and enjoyed their treats. Once they were finished, they practically glued themselves to Lisa's side, hoping they'd be rewarded with another goodie. Brown-nosers.

For the next fifteen minutes, we followed Jillian's manager around the display, listening intently as we were schooled on everything one needed to know to observe this traditional Mexican holiday. First and foremost, it wasn't anything like Halloween, even though it did fall on the day after. And, much to my surprise, one didn't need to be of Mexican heritage in order to celebrate the holiday. It helps, yes, to have someone explain what is what, but it certainly isn't required. After all, this was a day meant to honor loved ones who have passed away, regardless of ethnicity. That was why, Lisa explained, there were so many bright colors. We weren't supposed to be feeling sorry for anyone. Quite the contrary, this was when the spirits of the dead were actually welcomed back, with open arms.

I pointed at a few of the cooked dishes on the table.

"Oh, so that's why there's food present? To entice them to return?"

Lisa nodded. "They're *ofrendas*. Offerings. People will make their loved one's favorite dishes, in the hopes that they will be visited by their spirits."

Jillian turned to point at one of the animal figurines. The painting scheme was just as colorfully executed as all of the skulls.

"I see several animals, Lisa. I remember you telling me they were, what, spirit animals?"

Lisa nodded again. "*Alebrijes*. Spirit guides. They can come in many forms. Pedro Linares, a folk artist living in I City in the 1930s, came up with the idea. He was sick with fever, and claims he started hallucinating when he passed out. He insists he saw a forest with strange animals, with elements from multiple creatures."

Intrigued, I leaned closer. "You mean, head of a lion, body of a goat, that type of thing? That's why this cat-thing has wings?"

Lisa grinned at me. "Precisely. *Alebrijes* literally translates to *fantasy*, or *imaginary*. Therefore, Pedro theorized these mystical animals were there to guide the spirits from one side to the other, and back again."

"I've always seen those decorated skulls," I said, as I jammed my hands in my pockets, "but never knew the story about them. We appreciate the history lesson, Lisa."

"Indeed, we do," Jillian agreed. "Now, would you care to tell us why you wanted the four of us out here?"

My head jerked up. "What? She's the one who called us out here? What in the world for? Next, you'll tell us that the spirits are here, and you need them gone."

Lisa laughed. "Not quite, I'm afraid. Oh, let's see. How do I put this? Well, here we go. Some of my *ofrendas* have gone missing."

I blinked a few times. "Your ... offerings? From the table? They're, uh, missing? Man, I was totally joking earlier."

"What's gone missing?" Jillian wanted to know. "Are you sure someone didn't just walk away with it?"

"The first thing I noticed was my mother's hand-knitted scarf. She made it for my *abuela* many years ago. It was her favorite."

"Her *what*?" I whispered in Jillian's ear.

"Her grandmother. Now, shush."

"Yep. Sorry."

Lisa leaned forward and tapped a section of the table next to one of the skull candles.

"I had it here, next to her picture."

"When did you last see it?" Jillian wanted to know.

"Yesterday. I went to straighten the table and refresh several dishes and noticed it was missing."

"What else has been taken?" I asked. My notebook had found its way into my hand and, in proper police consultant fashion, I was taking notes.

"Several small, hanging pictures."

"Hanging pictures?" I repeated, looking up.

"Yeah, you know, the kind that are homemade?"

"Like homemade ornaments?" Jillian asked, coming to Lisa's aid.

"Yes, exactly. And, then there's the food."

It was Jillian's turn to look surprised.

"Food? What about the food?"

"Several plates have been tampered with," Lisa reported.

"As in, tainted?" Jillian asked, horrified.

"More like … sampled," Lisa corrected.

Jillian's look of horror switched to one of anger.

"Oh, that's unacceptable."

"I couldn't agree more, Mrs. Anderson. If I didn't know any better, then I'd either say we have a vagrant living somewhere inside this house …"

"… which we know we don't," Jillian interrupted.

"Yes. Either a vagrant, or …?"

"Oh, no you don't," I scolded, becoming stern. "Don't *even* go there. You're not going to tell me one of your spirits is now living in Highland House. You're not, are you?"

"I was going to say that, perhaps, our *ofrendas* are too tempting to ignore. Perhaps we have one—or more—of our dearly departed walking among us?"

I felt a chill creep down my spine and ended up shuddering.

"Well, this little outing has taken an unexpected turn," I grumbled.

Jillian swatted my arm. "Oh, Zachary. Don't start believing everything you hear. You can't possibly be afraid of ghosts, can you? No? Good. There's simply no way there could be ghosts here. I don't believe in them."

"I may not believe in ghosts, my dear, but I do have my concerns about any type of unexplainable phenomena. Besides, you have to admit something to me."

"What's that?" my wife wanted to know. I also noticed Lisa was listening intently.

"If there *was* going to be a house that was haunted, you and I both know it'd be this one."

Both Jillian and Lisa broke into laughter.

"Will you look into this for me, Mr. Anderson?" Lisa asked, a few moments later.

I looked at my wife, and then down at the dogs, who were both snoozing at my feet. However, at the exact instant I looked down, Sherlock awoke, looked up at the table, and did something that made my eyebrows shoot up.

Woof!

Just like that, both corgis were on their feet and were staring, suspiciously, at the table and the many offerings it held.

"I guess that means we'll take the case," I announced. "I always wanted my very own proton pack!"

"What does he want?" I heard Lisa quietly ask Jillian.

"He thinks he's a Ghostbuster now," Jillian explained. "Best to just humor him. That's what I always do."

"I heard that, lady," I scoffed, although anyone who knew me would know I was just teasing. I don't think I've ever raised my voice to Jillian in all the time we've been together. Oh, don't get me wrong, I'm sure we can each get on the other's nerves, but when you're in a relationship, who doesn't?

So … now I'm a Ghostbuster. This should be fun!

2

My first official day as a paranormal investigator didn't start until later in the afternoon. After all, I *did* have to get some gear together, didn't I? However, the only thing you'll find stuffed in my backpack would be a pair of latex gloves, two N95 face masks, disinfectant spray, my palm-sized video camera, and a bag of doggie biscuits.

Ghostbuster, I am *not*.

Actually, what I really should have packed was a change of clothes, 'cause I'm pretty sure I'm going to pee myself if I do come face to face with a ghost. Yes, I know; I'm being irrational. I know there's no such thing as ghosts or spirits that have yet to move on. Well, let's make that ninety-nine percent certain. After all, it's a mighty big world out there. How do we know for certain that some form of energy doesn't linger behind after a person passes away? It's that one-percent I'm worried about.

Yep, there you go. I'm a writer. These are the sort of morbid things I think about. And, based on my present situation, I've been thinking about them a lot.

"You two are up," I told the dogs. "Where do you want to go first?"

Neither dog bothered to look at me. Both of them were on their feet and promptly headed for the stairs in the middle of the house. Gently tugging them to a stop, I pointed left, toward the display we saw earlier in the day.

"I think you want to go that way, don't you? After all, isn't that the scene of the crime?"

Sherlock turned to give me a look that spoke volumes. With one glance, my tri-colored corgi pretty much told me that if I didn't want the help he was willing to give, then I had no business asking for it in the first place. As for Watson, well, she didn't seem to care, and was content to look wherever her packmate indicated.

"Fine, you win. Let's go upstairs. We'll see what we can find."

There were four bedrooms upstairs, not including a huge suite which took up the entire western side of the second floor. The suite seems to be the most popular of the rooms, since Jillian confirmed there's usually a two month waiting list to make a reservation. I've been in that particular room before. It was Dame Hilda's master bedroom. That one room alone probably has the largest closet I've ever seen before. This particular closet contained not one, nor two, but three different hidden compartments, thus increasing the closet's overall square footage to something larger than most apartments. Then again, not many closets had dedicated attic space, and a hidden pull-down ladder for access.

Everything had been lovingly restored. Jillian spared no expense. If it was something that existed during the house's heyday, even though it might have not been originally installed, it was then added to the house plans. Door knobs, hinges, light fixtures, everything.

Upon reaching the top of the stairs, the dogs turned to look left, toward the main master suite. Then, they collectively turned right and started heading down the hall as though they owned the place. The door on the far right corner led into one of the floor's four identical bedrooms. Sherlock lifted a paw and acted like he was going to scratch the door in order to get me to open it. Anticipating his move, I stepped in front of the door before he could do any damage.

"What have I told you before? No more scratching on doors, pal. That goes for you, too, Watson. We are here as guests." Spinning in place so that I was facing the door, I knocked a few times. "Umm, housekeeping?"

The door opened and a matronly woman appeared. "We don't need any service at the moment, thank you. My, I can't remember the last time I saw a male housekeeper. Oh. Oh! Look at the dogs! I know you! You're Mr. Anderson! These two are Sherlock and Watson, aren't they?"

Two corgi derrieres were wiggling so much that their whole bodies sort of *writhed* in ecstasy. I held out a hand.

"You have the advantage, Ms. …?"

"Marjorie Whitfield. My husband and I are celebrating

our fiftieth wedding anniversary today. We both live in town, but wanted some time away from home. Oh, I wish Herb was here. He loves your dogs, too. Did you really meet the Queen of England? Oh, that must have been wonderful!"

"The Queen is a very remarkable woman, Mrs. Whitfield," I said, nodding. "And yes, those two are Sherlock and Watson."

"You're not really with the housekeeping department, are you?" Marjorie wanted to know.

"No, we're just, er, ... ?"

Marjorie's eyes widened and lit up.

"The thefts! You and your dogs are investigating the thefts! Well, may I add something else to the list?"

It was my turn to stare.

"Have you, uh, noticed something missing?"

"I have, yes."

I pulled out my notebook. "All right, hit me with your best. What's missing?"

"It's really nothing," Marjorie was saying. "It's just that ... I can't find one of my mittens. Herb seems to think I simply forgot it at home, but I didn't. I wore them last night, so I know I brought them."

"Where *is* Mr. Whitfield?" I politely inquired.

"He's playing golf. I know it sounds strange, us celebrating our anniversary here, together, only we're not together. Well, I can't stand golf, and he doesn't particularly care for shopping, so we each agreed to meet up for lunch at the Lonely Gringo."

"They've got fantastic food," I confirmed. "Hey, out of curiosity, since I know there aren't any golf courses here in PV, where did Mr. Whitfield go to play golf? Medford?"

Mrs. Whitfield was shaking her head. "No, it was a city by the name of Eagle Point. It's not too far away."

"You're right, I've driven through that particular golf course. It's only about twenty minutes from here. It's a great area. Okay, back to your mittens. You were wearing them last night?"

"Oh, yes," Mrs. Whitfield said. "I'm always cold, and my hands get just like ice cubes. It drives Herb nuts. So …" Mrs. Whitfield held up a finger, signaling me to wait, and hurried around a corner. Moments later, she was back, holding a lone orange mitten. "I knitted these myself. On top of which, I've been through all our things. I can't find the second one anywhere."

"Umm, do you have any ideas who could've taken it?"

Mrs. Whitfield nodded and, if I'm not mistaken, turned pale.

"I know *exactly* who took it."

Relieved, I offered the matronly woman a smile. "You have no idea how glad I am about that. So, curiosity kills. Who did it?"

"My mother. She always said I couldn't knit a proper sweater even if I had someone there telling me how to do it."

Sherlock and Watson chose that time to give themselves a good shake before sinking into down positions. In unison, they watched the two of us converse. Smiling at the dogs, I looked up at Mrs. Whitfield and paused as I tried to determine the best way to phrase my objection.

"Umm, er, is your mother here, now? Which room is she in?"

"Oh, she's here, I'm certain of it. She never could stand to see me happy."

Right then, the cobwebs cleared out of my brain and I realized what Mrs. Whitfield was talking about.

"You're not suggesting your mother is here because of *Día de Los Muertos*, are you?"

"Well, of course! Ms. I said if I were to bring a picture of a departed loved one, that she'd take ten percent off the price of our stay. Oh, and something about her favorite dish."

That's just great. This woman thinks her dead mother stole her mitten? Seriously?

"I can see that you don't believe me, Mr. Anderson," Mrs. Whitfield said, frowning.

"No, I'm sorry. My wife tells me I need to be more open-minded. Still, I'm having a hard time believing a ghost is responsible for this."

"I'm not the only one!" Mrs. Whitfield insisted. "The lovely young couple down the hall were telling me that they have things missing, too."

I turned to gaze back at the hallway. "Down there? Are you talking about the suite?"

"Yes."

"Were they offered the same promotion as you?" I asked. "Did they bring a picture of someone they've lost?"

Mrs. Whitfield was already nodding. "They did."

"Hmm. Well, thank you for your time. Rest assured, I'm going to get to the bottom of this."

"Thank you, Mr. Anderson."

The door closed and I looked down at the dogs, who slowly rose to their feet.

"What do you think? Do you want to go check it out?"

The two corgis answered by tugging on their leashes and walking back, across the hall, to the western side of the house. The B&B's pride and joy, the Roaring Twenties Suite, appeared before us. Glancing down at the dogs, to check whether or not this was what they wanted to do, I saw that both corgis were now sitting, which confirmed we were in the right place.

"There's no such thing as ghosts," I softly intoned, before knocking on the door.

A young man in his early twenties answered the knock. He was much shorter than me, around five-foot-six, had short brown hair, and was wearing a green-collared Polo-type shirt with khaki pants.

"Yes? Can I help you?"

A woman appeared next to him. She looked to be around the same age, had long blonde hair pulled up in a high ponytail, and was wearing black slacks with a blue blouse. Both husband and wife heard Sherlock's soft snort and immediately looked down. The wife's eyes lit up with recognition first.

"Wh-what's this? Aren't you two Sherlock and Watson? David, did you set this up?"

David, the husband, shook his head. "Er, no. I have no idea what's going on."

"Hey there," I began, once the two of them were looking my way. "I'm so sorry to bother you. I'm Zack Anderson and these two are … well, you guessed it. This is Sherlock, and that's Watson."

"Oh, they're so adorable!" the wife gushed.

The man extended a hand. "David Sorrenson. This is my wife, Anya. Is there something we can do for you?"

I picked up the accent right away. Norwegian? Swedish? I figured it was from one of those Scandinavian countries.

"I'm really sorry to bother you. My wife owns this place

and she asked me to check out some reports of missing items. I was talking to ..."

"Of course!" Anya exclaimed. "Your dogs are famous detectives! We recognized them from television!"

Nodding, I held my hands out, as though I was presenting the corgis to the world.

"Yep, there they are. Where are you guys from?"

"Stockholm," David answered.

"You're a long way from home," I observed. "What brought you guys out to our neck of the woods?"

"Sightseeing," Anya reported. "Plus, we were really hoping we'd be able to meet those two adorable boys down there."

"You came all the way here just to meet the dogs?" I asked, incredulous. "And, for the record, Watson is a girl."

Anya dropped down to the ground and stroked Watson's fur. "Oh, that's no name for such a pretty girl, is it?"

Watson stared at her new admirer for a few moments before dropping to the ground and rolling over. Not to be outdone, Sherlock wedged himself up against Anya's leg and did the same.

"They don't like people at all, do they?" David joked. "But, to set your mind at ease, we've always wanted to explore this part of the United States. The fact that my wife's new obsession happens to live here is just icing on the cake. So, you're here to look into the thefts?"

I nodded. "What was stolen?"

Anya held up her smartphone. "My charging cable."

I looked at David for confirmation. "Okay. Umm ...?"

"I know it sounds trivial," Anya was saying, "and I'm really not going to make an issue of it. But, I left it right there, on the little table next to the bed."

"When did you see it last?" I inquired, as soon as I pulled out my notebook.

"This morning. After breakfast, David and I headed out to explore the town. When we came back, it was gone. The charging cube was still in the wall, but the cable was gone."

"We checked with housekeeping," David said, correctly guessing what I was thinking, "and they assure us they didn't take anything out of the room."

"Did you ask whether or not they saw the cord in here?" I asked, without looking up from my notebook. When I didn't immediately get an answer, I looked up. "It'd be nice to know *when* the cord vanished."

David turned to his wife. "I don't recall asking that question."

Anya nodded. "I did. They claim there were no cords draped across the table, like I left it."

"What time did you guys head out for the day?" I asked.

"Around eight in the morning," David recalled.

"And the cleaning lady tells me she was here around ten," Anya added.

"So, sometime in that two hour window, someone came in here to steal … a charging cable. Hmm."

David grinned. "Doesn't make sense, does it?"

"Those cables are, what, no more than ten bucks?" I scoffed.

"We each have spare cables," Anya pointed out. "That's why we didn't bother reporting it. It's just that, well …"

"… why in the world would someone break in here and take a simple cable?" I finished for her. I looked down at the dogs. "Is there anything you guys would like to look at?"

I swear I saw Sherlock shrug and nod. He gave himself

a solid shaking and immediately headed to the desk near Anya's side of the bed. He sniffed it a few times before turning to look at the window.

"What do you see, pal? Hmm, nope, it's just a window. Nothing spectacular. Wait. Are you suggesting whomever came in here did so *using* the window?"

"We thought of that, too," David confessed. "However, if you look at those windows, you'll see that yes, they swing out, but no, there's no way anyone could make it through."

I saw the small casement crank and looked questioningly at the room's occupants. "Do you mind?"

David waved a dismissive hand. "Please. Help yourself."

I rotated the crank and watched both sides of the window slowly swing out. It would seem Jillian had replaced the windows in the Roaring Twenties Suite, and seeing how she didn't want to obscure anyone's view, had opted for French Casement windows. The first thing I noticed about the windows is that there wasn't a screen on it.

"Where's the screen?" I asked, as I leaned out the window to inspect the ground. This was only the second floor, so the ground wasn't too far away. However, there also wasn't anything a burglar could climb onto in order to make it up here. No trellis, or drain pipes, or even any footholds could be seen on the building's exterior. "You'd need a ladder to get up here, and I would think it'd be blatantly obvious that he was up to no good."

"Especially during the day," Anya reminded me. "What about flying?"

I looked up. "Flying?"

Anya nodded. "That's right, flying. Or floating, which-ever you prefer."

I hesitated as I studied her face. Was she serious?

Thankfully, her husband broke out laughing, although to be honest, it did sound a little forced.

"Stop your teasing. You know it has nothing to do with the festival downstairs."

Anya looked at me and shrugged. "I will say we had the window open, seeing how the weather was beautiful today, and we wanted to let some fresh air in the room, but the windows weren't open by that much. Maybe ... six inches?"

I scribbled some notes. "That's helpful, thanks. Sherlock? Watson? Anything else in here you want to check out?"

Both dogs headed for the door.

"Apparently not," David laughed. He held out a hand. "Thank you for stopping by, Mr. Anderson. It saves us having to track you down so Anya could meet the dogs. *Min kära?* Is there anything else you'd like to say?"

Anya pulled out her cell phone. "Could I take some pictures?"

Ten minutes later, the dogs and I were back downstairs. Since I know there was no unauthorized access to either of the rooms upstairs, especially since Jillian had sprung for the state-of-the-art door entry systems that top-end hotels use, I decided to investigate the exterior of the house. It's the only way someone would have made it in. Even though Anya had said she only left a gap of around six inches, that would be more than enough room for someone to conceivably reach through the opening and spin the crank, thus opening the windows even wider. I just had to see for myself what it would take to make that possible.

"Oh, there's no way, guys," I moaned several minutes later, as Sherlock, Watson, and I stood outside on the lawn, gazing up at the western side of the house, where the suite overlooked the vast lawn. "If someone tried to put a ladder up against the house, then they'd be seen. I mean, look at this. You can totally see the street from here. Yes, there's a small window sill just outside of that window. Yes, the tiny ledge does connect the windows on that floor, but no, there's no way for someone to walk along that. Not unless they were Tom Thumb, that is. No, that's not the way they were getting in there. I just don't know what that leaves us."

Both dogs were sitting on the cool grass and panting.

"Any help here would be swell, guys."

I continued to be ignored. In fact, both dogs settled down and closed their eyes.

"Sherlock? Watson? Could I possibly tear you away from your refreshing nap and focus on the problem at hand? How is this person making it inside the rooms? Could there be a hidden room or secret door we missed?"

I can't even count how many rooms, doors, hallways, and hidden compartments had been found inside that house when it was fully remodeled. But, the idea was sound. Could there be something we missed?

Both dogs suddenly perked up. Sherlock jumped to his feet and strained at the leash, intent on checking out a small row of shrubs decorating the base of the house. Watson joined him moments later, and if I wasn't too far off the mark, I'd say both dogs were close to …

WOOF!

Yep, there it is. Was there something in the bushes? Right on cue, the nearest bush rustled. I looked at the corgis and saw both had their ears sticking straight up and trained on the shrubbery.

"What is it?" I whispered. "There must be something

there, 'cause I can hear it moving around."

"Awwoooo," Sherlock agreed, using one of his low, soft howls.

"Are you going to check it out?" I asked the dogs.

Neither one budged an inch.

"Oh, come on. There's something in there. Don't you want to, you know, spook it out of there? What's the phrase, flush it out?"

Neither corgi moved, nor did either make a sound.

"Thanks a lot, guys. Fine, I'll take a look. If something leaps out at me, then you and I both know you're gonna be in the doghouse, got it?"

I crept forward and placed one knee on the soft grass. With the leashes held tightly in one hand, and the other making certain I didn't execute a face plant onto the ground, I leaned as low as my shaky arm would allow, trying to peer under the thick row of bushes and shrubs.

"Uuuunnnnggghhh!!" a loud voice suddenly moaned.

I'm ashamed to say that I came *thiiiiiiiiis* close to wetting myself.

3

"Son of a biscuit-eater!" I bellowed out, throwing myself backward and executing a half-roll, to land on my back. "What the fracknoggin' …?"

"Such harsh language," a familiar voice teased, not bothering to hide the amusement in his voice. "Whatcha doin'?"

Vance Samuelson, senior detective at the local police department, and a good friend of mine, leaned over me and looked down.

"Dude," I started sputtering, "I'm gonna … I'm gonna …"

"… need a new change of underwear?" Vance teased, as he gave me a hand up. "I was driving by and saw you on the ground, so I thought I'd check to see what you were doing."

"Besides giving me a heart attack? I'm just doing a little hostbusting', that's all."

Vance regarded me for a few moments.

"Seriously?"

"It's the Day of the Dead," I explained. "And, wouldn't you know it, a few things have disappeared from the house. We were brought here to try and figure out what's going on."

Vance stepped around me to gaze at the front entrance of the house, which was nearly twenty feet away. He took a few more steps as he studied the contours of the house, then he turned back to me. Then, his eyes dropped to the dogs, who were both chomping at the bit to be allowed to say hello. Eyeing Vance, who nodded, I gave both dogs permission and watched as they raced each other to see who could get to him first. For the record, Watson won this round.

"Hi, guys!" Vance cheerfully greeted, as he squatted down to give each of the dogs a scratch behind the ear. "Look what I've got for you!"

Doggie biscuits were produced. Two corgis were suddenly behaving so angelically that I'm surprised halos hadn't appeared over their heads. Both dogs sat. Sherlock even raised a paw, as though he was expecting to be asked to *shake* in order to earn his treat.

"Enjoy, guys. So, you're checking out, what, some burglaries?"

"Yeah, people have reported several missing items."

"Izzat so? Anything I need to know about?"

"It's just piddly stuff. Someone lost a scarf, another a mitten. The couple in the room up there lost the charging cable for their phone."

"You're right. It doesn't sound like you need my help at all. All right, I'll leave you to it. Let me know if that changes."

"I will. Thanks, pal."

Once my detective friend was gone, I dropped to one knee next to the dogs.

"That's what you get for living in a small town like this. Friends can drop in at any time. However, I have one request: how about a little bit of a warning next time? If you see someone sneaking up on me, which means the person who feeds you, takes you for walks, and buys you goodies at the pet store, is about to get the bejesus scared outta him, then what about letting out a few warning woofs? Remember, you're on my side, not his."

Both dogs barked, in perfect unison.

"Okay, that's just a little creepy. I didn't expect an answer. And Watson, you rarely bark. Sherlock? Just … keep doing what you're doing. Come on, this mystery isn't going to solve itself. Guys, now's the time to work your magic. What are we dealing with here? Do we have a thief on the property, a ghost haunting the place, or is there something else at work here?"

In response, Sherlock promptly headed back for the

main entrance. Watson and I trailed behind.

"Well, I *did* ask for this," I said to my little girl, as we both followed Sherlock up the porch steps and into the foyer. "We were already here. What'd we miss?"

We approached the staircase and, assuming we were heading back upstairs, I was surprised to see Sherlock and Watson veer right. Then, they stopped at the first door on the right, which led to a room that was originally a den, but had since been turned into a mini-library. And, for the record, a complete set of my works was in there, along with a number of other titles, all for the enjoyment of Highland House's guests.

"What do you want in here?" I asked, as I pushed the door open.

This room, I knew, was hiding several secrets most guests would never know about. Yes, this was the new library, and yes, practically every wall was covered with books. However, I knew that the picture on the left, which happened to depict a small, thatched cottage with a young woman sitting at a loom, hid a secret passageway. Grinning, I gently slid my fingers along the bottom of the frame and felt the tiny, recessed button. One press would open a rather narrow corridor, which would lead directly to the area off the kitchen, known only as the servant quarters.

Moving to one of the bookcases, which looked no different than the others, I paused again. This one, I knew, was hiding one of the many compartments the previous owner had used to hide contraband.

Detecting movement, I watched both dogs sniff along the base of the walls, hesitating at the painting and again at the bookcase. Thirty seconds later, after making the rounds, Sherlock moved to the center of the room and fell silent. Watson joined him and, together, the two corgis became as still as statues.

"What are you doing?" I quietly asked them. "Knock it off, would you? You're creeping me out."

Neither dog budged, nor did they make a sound.

"Not funny, guys. Sherlock? Watson? Do something. Shake your collars, bat an eye, woof, anything, huh?"

Sherlock finally looked at me, then at his packmate, and then back at me. Moments later, he sank into a down position. When I started for him, he quickly rose to his feet and trotted to the large painting hiding the hidden passageway. As I stood there, watching the dogs watch me, I realized what they were doing: they had found something and wanted me to look. But ... in the center of the room?

"There's nothing here, guys," I announced, as I stepped into the middle of the room and slowly spun in place. "Everything is as it should be. There are no trapdoors here. It's the original hardwood floor, all right?"

Jillian had pulled out all the stops in restoring the floor to its previous glory. It had been stripped, repaired, sanded, filled, and stained. Yes, the floor was gorgeous, but that didn't mean it didn't have ...

Wait.

Let me interrupt myself and pose a question. Are you the type of person who is able to relax their eyes and let small details jump out at you? Something that doesn't match the others and therefore stands out? Well, I don't know why I did it, but that's exactly what I did, and much to my surprise, something *did* stand out. Plus, it was right smack in the middle of the room. I just had to move something out of the way first.

Eyeing my two dogs, I knelt down to inspect the floor.

A thin, gray area rug took up much of the room. Since I know the dogs weren't looking at the geometric patterns, I could only assume they wanted to see what was beneath it. It only took a few moments to roll the rug up and shove it against the opposite wall.

This particular floor was comprised of stripped, sanded, and refinished hardwood. At least, that's what I originally thought. Now that I was standing in the middle of the room, staring downward, I saw right away that the pattern of planks was off. Just like bricklayers when they're working, bricks won't ever sit directly over the stone below it. That would mean their grout lines would be straight up and down. Bricks are toggled, so that it increases the wall's durability. In this case, the wood was arranged in a similar pattern, but for some reason, it didn't apply to the center of the room.

Directly where I was standing was a section of the floor which didn't conform to the rest of the pattern. Oh, it was subtle, there was no doubt about it. To any outside observer, the change in pattern wouldn't be enough to stand out. But, as I stood in place, studying the wood planks, I could see that there was an area roughly six feet square where the lines were all different. Squatting on one knee, I saw that there was no symmetry in what I was starting to refer to—in my head—as the center box. Some pieces looked longer than others. Some were larger squares. Then, there was a smaller square, set in the direct middle, too. It was almost as if the carpenter was trying to create a mosaic out of leftover scrap pieces of wood, couldn't make it work, and just threw everything together.

"Well, well," I murmured, as I ran my finger along the grooves in the floor. "What have we here?"

My eyes were drawn to a small square piece of wood directly in the middle of the center box. There was something ... *off* about that piece. The surface felt coarse; rough. It was nothing like the rest of the floor, which was almost as smooth as glass. So, what was different with it?

A quick poke had my eyes opening wide. It *moved!* Well, it was more like a slight wiggle. I gently pushed the small square. Nothing happened. I tried moving it left, or right. Again, nothing happened. Then, noticing the tiny piece of floor was just marginally thicker than the rest of the wood pieces, I checked to see if I could pry it up.

My eyes widened with surprise as the square block of wood easily popped off. That's when I noticed it really wasn't wood, but a piece of tile made to resemble wood. Bemused, I stared at the empty square space on the floor. My eyes then took in the overall shape of the anomaly, and the empty square, and was immediately reminded of those childhood sliding puzzles, where the player had to arrange the numbered tiles in order. Poking a finger at the closest piece of wood that was of similar size, I gave it an experimental shove. It moved, too! It was a good thing I wasn't drinking anything, or else I'd have spewed it on the floor.

While similar to those sliding puzzles, I quickly discovered that what I had before me wasn't quite the same, although it was close. Once I managed to get a piece of the floor puzzle in the right position, then whatever was holding it let go, and I was able to lift the piece out of the way. Using this technique, it took me nearly twenty minutes to clear all the pieces out of the way. Once I did, I looked back at the dogs and gave them a mock salute.

It was a trap door!

4

"You two are something else. Check it out! How in the world did you know this was here? You know what? Scratch that. Let's see what's behind door number one, shall we?"

Lifting the heavy wooden door up, I propped it open with a thin, wooden pole found on the side of the opening. Once I was sure the door wouldn't come crashing back down on me, I activated the flashlight on my phone and took a long look at what lay before me.

It was a secret staircase!

This one wasn't one of those super-narrow, steeper-than-you-can-climb types that would require climbing gear just to make it down the stairs. Instead, what I saw were stone steps, descending into darkness. Eyeing my phone, I made the executive decision not to try the stairs until I had a source of light that was *much* stronger.

Lowering the trapdoor back into place, I took the dogs and headed toward the check-in counter. Lisa was there, talking with one of the two staff members handling the guests checking in. The manager caught sight of me and waved me over.

"Mr. Anderson! How are things … ? You found something, didn't you?"

I pointed at the dogs. "They did, I didn't. Hey, do you have a flashlight I could borrow?"

Lisa nodded, ducked below the counter, and came up with an 18V Lithium-Ion cordless, rechargeable LED light. According to the side, it was capable of spitting out 200 lumens of light. In comparison, my cell's flashlight will probably put out no more than 50.

"Will this work?" Lisa asked me.

I clicked it on and promptly blinded myself. "Yep, this'll do. Thank you. Hey, as long as I'm thinking about it, can you put an Out of Order sign on your library door? I'm going to have the trapdoor propped open, and I wouldn't want anyone falling in."

"Trapdoor?" Lisa incredulously asked. "You found another hidden door in the library? Ooo, I have to see it!" Highland House's manager followed me into the library and whistled once she saw the missing floor pieces and the outline of the door. "Geez, how long has *that* been there?"

"Years and years," I confirmed, as I pulled the door back open and made sure it was locked in place. Clicking on the flashlight, I looked back at Lisa. "You'll make sure no one else comes in here?"

"I'm on it. Good luck down there. I hope you find our missing stuff."

"I hope I can figure out why it was being taken in the first place," I countered.

The stairs were shallow enough that the corgis could take them themselves. With the light held high, we emerged into a room the size of one of the second-floor bedrooms and looked around. Were we completely underground? After all, there were only a dozen steps or so. I did notice one corner of the room was brighter than the others. There must have been a small window up there, hiding behind some type of tarp. Stacks of crates were everywhere, and judging by the amount of accumulated dust in the room, no one had been down here in decades.

Sherlock led me to the closest crate. Seeing how it wasn't sealed, I leaned over it and shone the light to see what it contained: bottles. Row after row of dusty bottles, with no labels, could be seen. Lifting one up for a closer inspection, I turned to Sherlock and held it out to him. Both dogs sniffed once, snorted at the same time, and lost interest. At least, Watson did. Sherlock, about to turn around, sniffed once, and returned to the crate. He reared up on his hind legs and whined.

"It's booze," I told the corgis. "I'm certain of it. All these crates are probably loaded with them. Quite frankly, I'm surprised. I thought for certain we had located all the hidden rooms during the renovation. I ... you're whining again. Why? Do you want to see inside? All right, just a moment. There, the crate is on the ground. What do you think?"

Sherlock jumped up, so that his front legs were resting on the rim of the crate. He lowered his head and nudged a bottle. Looking back at me, he whined again and nudged the very same bottle.

"Color me intrigued," I said to myself, pulling the bottle out. I held it up to the light and was surprised to see it didn't contain any type of liquid. Instead, I could see something inside. Something metallic. "I think we might have found another piece of Dame Hilda's missing jewelry. Sherlock? Check the other crates. See if there's anything else, would you?"

Just once, it would have been nice to see Sherlock doing what I wanted him to do. Then again, what was I expecting? For him to completely understand what I wanted him to do and say, *Sure, Dad, let me get right on that*. Did he? Nope. He did wander off, though, to slowly inspect the room. Seeing how there was only one way out of this subterranean room,

I felt it was safe enough to drop their leashes.

Sherlock immediately went to the far corner, where the faint light was trying to squeeze through a dirty towel hanging on the wall.

"There's probably a small window up there," I told the dogs, as I wrestled with the cork. "You can see from the size of that rag that there's no way a human could fit through it. Just let it go, okay?"

The cork came free and, with genuine flourish, I emptied the bottle into my hand. When I saw what I was holding, I almost dropped it on the floor. It was a gold diamond necklace. Holding the piece of jewelry up for a closer inspection, my eyes widened as I noticed the size of the stones. These weren't teeny-tiny filler stones. Each gemstone looked to be at least a half carat in size, and judging by the number of stones, I'd say the total carat weight to be somewhere in the vicinity of thirty or so.

I know I'm not a jeweler, and I have no business giving out an uneducated guesstimate on what this necklace must be worth, but as a married man, I've done my fair share of pricing out pieces of jewelry for Jillian. Tennis bracelets could easily run several thousand dollars. This, however, was a necklace, and I'm pretty sure a ballpark value for this thing was probably in the fifty-thousand range.

"We're just gonna tuck this bad boy away," I breathed, as I slid it into my pocket. Holy moly, I did *not* like carrying around something that valuable. But, I couldn't leave it down here, either.

"Woof!"

Looking over at Sherlock, I could see Watson had joined him and, together, they were staring up at the ratty towel.

"What's the deal, guys? Why are you so fascinated

with that thing? All right, fine. Look, I'll pull it down for you, okay? There. This disgusting piece of garbage can be thrown away. I ... will you look at that? My bad, guys. As usual, I should've been paying attention."

With the removal of the rag, the source of light was revealed. It *was* a window, and a small one at that. However, what caught my attention was that it was broken. And, the window may have not been cleaned in over fifty years, but I could still tell that it was above ground, probably behind one of the clumps of shrubs: I could barely see any daylight at all.

There were several stacks—of varying sizes—of crates next to the window. Sherlock moved to the closest and indicated I wasn't done with my inspection.

"Awwoooowoooowooo."

It wasn't loud, nor was the howl accusatory. Sherlock simply wanted to draw my attention. Well, he had it, but I didn't know what he wanted me to notice.

"Watson? Would you care to translate? There are more crates here. Should I start taking them down?"

Sherlock had the tenacity to turn in place and stare at Watson, as though they were having a silent argument. I can only imagine what was being said.

"How many times are we going to have to do this? How can we make it any easier?"

"He is human, after all. Don't be too hard on him."

"I've done what I can for the lumbering idiot. It's your turn now."

"Swell. In that case, let's try something a little more obvious, shall we?"

My little red and white girl actually lifted a paw and scratched at the base of the smallest stack of crates. Then I felt my heart stop and my breath lodge in my throat as the tower of crates rocked to the left, and then the right, and I knew if I didn't intervene, it was going to topple over. Holding the crates in place as the tremors stopped, I looked at Watson and wagged a finger.

"That really wasn't necessary, was it?"

Unbeknownst to me, an adjacent stack of crates was still quivering, and it was just enough to send the top crate crashing down at my feet. I have to admit, my jump was pretty impressive. I figured it was at least two feet high and at least that many feet backward. *And* ... I managed to stick the landing.

Neither dog flinched, which wasn't surprising, as Watson was the one who got the stacks moving in the first place. Clearly, though, the majority of those crates had to be empty, or else it wouldn't have been that easy to force them off balance.

Intent on using my foot as a broom to sweep the broken pieces of crate to the side, I noticed a flash of orange on the floor. Stooping, I picked up an orange mitten. Orange mitten? Didn't one of the guests say she was looking for an orange mitten? Holding the light out in front of me, I inspected the rest of the clutter that must have been inside the crate. Seeing a white USB cord in the dust, I picked it up to reveal it was the missing charging cable from the couple in the Roaring Twenties suite. I also found a handful of homemade pictures, complete with pieces of string still attached.

"We found the thief's hideout," I whispered to the dogs. "However, I have no idea how they're getting in here. There's no way out except the stairs. And that small window, I suppose. Unless you're only two inches tall, that isn't gonna work. Come on, let's gather everything up and get out of here. This place gives me the creeps."

Gathering up the mitten, cord, pictures, and a scarf that was probably Lisa's missing family heirloom, and a few other things that looked out of place, we hurried up the stairs and closed the trapdoor. Seeing the jumble of wooden floor pieces around the hidden door, I sighed, dropped what I was holding, and spent the next fifteen minutes putting the floor back together. Once it was, I gathered the stuff and—with the corgis leading the way— approached the front counter. Once the pilfered items had been dumped, I waited for Lisa to look my way. She did, and when she saw her grandmother's missing scarf, her eyes filled with tears.

"You found it! Oh, I'm so relieved! Thank you so much! I'm so confused. I wonder how it made it into that hidden room in the library. And you've found the rest of the stolen items! Oh, this is such good news!"

I pointed at the variety of items on the counter. "I think we've found everything. I spoke with several people upstairs. One was looking for this mitten, and another, that is, the couple in the suite, reported a missing charger cable."

Lisa held up the USB cable. "Who would want to steal this? This is, what, worth maybe five dollars?"

I shrugged. "Whoever did it has a secret method to get into that room, 'cause there's no way they used those stairs to do it."

"Woof."

The bark was soft, and as a result, I totally missed Sherlock's attempt to get my attention.

"There's a window down there," I continued, "and it's broken, so it's open, only it's somewhere behind the shrubs running around the base of this place."

Sherlock tried again. "Woof."

"There has to be some explanation," Lisa insisted.

"*WOOF!!*"

Both Lisa and I turned to look down at Sherlock. The feisty corgi wasn't looking at me, or Lisa, or even Watson. Instead, he was facing the foyer and was anxiously pulling on his leash, as though there was something—or someone—over there he had to greet.

"You're not going anywhere," I announced, as I wrapped the leash around my hand. "You are going to behave yourself."

Exasperated, Sherlock looked at Watson, and I swear she shrugged. Moments later, she, too, was pulling at her leash.

"Excuse me a moment, would you?" I said, offering Lisa a smile. "I'm not sure what's setting him off. We're going to go check it out."

Heading back to the foyer, with the front door visible directly in front of us, we came to a halt as Sherlock decreased his speed so much that he was moving in a very slow walk. Noting how I've seen him do this maneuver before, and it typically meant he was trying to sneak up on something, I gave him his slack and let him lead the way.

Stepping through the front doors, and about to head down the porch steps, our little group came to an immediate halt. There, in the middle of the stairs, was an orange and white tabby cat. Its leg was lifted high as he worked to, uh, clean himself up. The cat then noticed the three of us staring at him. If possible, the leg was lifted higher and the cat went back to work.

I looked at the cat, then at the dogs, and I finally

realized what I was looking at.

"Is everything all right, Mr. Anderson?" Lisa asked, as she arrived behind me.

I pointed at the cat. "We seem to have found a cat."

"Who, him? Oh, that's just Snipper. He's a friendly boy who has taken up residence in the house. I've told Jillian about him, and she assures me it's okay to let the cat stay here. He makes sure the mice population remains nonexistent, and the patrons love finding him in their rooms."

"In their rooms," I slowly repeated.

Lisa's eyes widened. "No. Are you telling me Snipper is our thief?"

I handed Sherlock and Watson's leashes to Lisa and sat down next to Snipper. The big cat eyed me a few moments before deciding I must be harmless. He started purring and rubbed himself against my leg. That's when I noticed tiny bits of broken twigs and leaves on his fur. *That* was what he had been cleaning off his coat.

"Snipper is using the window," I said, sporting a grin. "Mr. Klepto here has been taking stuff he finds and then heads outside, where he pushes his way through the shrubs and enters the underground room through the broken window. That's how the stuff is disappearing. Look at the mitten and your scarf. They have little bits of leaves and such on them, don't they? Don't you see? Snipper had been dragging them along the ground. I told you there was no such thing as ghosts."

Snipper chose that time to cease his cleaning session and return our frank stares. After deciding he was clean enough, the tabby cat rose to his feet and sauntered down the steps to the sidewalk. After giving the cat a decent enough head start, the dogs and I followed, intent on seeing whether or not Snipper wanted to return to his hidden lair. Sure enough, he turned left and, with us hot on his tail, disappeared into the shrubs. Sherlock and Watson sniffed at the southeastern corner of the house before turning to look at me.

"Zachary!"

The three of us turned to see Jillian walking toward us.

"How are things going? Any progress?"

I nodded and pointed at the shrubs. "Yep. We just followed the thief over here and have confirmed he's now hiding in his lair."

My wife was quiet for a few moments as she digested this bit of news.

"You found the thief, and you know where he's currently hiding?"

"Yep. He squeezed through a hole in a broken window and is currently noticing all of his stolen goodies have been confiscated."

"Shouldn't we be calling the police?"

"On a cat? Probably not. I'm pretty sure we'd be laughed at. Vance already laughs at me enough. I don't need to give him any more ammo."

"The thief is a cat? But … Snipper! You're telling me Snipper is our thief?"

I nodded. "That's exactly right."

"And that's where he's been hiding? In the basement?"

"Yes, but not the one you're thinking of. We found a secret staircase in the library, and it led down to yet another unexplored room."

"You found a secret set of stairs?" Jillian sputtered. "In the library? Heavens, how long have I been gone?"

"Not long," I grinned. "Oh, hey, that reminds me. You might want to put this in our safety deposit box at the bank. Sherlock found it, and I personally don't like carrying something like this around with me."

Jillian's eyes threatened to bulge out of her head when she saw what I had deposited onto her hand.

"Is this …? Are these diamonds?"

"They were found in a hidden room at Highland House. I can pretty much guarantee you they're genuine."

"Zachary, look how many stones there are! This must be worth a fortune!"

"Which is why it needs to be secured," I said, dropping my voice and pushing her hand, still clutching the necklace, down toward her purse.

"Where did you …? How did you …?"

I slipped my arm through hers and, together, we walked down the sidewalk, each holding a leash.

"I'll tell you all about it, over dinner. You know what? I think we should go to the Lonely Gringo. I'm in the mood for some Mexican food."

About the Author

Jeffrey M. Poole is a professional author living in Oregon with his wife, Giliane, and their Welsh corgi, Kinsey. He is the best-selling author of fantasy series Bakkian Chronicles, Tales of Lentari, and Dragons of Andela, in addition to the mystery series Corgi Case Files.

Jeffrey's interests include astronomy, archaeology, archery, scuba diving, collecting movies, and tinkering with any electronic gadget he can get his hands on. Fans can follow Jeffrey online at his blog.

Sign up for Jeffrey's newsletter to get all the latest corgi news—AuthorJMPoole.com

Books in the Corgi Case Files Series

Case of the One-Eyed Tiger
Case of the Fleet-Footed Mummy
Case of the Holiday Hijinks
Case of the Pilfered Pooches
Case of the Muffin Murders
Case of the Chatty Roadrunner
Case of the Highland House Haunting
Case of the Ostentatious Otters
Case of the Dysfunctional Daredevils
Case of the Abandoned Bones
Case of the Great Cranberry Caper
Case of the Shady Shamrock
Case of the Ragin' Cajun
Case of the Missing Marine
Case of the Stuttering Parrot
Case of the Rusty Sword

Praise for Jeffrey Poole and the Corgi Case Files:

"I can't wait for the next book. I love mysteries and animals, so these books are perfect reading for me. Sherlock is a small furry Jessica Fletcher." – H. Dudley, 5 stars online review

"A great introduction to the characters in the Corgi Case Files mystery series. Sherlock is brilliant!" J.D. – 5 stars on Amazon (on *Case of the One-Eyed Tiger*)

"The best thing--this guy loves the corgis, as I do, and he describes their behavior very well. Looking forward to future stories." – 5 stars, Amazon

"An intriguing story with a wonderful cast of characters. The plot was excellent and filled with twists and turns it kept my interest to the very end!" – 5 stars on Amazon

"I absolutely love this series. If you like a good story, great characters and seriously smart and lovable canines, you'll love this book. Start with the first book and work your way through the Corgi Case Files. They just keep getting better." – K. Underwood, 5 stars online review

The Birdless Thanksgiving Affair
An MG&M Detective Agency Short Story

By Rick Adelmann

~ ~ ~

November 30, 1922

I'm attempting to hide my excitement, but failing. This is the first time the entire west coast family has spent Thanksgiving together since we moved to Beverly Hills, California. I'm Major James Mallory. My wife Anneka and I took on the pleasure of hosting this year's celebration. Being members of MG&M Detective Agency can be quite time-consuming. We, along with our partner, Woodie Garth, never know when we'll be called out to solve a crime, search for missing persons, or spy on an unfaithful spouse. So, if I'm pleasantly excited about the holiday, so be it!

Our agency's calendar was clear for the holidays. Woodie had just arrived with his fiancée, Victoria Davis, sharply at six p.m. Miss Davis is a successful jeweler in San Ricardo. She had been a carefree flapper until meeting the handsome, charming Woodie Garth. Vicky now seems ready to put on the shackles of marriage with our partner. Anneka and I, as well as the rest of our close-knit family, are simply waiting for the wedding announcement. However, married or not, she will continue to be a vivacious, fun-loving woman.

Vicky is the perfect fit for Woodie. In his years in New York City, he was the quintessential 'Man About Town.' As my partner at the agency, as well as my friend, I could see his transformation into a one-woman man. Due to the influence of Anneka and me, more importantly, he met a woman he could trust with his heart.

They entered through the double doors of our palatial hacienda-style home above Beverly Hills. Vicky is always dressed to the nines for special occasions. Tonight, she wore a metallic lace dress. The torso went straight to the hip. The entire dress was covered in an elaborate floral motif.

My wife of four years, Anneka, greeted them as Fred led them to the front room. "Vicky!" Anneka giddily hugged her friend. "You look smashing, as usual." She took both of Vicky's hands. Her eyes scrolled down Vicky's outfit.

Anneka looked just as becoming. She wore a navy-blue velvet evening dress that hugged her lovely figure in all the right places. It had a plunging neckline with a long string of pearls which wrapped around her neck, falling discreetly over her bosom.

"Oh, this old thing?" Vicky glanced down at her dress. "I meant to throw it away last season, but it comes in handy for family gatherings." She waved her hand, dismissing Anneka's compliment.

"What are you talking about?" Woodie barked, hearing her comment. "I just bought the outfit for you last week."

"Woodie! You know nothing about socializing in polite company." Vicky shook her finger. "I'm trying to be coyishly unpretentious. Then you go and ruin it."

"Sorry, my dear," Garth mumbled, not sounding at all sorry. "Do you want a drink?"

Vicky laughed, shaking her raven-colored bob. "Of course. You know what I like."

Garth and I walked across the large family room to the small bar under the staircase. "Well, you know how to put your foot in it, don't you?" I asked.

"Why the heck do women dress in their finest clothes, then brush away compliments?" Garth shook his head.

"Don't ask me." I shrugged as I pointed out Fred, my life-long well of wisdom. The old guy was acting as a bartender at the moment. Clint Rogers, my rancher brother-in-law, was being served a frothy beer. "He's the guy to answer that question."

"Hey, fellas," Fred said, trying to sound like a British saloon keeper. "What will be your pleasure?"

After giving him our order, I told Garth to repeat his question. He did so with Clint listening in.

"Ha!" Clint slapped his knee, almost spilling his beer. "Y'all can tell you're a single man, Woodie."

"Why?" Garth frowned at him. "Do only married men understand women?"

"Hell, no," Fred interrupted. "We married men know better than to ask foolish questions like that. Ain't no man, married or single, can understand the ways of the feminine gender. So, just love them, pamper them, and let them think they deserve the pampering. You'll live a long, happy married life."

"So, that's the secret," Reed Bennett, my other brother-in-law and police captain with the San Ricardo PD said. "I thought it was good sex."

"Well, that too." Fred grinned. The five of us laughed, looking around for our better halves. They were all waiting for us on the cushions in the bay windows, which looked out on several large oleander plants and over the front lawn of our home.

"We better take the drinks over to the ladies." I nodded toward the women. All were smiling or laughing, dressed in an assortment of bright colors. The twins, Greta and Gerda, weren't sticklers for the latest styles, nor did they follow the expected trend of wearing identical wardrobes. Instead, they wore what pleased them and their husbands.

Anneka was looking in my direction. I smiled, holding up her glass of red wine. The others had grabbed the drinks and headed to their ladies. Above me, I heard the voice of our adopted daughter, sixteen-year-old Emma, standing on the steps. Her sandy hair was cut in a shingle bob. Her arms were crossed as she leaned over the railing. She frowned down at me. "You men sure don't know anything about women, Papa Jim. You're all lost." She gave up the frown and giggled. Then, flashing the smile I loved to see on her pretty face, she added, "Don't worry, I will not tell any of the ladies what you men said."

"You shouldn't be spying on us like that, Emma," I said softly, peering up at her. "You can get yourself in all kinds of trouble. What did I say that was wrong?"

She ignored me and bounded down the steps, circling around the bar to join me. "Can I have a sip of Anneka's wine?"

"You're too young," I growled. "Ask me again in a couple of years."

The growl didn't seem to scare her in the least. "Oh, come on. Just a sip. I never had wine before." She pouted at me. Her eyes were half-closed, her bottom lip out. "Please. It's Thanksgiving. I should be old enough for a sip."

I looked around. No one was watching. "Okay, just a sip." I handed the glass to her. Instead of a sip, she took a hearty gulp. "Ah, that hit the spot." She handed me the half-empty glass and skipped off laughing.

I'll have to have a long talk with Anneka about that girl, I thought as I refilled the glass. I joined the others, handing Anneka her drink.

"There's a spot of lipstick on my glass," she said, holding the glass up to the sunlight streaming through the front window.

"I'm gonna have to talk to Fred about cleaning them better."

"Did you let Emma have a sip of my wine?" Anneka put her fist to her hip, frowning at me.

Reed overheard us. "It sounds like Emma outsmarted you too, Major." He laughed. "Don't worry. She did the same to me the last time she visited Greta and me in Venice Beach."

"She got you to give her a sip of wine?" I asked.

"Naw. A chug of beer. She had half the mug down her before I grabbed it back. She does it for the fun of getting away with it. You know how young people are."

"Not really," I mumbled. "Gerda and Greta were all grown up when I met Anneka. Emma has only been with us for two years. So, I'm out in the cold regarding girls of that age."

"Still." Anneka placed her hand on my shoulder. "Maybe you'd better let me deal with her discipline from now on."

"Don't worry, Jim." Greta laughed. "She's just having a

bit of fun at your expense. She'll get over it when she starts to mature."

Fred's wife, Liz, a beloved mother figure to me, came in from the kitchen through the foyer. "Dinner is just about ready," she announced in her pixie-like voice. "Why don't you folks head to the dining room? You can find your places." She wiped her hands on her apron as she returned to the kitchen.

Our dining room was to the rear of the house. A knotty-pine rectangular table could easily seat twenty or more guests. The Western-style high-back chairs were pulled out for us.

Liz had gone out of her way by placing nameplates on the table at each chair. I found Anneka's and mine at the head of the table, facing the floor-to-ceiling windows overlooking the valley below the hills. During daylight hours, it gave us a magnificent view of the cities below us and the ocean many miles away. I helped Anneka into her seat. She looked lovely this evening. Her navy-blue evening dress perfectly accented her shoulder-length strawberry blonde hair.

To my left, Garth sat with Victoria. Reed and Greta found their seats next to Woodie and Vicky. On Anneka's right was our prankster, Emma, then Clint and Gerda sat with a highchair holding their six-month-old, Tyrus Rogers, between them. At the far end of the table sat Liz and Fred. However, only Liz was seated.

Greta and Gerda were identical twin sisters. They were ten years younger than their elder sister, Anneka. In my estimation, all three were gorgeous women.

"What happened to Fred, Liz?" I called out.

"I'm not sure." She looked around, seemingly puzzled.

"I hope he's bringing in the turkey. He should know I can't carry a twenty-four-pound bird all the way from the kitchen into here." She pursed her lips.

"Twenty-four pounds?" Clint called out. "We only have a few calves that size." He laughed as baby Ty started banging his utensils on his tray.

"Well, I knew you were coming over, so we searched all of California to find one of the biggest birds we could find," Liz grinned.

"That was smart of you, Aunt Liz." Gerda elbowed her husky husband. "You should see the way this guy eats at home. Kitchen sink and all." The rest of us at the table laughed uneasily. The table was set with the usual trimmings of a Thanksgiving dinner, except the turkey. Steam rose from the white, blue-trimmed platter of yams. Mashed potatoes were piled high. Creamed baby onions sat in front of me. A plate of asparagus sat close to Emma. I couldn't see what sat at the other end of the table, but there was a big empty spot in the center where the turkey would go.

"You even eat the iron pump handle, Clint?" Emma asked with a big grin.

"Sure do, but the handle gets caught in my teeth."

Emma started laughing. "Do all cowboys eat so much, Clint?"

"You bet, little lady. We've got a lot of hard work to do out on the ranch every day."

"Even Dale and Aaron?" Clint's younger brothers worked the ranch, but had different aspirations for the future. However, what proved to be most discomfiting was both had designs for Emma.

"No, Dale would rather have his nose stuck in law

books. Young Aaron would rather be reading and studying the Bible." Clint nodded to Emma. "I'm proud of both my brothers. We each have our calling."

"So, your brothers plan to move out after handing the ranch over to you?" Reed asked from across the table.

"Me, Ty, and any other young'uns coming along," Clint answered as Fred entered the dining room from the front hallway.

He stopped in the doorway, gazing around the room. "You all waitin' for me?"

Liz turned in her seat to face her husband. "We're waiting for you to bring in the monster turkey I cooked so you can carve it out here."

"Sorry, I didn't know you wanted me to bring it out." He rubbed his bald head. "Why couldn't Jim boy bring it in? He's strong enough." He glared at me as he walked toward the kitchen door.

"Never you mind about Jimmy. He's the master of the house, not a servant," Liz scolded. She stood and accompanied her husband to the kitchen. They left a room full of laughing guests.

A few minutes later, they were back in the dining room. Liz looked stunned. Her mouth gaped in surprise. "It's gone! Someone stole the twenty-four-pound turkey right out of my kitchen."

"What do you mean, it's gone?" I stood up and approached them.

"Just what she said, Jim boy." Fred pointed toward the kitchen. "Liz left it on the kitchen shelf, below the rear window."

"Like I always do. It was hot coming out of the stove, so I wanted it to cool before bringing it to the table." Poor

Liz was all flustered. She wrung her hands, and I heard a sob catch in her voice. "I've never had that happen before."

"Okay, Liz, relax. Let's go see what happened to our turkey." I waved to Woodie and Anneka to follow me into the kitchen. "This is a case for MG&M." I tried to be light-hearted about it. Nonetheless, I was starved. I was looking forward to the meal.

Emma followed us. "I want to see what happened. If there is a turkey thief in the neighborhood, I want to catch him."

We all grinned at her dedication to crime-solving. Then, entering the kitchen, Liz pointed out the wide shelf to the left of the stove, on which she'd left the bird. The open window faced the backyard, where the swimming pool and the pool house stood.

"It looks like some vagrant must have smelled the turkey as it cooled. He or she couldn't help themselves," Anneka surmised. "The poor creature must have been starving."

"That must be it," Emma chimed in happily. "We should let him keep it."

"For heaven's sake, child. It's our turkey." Tante Liz frowned. "It's stealing. We can't allow it."

"Besides, we've got family waiting in the dining room. Let's go to the backyard. We need to see how this happened." I led the way toward the door leading to the sunroom.

Fred stopped us. "I'll go back to the dining room. Someone should explain to our guests what's happening. Maybe they'll want to start without us."

"Sounds good, Fred." Garth glanced over to Fred's left. "Miss Liz, why don't you join him. If there is a vagrant out there," he nodded toward the backyard, "he may prove to be violent."

"Oh my!" Liz put her hand to her mouth, "I never thought of that."

Fred put his arm around her short frame, guiding her back into the house.

"If there's a thief," Anneka stopped us, "we should be armed. I'll go up to our room and find my .38 and your Colt, Jim."

Garth, Emma, and I went out to the rear of the hacienda. It was a chilly, overcast evening, but still light enough to see the entire yard. We went to the window where the turkey had been.

Three wooden chairs sat against the wall under the window together.

"I see how this could have happened," Garth said. "The chairs would have been high enough for someone to climb on them and reach the bird." He looked down to the ground around the window. "There are stone steps, and the ground around them is too hard to leave prints."

Anneka joined us. She handed me my Colt, which I tucked behind my belt. "I thought we may need a flashlight as well." She passed a large one to Garth. Anneka then looked around the scene of the crime. "He, or she, wasn't very strong," Anneka mentioned.

"Why do you say that?" I asked.

"Well, look. The person didn't lift the prize from the shelf, but dragged it." Anneka pointed at a line of grease and fatty skin on the windowsill leading to the wooden chairs.

"The thief must have been so hungry they couldn't lift the turkey," Emma laughed, looking at us.

Garth was farther away from the window and gazing down into the grass. "He must have been in poor shape. Look at this." He pointed down. "The grease marks from the bird's skin left a trail over the stepping stones."

We went over to where he stood. "Extraordinary!" I nodded. "There it goes, toward the pool house." All four of us ambled, our eyes on the ground, following the trail. "I hope this guy isn't armed," I muttered.

"Don't worry, Papa Jim. He is not armed."

We stopped. Our eyes glared down at Emma. Garth asked her, "How do you know he's not armed?"

She looked flustered. "I, I, just feel that way." Her eyes were wide as she watched our reaction. "A person who steals food probably wouldn't have a gun or something."

Garth, Anneka, and I remained silent but looked at each other. I raised my eyebrows. "Okay, let's continue." The line of fat led to the open door of the pool house, then inside. Finally, it ended at an opening in the tile floor.

We stepped into the small building. I went in first, then stepped aside for the others to join me. The back of the building contained four curtained changing rooms. The south wall held an ice box for refreshments. Four folding chairs leaned against the north wall. But what surprised me was the trap door in the center of the pale blue tile floor.

"What's this?" Woodie squinted as he gazed down into the blackness.

Both Anneka and I joined him. We looked down through the opening. The gap was about four feet square, and the first step of a staircase was showing. "I've never seen this before. Fred and Liz found the house for us. They never mentioned this secret staircase."

"No, they haven't," Anneka shook her head. "But it

looks like our intruder knows about it."

"Yes, the trail of turkey fat leads right to it," Woodie said as he peered into the darkness below. He looked at Anneka and me. "Do you want to go down?"

I was a bit apprehensive about what we might find. "I suppose we've got to. Hand me the flashlight, Woodie. I'll lead the way."

"I'll follow," Garth offered. "Anneka, it might be best for you to stay up here with Emma."

"Usually, I'd argue with you, but I'll stay in the pool house for Emma's sake." Anneka put her arm around our young lady's shoulder.

I turned on the flashlight as I slowly stepped down into the abyss, descending one step at a time. The steps were narrow, but the angle was wide. I counted each step, twelve in all. The flashlight beam gave little light in the complete darkness. When I reached the dirt floor, I felt Garth at my heels.

"Do you see anything, old man?" he whispered.

"Not a damned thing." I stood still, listening intently. There was a sound, a growl, not far ahead. "Do you hear that, Garth?"

"Faintly. Step aside, let me move ahead."

Garth stepped forward with the flashlight. I reached out and my hand touched a concrete wall. "I can feel the side of the swimming pool on our left, Woodie."

"Yes, I felt that as well. I'm going straight. The sound you heard is dead ahead. From what I can see, this tunnel weaves away from your home to the south."

I caught up to him in the narrow tunnel leading to the cliffs behind our property. "I have to agree." Then the low growl echoed again from beyond. I felt a shiver run up my spine. I stood perfectly still. "It sounds like an animal of some sort. Be careful. It may be a wild beast."

"I didn't bring my weapon, Jim," Garth whispered through the darkness. "Maybe you should lead."

"Not a bad idea." I was relieved that Garth was as nervous as I was about what might be down there.

"I'm right on your tail," Garth replied from behind me. "This is one hell of a way to spend Thanksgiving," he muttered.

"I know." My foot hit a rock that jutted off the cement wall. "I don't believe we'll be eating the turkey even if we retrieve it."

"Very astute of you, old man." Now Garth sounded like his sardonic old self again. He irked me when he got that way. "You always have words of wisdom, don't you, Major?"

"No need to be sarcastic," I snapped. Then, turning around, I flashed the light into his face. "Here, maybe the light will help you see more clearly!"

"Give me that, Major!" He grabbed for the flashlight.

I wasn't about to relinquish it so easily. "If you think you're man enough to take it from me, give it a try!" In the back of my mind, I knew I shouldn't have been acting that way, but— my childish alter-ego took over. I held on tight as he grabbed the head of the flashlight. We yanked and pulled at the flashlight like two little boys fighting over a toy. The beam of light flashed around the walls and floors. It made the tunnel look like a piece of abstract art. The experience brought on a sense of surreal images.

Garth was getting angrier by the second. He swore at me as he fumed, using words I'd never heard him use before. But he couldn't wrench the tool away from my solid grip. Well, not until I fell against the wall opposite the concrete wall. It was constructed flimsily of loose gravel. When I hit it with my bulky body, all the earth slid to the floor, taking me with it. My grip came loose as Garth yanked the flashlight from my hands. Unfortunately, he pulled it too hard. The flashlight flew out of our hands, hitting the concrete wall behind him. It made a horrible glass-breaking thud against the floor. We were now in total darkness.

"Now, see what you've done!" Garth bellowed.

"What I've done?"

"You tried to blind me, then childishly fought over the flashlight. Look at the results. You left us in total darkness."

I heard his voice but couldn't see where it was coming from. "Don't put the blame on me." I wasn't about to let him win this one. "If you weren't being such a sarcastic ass, I wouldn't have needed to defend myself. Thus, it's your fault we're lost in total darkness!"

"You're not lost," Anneka said, her voice miffed yet controlled. "I've got the candle holder from the pool house. I can lead you out."

"How did you know we needed help?" I uttered, looking away from the candle's light.

"That's a foolish question, Major. How could she not know with you roaring like a lion in heat."

"Me! Your foul language would have embarrassed the demons in hell—"

"Both of you, dummy up!" Anneka growled, the candle holder trembling in her hand. "Emma and I could hear the two of you echoing through the tunnel. You scared the poor girl. I don't know what the problem was, and I don't care. Grow up! Follow me!" she ordered, carefully turning so the candle would stay lit.

I looked at Woodie in the dim light. He turned to me with a flustered scowl. "I suppose she's right, Jim. Maybe we should go upstairs and eat crow for dinner."

I had to smile at his comment. Even though I felt as ashamed of my conduct as he seemed to feel. "Come on, let's have some stuffing—"

"I'm afraid the stuffing was still in the turkey." Garth stopped me. "Fred was going to extract it before bringing the bird to the table."

"Damn!" I always enjoyed Liz's special stuffing. She included raisins, diced apples, onions, and walnuts. "All right then. We'll have a vegetarian dinner."

We reached the secret staircase without conversing along the way. Anneka was unnaturally quiet as she led the way. I assumed she was still angry with us. Knowing the woman as I do, she'll stay miffed for a long time.

"Did you find it?" Emma's eyes were wide as she leaned over the opening. "What did you find?"

"No, we didn't find the turkey," I mumbled.

"I'm afraid there's a monster down there who ate it," Garth lied. "So, don't sneak out of the house and go down there, young lady."

I looked over at Garth. I saw a glimmer of light on his dirt-smeared face. I assumed it was his way of keeping Emma from getting adventurous.

"Monster?" She stood straight, placing her fists on her hips like Anneka does when she feels insulted. "I am sixteen, Uncle Woodie. Do you really think I'd fall for that fib? For heaven's sake. I'm not a child anymore."

Garth climbed out of the opening, stepping aside for me to come up. He looked at Emma, nodding. "I suppose you're not. You look all grown up."

"Thank you." She relaxed her stance, uncurling her fists. "So, what did you find?"

"Nothing, really. Just a dirty long tunnel." He looked at me for a second. "We didn't get to the end. I foolishly broke the flashlight."

"Is that what all the noise was about? It sounded like you were fighting with somebody." Emma looked from Garth to me. "I knew it was not a fight between the two of you. True friends, like you two are, do not get into such fights."

Garth and I sheepishly looked at each other.

"You're partially right, Emma." I glanced back at her. "Friends quarrel but apologize, then move on. Right, Woodie?" He nodded in agreement.

Before leaving the pool house, we closed the trap door and slid a heavy bench over the top. If there was a beast below, he couldn't escape through the pool house.

"Before we go back for dinner, I have some questions, old man." Garth stopped and turned to me. "How is it you didn't know about that tunnel, Major?" He walked out of the pool house, heading toward the main house.

"I really haven't spent a lot of time in there," I explained. "Whenever I go swimming, I dress and enter through the door leading to my basement gym."

"I can give you a better handle on that," Fred said when he met us near the house. "Anneka came running in asking about the staircase while you were down there. I got curious myself and then remembered." He waved a small folder at us. "We have paperwork on the swimming pool. The stairs and space below were added for the workmen. They needed an easy access to the pool's pipes. The trap door was cleverly built to blend into the flooring of the pool house."

Garth took the folder and looked at the diagram. "Seems simple enough. But it shows a rather small area below."

I looked over his shoulder and saw he was correct. "Yeah, we went further than this small area. Who added the tunnel leading south toward the rocky cliffs?"

"That, I can't tell you," Fred replied, snatching the folder from Garth's hands. "There's only been two other owners in the past eight years. One of them must have added on?"

"What about the growling creature in the tunnel?" Anneka called to us as we walked away.

"Later, dear. You can't hunt for a monster in a dark tunnel on an empty stomach. Right, Emma?"

"Right, Papa Jim." She smiled hesitantly, before grabbing my arm and pulling me to a stop. "I have a confession to make." Her eyes darted from Garth to me, then to the ground. "I sort of know what happened to the turkey."

"You do? Then kindly explain it to us." I looked down at the squeamish girl as she shuffled her feet.

"I'd rather show you. It would be easier to explain."

"All right," I nodded. "Let's get some light and go back." I was hungry for dinner but I hoped this wouldn't take long; I wanted this cleared up. It was fully dark now, so we collected two more flashlights from around the house before returning to the staircase.

The exploration team consisted of Garth, Emma, and

me. She appeared to be nervous about what was below. We stopped before entering the pool house. "Emma, what has you so jittery?"

She looked up at me, her big brown eyes moist. "I'm okey dokey, Papa Jim." Then her forced smile faded. "It is just that I don't want anyone hurt."

"Uncle Woodie and I will be fine." I grinned. "No one is gonna hurt us. Remember, I'm packing my Colt with me." I patted my weapon in its holster to my rear.

"Are you worried about the intruder down in the tunnel?" Garth held a frown on Emma.

A long pause ensued as Garth and I waited for an answer. Emma shifted her feet back and forth as she held her head down. "I know who took the turkey," she mumbled.

Garth and I let out a sigh. I'm not sure if it was a sigh of relief or of disappointment. I frowned down at her. "You kept this secret for all this time? Why? Who is it?"

"It is hard to explain, Papa Jim. You'll understand when I go down and find him."

"Him?" Garth's eyes widened. "You hid a boyfriend down in those nasty tunnels?"

Emma couldn't help but laugh. Even under the harsh circumstances, her sense of humor prevailed. "No! Uncle Woodie. I would not do that. Give me a flashlight; I will show you."

I reluctantly handed my light to her. "Are you sure you'll be safe down there?"

"I've been in the tunnel many times. I'll be fine." She grabbed the flashlight and turned it on. "Good, you gave me a working light. I'm glad you didn't break it like the last one you had." Her curls shook as she laughed. "You wait here. I'll be back in a few minutes."

When she said 'right back', I assumed maybe five minutes. However, twenty minutes went by. There was no Emma or the person who ate my turkey. By this time, the rest of the family had wandered out to the pool house. Still chewing on the stem of his pipe, Fred muttered, "What are you waiting on?"

"We're waiting for Emma to return from the tunnel." I paced in front of the door to the pool house. "She's been down there for over twenty minutes."

"You let our little girl go down there on her own?" Anneka glared at me. Her voice rose to a fever pitch.

"It was her idea."

"Before any of you begin to worry," Garth raised his hands in our defense, "Emma admitted she knew the culprit. So, I believed she'd be safe. But it's been a while. I'm beginning to worry."

"Well, then, we better check on her," Reed said. "Give me your flashlight. I'll go down."

"Yeah, I better go with him," Clint added. "There may be trouble. I don't know why you let her go alone, Jim."

We sure made a mess out of this whole affair, I thought. *Garth and I failed to find the damned turkey, we fought over a stupid flashlight, and now we've put young Emma in danger.* "All right, you two go down—"

"No need for that," Greta called from inside the pool house. She, Vicky, and Gerda, with baby Ty, were standing by the tunnel opening. Since the pool house was relatively small, everyone stood outside, peering through the window as Anneka and I went to the door.

Reed and Clint had returned, and Emma emerged behind them.

"Okay, Emma, where's the thief?" I blustered.

"Don't sound so gruff, Papa Jim. You'll scare him." Emma frowned at me.

"Well?" I tapped my foot.

A brown and black furry face slowly emerged from the secret staircase. His black nose twitched as he took in the new scents of the people around him. His big brown eyes with thick black eyebrows scanned the strangers. He blinked slowly and a terrified whimper escaped him.

Emma gazed down, speaking gently, "Come on, Rascal, no one is going to hurt you." She scratched behind his short, floppy ear, coaxing him up. Rascal emerged from the staircase, showing himself to be a puppy. He appeared no older than six months. The poor guy was shaking and leaning against Emma's leg.

"You mean to tell me our culprit is a damned dog?" Fred barked, which made Rascal jump. "I thought it was a raccoon, or a coyote, or maybe even a bear."

"Be nice, Uncle Fred. You scared him," Emma admonished.

"The poor thing is scared to death." Liz's eyes misted over.

I slowly walked into the pool house and crept up to the dog. From there, I could see how filthy he was. He had scratches on the side of his head with bite marks on his legs and neck. He was malnourished, despite devouring our turkey. So much so that I could see his rib cage. I reached out my hand, holding it to his muzzle. "There, there, boy," I whispered calmly. "No one's gonna hurt you." Rascal looked up at my face as he sniffed my fist. Then, after a few moments of analyzing my character through his nose, he stood straight, gave my fist a lick, then walked up to me, wagging his tail.

"He likes you, Papa Jim!" Emma laughed as she rubbed Rascal's head.

"Sure he does," Woodie said. "It takes a dog to know another dog."

I smiled. "Rascal has been through some rough times. Unfortunately, the wounds seem to have come from the fighting pit."

Garth looked over the dog's wounds. "You might be right. Some bastards put him in the pits to fight another poor animal." He turned to Emma. "Why didn't you come to Jim or Anneka sooner?"

Emma gazed at the floor. "I was afraid they wouldn't let me keep him. When I saw him in front of the house, he looked pitifully sad and miserable. A lot like what I must have looked like when I was brought here. I just couldn't take the chance of losing him." Emma remembered what happened two years ago when we freed her along with a large group of other girls from a brothel full of children. "I could see he was mistreated, just like I was."

"You should've known better," Greta admonished. "So, he's been living in that tunnel for how long?"

"It has been about two weeks. I have been feeding Rascal our leftovers, but he is still awfully *dunn*, or how you say, skinny."

"Don't worry, we'll fatten him up." Fred nodded his bald head, grinning. "But the turkey must have filled him for tonight."

"*Ja*, it did. He almost choked on a bone, eating it as fast as he did." Emma laughed. "We get to keep him, Papa Jim?"

I looked down into the eyes of the handsome beast. "I

guess so. We'll have to get him to a vet to check him out first thing Monday morning."

I thought about the duties of dog ownership. "Of course, he needs someone to pick it up when he messes in the backyard. He's a dog, after all." I laughed as we stepped inside. Emma didn't join in the laughter. Instead, she frowned.

I thought I saw Rascal smile as he looked up at me. That's if dogs can smile. "He likes you, Papa Jim." Emma stood beside me.

"It appears to me like Rascal picked a different master," Anneka nodded to me. "But he'll share the pup with you, Emma. Won't you, Jim?"

"Certainly. Emma is our official poopy scooper."

Gerda looked at me strangely. "Why did you say we would take him to the army for a check-up? Rascal needs a doctor."

"A veterinarian is an animal doctor, Gerda," Clint said. "Rascal ain't enlisting in the army."

"Where did you get the name Rascal?" Vicky asked as she took Woodie's arm.

"Oh, I gave him that name after he chewed through Tante Liz's clothesline pole on the side of the house."

Liz threw up her hands. "What? *Du dummer hund!*" Liz stomped off to see the damage as Fred followed her.

The rest of the family seemed to have forgotten all about eating as they stepped around the swimming pool, then walked through the sunroom door. I peered down at my side; there was the big puppy. He was trotting alongside me, acting as if he already belonged there.

After everyone had entered the sunroom, I stopped. Getting down on my haunches, I gave the pup a closer inspection. "First thing you need is a good bath, young man. You smell like a sewer."

"I tried doing that, Papa Jim. He's hard to handle." Emma was standing beside me.

"Oh, you startled me. I thought you had gone in. Well, I was hard to handle at that age too. We'll give Fred the dog bathing job later on," I responded, rubbing Rascal's head.

"There's something else I want to show you," Emma whispered and looked back toward the pool house.

"You mean in the tunnel?"

"*Ja*, something spooky. Even Rascal was afraid of it." Emma looked worried. I could see that she was serious about her findings.

"Okay, lead the way," I stood and noticed Garth had come back outside. "You coming?"

"No. I want to see who owned this place before you," Woodie said. "It should show the seller's name in the escrow papers. Then, maybe we can find out why the extra tunnels were dug."

"Good idea."

"Before I do that," Garth said, gazing down at Emma, "How did you know about the trapdoor to the secret staircase?"

"Oh, that was simple. I was giving Rascal a bowl of water next to the bench in the middle of the room. I got clumsy and spilled it. I saw the water run across the floor and trickle down the opening in the floor."

"Ah, you're quite observant." Woodie was impressed. "So, you moved the bench and, Abracadabra, there it was!"

"No, the secret door was there. I don't know what an abracad—I —is!"

"Sorry, that's a magic word, like poof! The door was

there," Garth explained.

"In that case, *ja*. I thought it would be a good place to hide Rascal."

"Okay, that makes sense." I lit a cigar as I listened to her explanation. Then I nodded toward Garth. "Fred's got the house papers. Go wake him up and see what you can find." I then looked at Emma. "Take our new friend and find him someplace to sleep."

"How do you know Uncle Fred is asleep?" Emma gave me a queer look.

"I know the old guy. He'll fall asleep any place at any time. So, I assume he needs waking up." I laughed as I gave Emma's shoulder a squeeze.

All three scurried off, leaving me alone in the sunroom. I realized that Anneka would frown on my smoking in the house, so I stepped out into the chilly night air. It gave me time to think about my family around me. The day wasn't a traditional Thanksgiving without a big gobbler to eat. But I could hear the laughter and talking coming from the front of the house and felt the camaraderie of my family. That was music to my ears. In Cleveland, I was always invited to my brother's place for the holidays. However, I felt as if it was an obligation, not a heartfelt invitation. So, my Thanksgiving dinners were usually held at my cold, stone mansion attended by Fred, Liz, and me.

"Are you ready to go exploring, Papa Jim?"

I jumped at the suddenness of not being alone and took a deep, unwelcome inhale of cigar smoke. Coughing the fumes out, I saw Emma standing beside me. "Why'd you scare me like that, little girl?" She'd changed into a wool sweater over a pair of trousers.

"Sorry. I thought you heard me coming up. I brought

a couple of flashlights." She stepped around to face me. Then, reaching forward, Emma forced a light into my hand. "Let's go."

"Just because I was thinking about the tunnels doesn't mean I want to go in there. Especially in the middle of the night."

"What is the difference if it's day or night up here." Emma shrugged. Her round brown eyes caught the moonlight just right. "It's always dark down in the tunnel."

She had a point. "True." I did want to see what other mysteries the tunnel held. "Were there any books or papers in there the other times you went down?" I asked Emma as we headed for the pool house.

"No, nothing to tell me why the extensions were dug there. It's a real mystery, is it not, Papa Jim?"

"I suppose so. I didn't get to see anything the first time I went down."

"It's really kinda boring when you first go in," Emma said, opening the door to the pool house. "But some turns in the tunnel take you to strange places."

We moved the bench out of the way and stood next to the trap door. I glared down at Emma. "What do you mean, strange places?"

"It's hard to explain. You'll see. Follow me." Emma lifted the trap door, letting it fall hard on the tile floor. Taking her flashlight, she descended the secret staircase quickly. Seemingly, she didn't have a care about what lay below.

I flipped on my light as I followed her. We walked along the tunnel, and this time I took the time to scroll my light along the walls and floor. However, most were bare. On one side was the concrete wall. Now I could see the pipes and handles leading to the pool. On the opposite side, the wall was dirty and slimy gravel. The bed of the floor was flat with a few stones for me to trip on. Emma had hurried ahead while I was gawking.

"Wait up, Emma," I called.

"Oh, I forgot, you haven't been here many times. I've been in the tunnels at least once daily, taking care of Rascal." She turned toward the unexplored area ahead of us. "Here's a cut to the left just ahead. You'll hear what is strange."

Outside the beam of our lights was black as pitch. Emma scampered along. Since I trusted her to know her way, I moved just as fast. I saw her turn down an arm of the tunnel to our left. I followed, but within a few steps, I bumped into her. She was standing in the tunnel with her flashlight off, standing still.

"What are you—"

"Shhh," she whispered. Because we were now engulfed in total darkness, I presumed she had her finger to her lips.

"Poor Rascal had to be in these dark tunnels by himself," I whispered.

"I left a flashlight on for him when I left. Now, shhh. Listen."

I stood perfectly still, barely breathing. I heard nothing. After a few moments of silence, my ears began to pick up on something. It rose in volume. Finally, I made out what the sound was: a woman crying, an eerie guttural cry. It was low, as if she was at the end of the tunnel. However, it slowly got louder. It was as if the woman in tears was walking toward us. The poor woman was sobbing pitifully now. I heard the sound of complete despair coming from her inner being. It wasn't just a cry, but more profound; a horrible, pitiful sound I'd never heard before.

The wailing came closer. The cry seemed to emanate from the walls themselves, all around us. "Emma!" I cried. "We've got to help this poor woman." I turned my flashlight on, aiming it straight ahead, down the tunnel. The sound stopped immediately. "Where'd she go?" I ran down the tunnel ahead of Emma. But it only went about twenty feet further when the tunnel ended at a rock wall.

Emma ran up behind me, grabbing my jacket sleeve. "There is no woman, Papa Jim. I've heard it before, just like you did. When I came down this branch of the tunnel, I found no one. She's not alone down here. I have heard other voices."

"Let's get out of here." I wasn't about to spend another minute down there. We scurried back through the tunnel maze and up the secret staircase, my legs shaking as I climbed. I grabbed the hatch, slamming it shut. We reached for the bench that had covered it before and slid it back into place. "I don't want you going down there anymore, Emma."

"Do not worry. The only reason I went down there now was that you wouldn't believe me unless you heard it yourself."

"You're right about that, little girl. I'll get a lock tomorrow. Let's not tell anyone about this. It'll spook them."

"What do you mean, spook them?"

"Scare the hell out of them," I clarified.

"*Ja.* I don't want to do that." We exited the pool house, walking toward the hacienda. Then Emma looked up at me.

As we walked in the door, Emma turned to me. "I

don't want Rascal to be lonely anymore, Papa Jim. Can he sleep in my room?"

"Sure. Just remember what we said about you caring for him and cleaning up after him."

We found that the clan had moved into the sunroom.

"You folks are not in the dining room. What happened? Another thief?" I looked around and saw everyone sitting leisurely. Fred had his feet up on the ottoman, smoking his pipe. Clint bounced baby Ty on his knee, with Gerda smiling gleefully at them. Reed and Greta were snuggled together admiring her sister's family.

Garth came barging out of the dining room, followed by Vicky. "I've got the answers for you," he announced. "I'll tell you about it over dinner."

"We're still going to eat?" Liz asked. "In that case, I better warm everything up." She hurried into the dining room and grabbed a couple of platters. "Fred! Get up and help me!"

The old guy tapped the ashes from his pipe. He grunted and groaned as he left the lounge chair and did as he was told to do.

"Where's Anneka?" I called out to whoever knew the answer.

"She's in the kitchen looking for a piece of meat to replace the turkey," Fred replied as he pushed his back against the kitchen door.

I scurried over and held the door for him, then entered. Greta was helping Liz get the yams, broccoli, onions, carrots, mashed potatoes, and gravy into pans. Anneka was bent over, her head in the icebox, rummaging through the items. I couldn't help myself; I stepped behind her and grabbed her hips.

Anneka squealed as her head went up and hit a shelf inside the icebox. She rubbed her head and, without looking around, said, "Fred! Not here in your own kitchen!"

I knew immediately she was kidding. But I had to play it. "Oh, so Fred's been playing hanky-panky, huh?"

She pulled out of the icebox, turned to me, and laughed. "There's nothing here to replace the turkey."

"Never mind that." I sighed, giving her a hug. "We can do without. Liz has made enough of everything else for an Army."

It was after nine that night before everything was prepared again. After we were seated at the table, I noticed that no one seemed to miss the turkey. Our plates were piled high with everything else. But, most importantly, we were enjoying ourselves. Conversation between our guests was amusing. The main topic of discussion was little Tyrus Rogers. We all called him Ty. Tyrus sounded too Grecian. But he was named after his great-grandfather on Clint's mother's side.

Ty was a good-sized baby, coming into the world at nine and a half pounds. And he hasn't stopped growing since. He's gonna be a big guy when he's all grown up.

Then, talk of our turkey snatcher brought on peals of laughter from all. Emma was indeed relieved that no one held it against either of them for losing the bird.

One more topic needed to be addressed this evening. "Woodie, what did you find out about the previous house owners?" I asked him.

"Good you brought it up, old man." Garth wiped his mouth with his napkin and cleared his throat. He glanced around the table at everyone. "You all might want to listen in. These findings are quite interesting."

The table got quiet, everyone anxiously waiting to hear the tale. From Fred and Liz across the table, to Clint and Gerda with their sleeping baby, to the opposite side of the table where Reed and Greta sat. Emma, our youngest, sat next to Anneka eagerly anticipating what Garth had learned.

Once Woodie got their attention, he started. "Has anyone here ever heard the name Mildred Von Kamp?" He looked at Reed. "You should have heard it, Detective Reed."

"Indeed, I have." He nodded vigorously. "That was about four years ago. She was a rich widow woman who went missing." He glared at Garth and asked, "Don't tell me it was from this house?"

"You got it, Reed. The house was built in 1914 by a movie producer. However, he never moved into it. The following year, he added the swimming pool and sold it to the wealthy Von Kamp couple." Garth held his hands in front of his chin and continued. "It was all in the deed of sale that Fred had tucked away. The two lived in seclusion here at the hacienda until 1918, when Peter Von Kamp died from natural causes. Soon after, she went missing and has never been heard from again."

"WOW!" Emma said. "So, Mildred Von Kamp is the weeping woman in the long tunnel."

"What weeping woman?" Greta said, frowning at Emma.

"Oh, I am sorry. You haven't heard her yet." Emma grinned.

"For heaven's sake," Anneka said. "Don't tell me we bought a haunted house!"

"Not house, dear. Haunted tunnel," I corrected her. "I

have heard the woman weeping as well. So, it's not Emma's imagination. Garth, did the deed say anything about who dug the lengthy tunnel?"

"No, just the staircase and short tunnel used to repair the swimming pool."

"It sounds like the extra tunnel was added to hide poor Mildred's body," Fred said.

"That stands to reason," Reed nodded to the bald man. "It looks like I might have to investigate and reopen this cold case."

"Not tonight, dear," Greta said, holding his arm. "It's not something one wishes to do on Thanksgiving."

"I agree," Vicky added. "But, before you policemen can start digging up the property, I want to go down there and have a word with Mrs. Von Kamp."

"Me too!" Gerda called out, almost waking the baby. "I've never spoken to a dead person before."

"Maybe later, after the investigation. If it turns out to be a crime scene, no one will be allowed there." Reed pointed his fork at his sister-in-law.

When we finished our Thanksgiving dinner, we went our separate ways. Reed and Greta Bennett went home to Venice Beach, where they had a cottage on the canal. Clint and Gerda, with baby Ty, headed east to their ranch in Chino. Fred and Liz were dead tired after their long day. The elderly couple went directly to their apartment here at the hacienda. Garth and Vicky were the last to leave—Woodie to his bungalow on the Santa Monica beach, and Vicky to her Victorian mansion farther north in Santa Monica.

Anneka was also bushed. So, she bade me good night as I stood on the back patio smoking a cigar. The puppy was no longer a threat. Emma convinced him to spend the night in her room.

The air was chilly; however, it felt invigorating. The night brought to life thoughts of my family. It had only been a few years since we came to California. But, in that short time, my immediate family has grown and has shown signs of growing more prominent. There's no telling where this loving group of people will be in the following years.

That's how our Thanksgiving went in 1922. I hope they remain as unexpected and fun as the years move on. I've never been one for traditional anything in my life. *Surprise me, Lord!* Each year I'd like to experience something different. The only constant I want is the love and companionship of my family around me. I believe that's what Thanksgiving is all about.

~ ~ ~

Books in the MG&M Detective Agency Series:

The Greek Coins Affair
The Hilltop Ranch Affair
The Blue Sky Affair
The San Carlos Affair
The Forgotten Murder Affair
The Irish Manor House Affair
The Amazing Esmeralda Affair
The Hanged Man Affair
The Missing Heiress Affair

About the Author

Rick Adelmann has always been a writer, starting at the age of twelve. He kept writing as he worked for a BA degree in history, taught school, acted in a couple of movies, repossessed cars, sold real estate, worked in security, and manned the cord boards at the phone company. And somewhere in there he spent a couple of years with the Cleveland PD, enlisted in the Air Force, worked at a Medina, Ohio radio station, then headed out to California to make his fortune.

All this experience gave him a zillion ideas for plots and characters. When not writing, he spends time with his lovely wife Gayle, greets people at his church, putters in his garden, watches baseball, and plays with his dachshund, Cookie. Visit his website at rickadelmann.com

Get a FREE MG&M short story. Visit Rick's website to find out how!

Connect with Rick on social media!

Visit Rick's website: rickadelmann.com
Facebook: facebook.com/rick.adelmann.752
Twitter: twitter.com/RickAwriter
Pinterest: pinterest.com/rickcnbike/
Instagram: instagram.com/ricksmysteries/

Hanukkah Sweets
A Samantha Sweet Holiday Short Story

By Connie Shelton

~ ~ ~

1

Samantha Sweet twisted the neck on the pastry bag and aimed the nozzle into the center of the puffy donut in her left hand. Red jelly filled the pastry's center, and she set it back on the cooling rack and picked up the next one, just as the back door at Sweet's Sweets opened to admit a puff of chilly air along with her friend Zoë Chartrain.

"Okay, everyone," Zoë said, holding out a covered plate. "Time for your opinions on my latkes. This is my fourth batch and Darryl says he's full up to here with fried potato. Hopefully I've got the recipe right this time."

Sam filled two more of the *sufganiyot*, set aside her pastry bag, and watched as Zoë removed the insulated cover and took out two small dishes of condiments.

"These are the toppings. Sour cream and chive here. And spiced applesauce here."

Julio, Sam's master baker, produced a couple of small spoons and four little plates. In a matter of seconds, he'd helped himself to two of the potato pancakes and a dab of each topping. Becky Harper, the bakery's decorator, called out to Jen in the front sales room and followed Julio's lead with the treats Zoë had brought.

"Well, I'm no expert on Jewish cooking," Becky said, "but these are wonderful."

Julio merely rolled his eyes, smiled, and took another.

"I agree," Sam told her friend. "I do think you've nailed it." She wiped her hands on a towel and held out the cooling rack of pastries she'd just finished. "These need a little dusting of powdered sugar, but what do you think?"

Three of the jelly-filled donuts disappeared in no time, with moans of pleasure all around.

"I'll do a chocolate-hazelnut version too," Sam told Zoë. "Was there any other filling the guests specifically requested?"

Zoë shook her head. "They'll be here for eight days. I'm sure we'll get more ideas while they're here. I hope I get the details right. I've had Jewish guests before, of course, but never for the holidays and never for eight days straight."

"It's a big family, right? There will probably be a variety of opinions and tastes."

"Four adults and three kids. The rooms were booked by Lazarus Nieman, and I get the impression the others are extended family." Zoë counted on her fingers. "A cousin of his, her married son and wife, and their kids. I'm sure once we meet, I'll be able to keep them all straight in my mind a little better."

Jennifer Baca had joined the group and was licking jelly off her fingers. "I think it's cool that they wanted to celebrate Hanukkah here together in Taos."

"My kids think we should become Jewish because they get presents for eight days instead of just one. I told them they'll most likely get eight gifts on Christmas Day, so they shouldn't sweat it. As long as all the grandparents and aunties come through, I think I'll be fine on that promise." Becky set her plate aside and washed her hands, heading back to the other end of the worktable where she had a wedding cake half decorated.

"I think the latkes are definitely a winner," Sam told Zoë. "And I've got rugelach and babka on my baking list for tomorrow, along with the filled donuts. What's on the guests' agenda for tonight?"

"They arrive around three this afternoon. We'll do a little welcome tray of snacks and offer some hot beverages. And I always have a big pot of chile on the stove for anyone who wants it. Lots of guests prefer to eat out and sample the restaurants, but this group will be tired from traveling, I'm guessing. They flew into Albuquerque from New York, which is never a direct flight, and then they've got the drive up here. At least the roads are decent."

The most recent snowfall had happened two days ago, so now there were clear roads and good powder on the ski runs. Sam promised to get the breakfast bakery items, which Julio would start on well before dawn, and deliver them to Zoë's B&B. Everything would be just perfect.

2

Sam carried three boxes of baked goods from her van as she approached Zoë's back door the next morning.

"I've got two more. Hopefully enough for today and

tomorrow," she said, handing off the first load to her friend. Three minutes later, she stomped the snow off her boots and stepped into the enclosed porch, just in time for Zoë to meet her again.

"Come on in. I'd like you to meet our guests and introduce them to Taos's finest baker. Your donuts were a huge hit last night."

They carried the boxes into Zoë's kitchen, where several serving plates were set out. Oatmeal and all the choices of toppings sat on the kitchen island, along with two pitchers of fresh juice and stacks of plates and bowls. A woman in her mid-sixties sat on one of the bar stools, but she jumped down when she saw Sam and Zoë with their arms loaded.

"Let me help," she said, reaching for the boxes Zoë held.

"No need, Elaine. You're a guest. Just relax a couple more minutes and we'll have everything set up in a jiff."

"Well, I didn't mean to imply …"

"Elaine, I want you to meet Samantha Sweet, my dearest friend, and owner of the most successful bakery in Taos."

Sam pulled off her mittens and extended her hand. "Nice to meet you. I understand your whole family has come up for the week?"

Elaine tilted her head, left and then right. "My son and his wife and kids. He's in a very prestigious position with the Metropolitan Museum in New York. That's where we're from."

As if the accent didn't give it away. Sam smiled and looked around.

"Oh, they're getting a late start," Elaine said. "Especially the kids. I tell you, kids today don't know what a full day's work is." Sam noticed that the woman was already dressed in a pair of warm navy blue slacks and matching sweater, her short graying hair neatly styled, and her makeup in place, even though it was barely past seven a.m.

"And don't forget your Uncle Laz," came a voice from the doorway to the dining room. "How's my favorite niece?"

The man who walked into the kitchen was slim and sprightly, white-haired, with a bristle of a mustache. He wore tan slacks and a plaid shirt buttoned clear to the throat. He walked over to the barstools, where Elaine had again taken her seat, and snaked an arm around her shoulders to give a squeeze.

Zoë paused in the middle of setting jelly donuts on one plate and Sam's freshly made bagels on another. She said good morning and introduced Sam.

Laz gave her a wink and turned his attention to the food. "Nice looking babka," he said to Sam, who'd removed her coat, washed her hands, and began slicing the fruit-and-nut-filled bread onto another platter. Did she imagine the old man's flirtatious tone?

She kept a straight face. "Thanks. I hope everyone enjoys the treats."

"Lazarus is the one who is treating the whole family to this week's vacation," Zoë told her.

"Laz, please. Just Laz," he added.

"Well, Laz, that's a very thoughtful gift. You must all be very close."

A sputter came from Elaine, but the woman had left her seat and picked up a napkin, ready to sample a slice of the babka. She now gave her full attention to the pastry.

Laz set one of the jelly donuts on a plate and took a seat at the counter, but whatever he was about to say was interrupted by a forty-something couple who came through the doorway, all smiles. She'd combed her freshly washed hair back from her face to let it air dry. He smelled of soap and an expensive cologne, and they both had that satisfied look that could mean there'd been early morning sex. Sam smiled to herself.

"Joe and Nina, this is Sam," Zoë said, holding up the coffee carafe.

"My handsome son," Elaine said, beaming toward Joe. "And where are the children?"

Nina spoke up as she picked up a mug and held it toward the coffee source. "The boys are sprawled out in their beds, snoring away, and will probably stay that way for a while yet. It's why I suggested we keep breakfast informal and let everyone help themselves. You really don't want a couple of teens who've had their sleep disturbed."

"It's the altitude," Zoë suggested. "People usually sleep like hibernating bears when they first get here."

Elaine sniffed a little and looked toward the dining room doorway. "Well, not our little sweetheart, I see." She held her arms open wide toward the dark-haired elfin kid who blushed when she realized all the adults were staring in her direction.

"Leah, come in and say hello. You know everyone here except Ms. Sweet, who baked us all these wonderful goodies."

The girl smiled up at Sam but didn't say a word.

"Have some oatmeal first, then you may have a *sufganiyot*," Nina said to her daughter.

"So, what activities have you planned for the week?"

Sam asked.

"Skiing!" Joe and Nina both said it at once, laughing.

"We've been to Vermont a few times, and the boys really love it. David is a total hot-dog on the slopes," Joe said. "Of course, Nina and I aren't quite so daring but we've talked for years about how we'd love to ski in the Rockies, so this is a real treat."

"Leah's newer at it, but we hear there's a great ski school here, so we've signed her up to work with an instructor for the first day or so." Nina stirred cream into her coffee and took a tentative sip.

"It's a piñon blend," Zoë told her when Nina made an appreciative noise.

"Mom and Laz want to see the sights," Joe said. "I suppose you can recommend some places? Museums and galleries would be to Mom's taste."

Elaine reached out and squeezed her son's hand. "Don't you worry about me. I visited the brochure rack at the visitor's center when everyone else went to the restroom yesterday. I've got a big stack of activities all planned." She turned to Sam. "It's our first trip out West, and I can't believe all these buildings made out of nothing but mud!"

Adobe construction was a little more complicated than that, but Sam didn't go into it.

"I notice you all arrived in one vehicle," Zoë said, "but there's a little shuttle that makes the rounds in town and I can show you where they pick up riders. Darryl doesn't keep any particular schedule, but he'd be happy to drop you off anywhere that's on his way."

"Where is your tall, handsome husband this morning?" Elaine asked.

"At the jobsite. Construction can get tricky around

here in the winter months, but he's got a remodel project that's all indoor work. I think today he was meeting the electrician's crew to get them started on wiring the owner's garage for an electric-car charging station."

Sam noticed Laz had filled a bowl with oatmeal and berries and carried it to the huge round breakfast table near the windows. He'd been steadily spooning it in and now the scraping of his spoon indicated he was finished. Zoë still had her hands full with coffee refills, so Sam walked over and offered to take the older man's empty bowl and see if he needed anything else.

He grunted permission to clear his place, then pushed his chair back and walked out of the room without a word. Funny man.

She carried the bowl to the sink and ran some hot water into it, then surveyed the kitchen. Everything seemed under Zoë's able control.

"Listen, I need to get back to the bakery," she said. "The holidays are fairly crazy for us. It was nice meeting all of you, and enjoy your day."

Zoë walked with Sam to the service porch, where she shrugged into her heavy coat. "Tonight's going to be the big dinner. You and Beau should come, if you guys don't have other plans—I know it's short notice."

"You're sure they don't mind? I'd assumed it would just be their family."

"Joe and Nina insisted. Last night, when I told them about you, they came up with the idea."

"Sounds like fun. What can I bring?"

"Nothing at all. Elaine has already offered to go with me to choose the brisket, and she's been through my spice rack to be sure I have the seasonings she likes to use. All of my practice making latkes may have been a waste. I get the feeling she'll be directing the whole show."

Sam chuckled. Having an overseer would drive her nuts, but she knew Zoë was one of those cooks who didn't mind having help in the kitchen. At any rate, it would be an interesting evening.

3

They arrived at six and Sam spotted another car in the parking area out front, one she knew. While Beau walked around the front of his truck to open her door, she picked up the Sweet's Sweets box. Earlier in the day she couldn't resist making sugar cookies in the shapes of snowflakes and dreidels, frosting and decorating them in blue and white.

The kitchen was warm and filled with women when they walked in. Zoë was pulling something from the oven and Elaine stood at the large six-burner stove, tending a pan of latkes. Sam spotted her daughter and granddaughter.

"Grammy!" Ana rushed over and threw her arms around Sam's legs before she'd even removed her coat. They went through their usual hug routine before Ana rushed back to Leah, who'd apparently become her new, instant best friend.

"Okay, kids out of the kitchen," Kelly said with a laugh, shuffling the two little girls toward the door.

"I'll take them," Beau said. "This is clearly not my domain."

"The guys are in the living room, or maybe the parlor," Zoë said over her shoulder.

A new face appeared at the dining room door as Beau and the kids walked out. Sam greeted Emily Plankhurst, the town's new librarian.

"I know. I'm standing in for Scott as Kelly's date for the evening," she told Sam with a laugh.

"My husband, once again, has a book deadline, so we cleared the house to give him some peace and quiet," Kelly said, taking a platter that Elaine handed to her.

"Let's get everything on the table, and we're ready," Zoë said. "Sam, you can go tell the men we are ready to begin."

Nina, Kelly, and Emily began picking up the bowls and serving dishes filled with sliced brisket, roast chicken, a variety of veggies, and Elaine's latkes. The table glittered with Zoë's best china and glassware, and fresh flowers filled crystal bowls. The males of the group didn't need to be told twice, including the two teenage boys Sam hadn't met yet. The older one, David, maneuvered his way around and made certain he got the chair next to Emily. Within minutes everyone else was seated.

Elaine began the ritual with the lighting of a candle on the menorah centerpiece and the chanting of a prayer. The ancient Festival of Lights ceremony touched Sam, as she watched this close-knit family celebrate their heritage.

* * *

An hour later, Sam checked in on the room Zoë liked to call the parlor. Darryl had lit a cozy fire in the fireplace, and lamps throughout the room highlighted the plush upholstery on sofas and chairs, and the spines of books on the bookcase that filled one entire wall. Joe and Nina relaxed with herbal tea, while the kids gathered on the floor to play dreidel, the visitors explaining to Ana how the game went. Laz was poking through the books, pulling out one after the other and setting them back.

She could hear Beau's voice coming from the larger living room, saying something to Darryl about the newest construction project. She walked in their direction, planning to ask whether either of them wanted coffee before Kelly unplugged and washed the pot. The question was hardly out of her mouth when there was a crash and a scream from the parlor.

Sam got to the door first.

A bookcase lay on the floor, revealing a gaping black four-foot hole in the wall behind. Her first thought was Ana, and she saw that Joe and Nina had already rushed to the kids, pulling all four of them away from the wreckage of the shelving and the scatter of books strewn everywhere. Spilled tea dribbled from Zoë's once-beautiful coffee table, which was now a broken heap.

"What the h——?" Darryl stood behind Sam, he and Beau crowding through the doorway. "What on earth happened here?"

Both little girls were crying, more from the fright and the grownups' reaction than any actual injury. As Sam bent to hug Ana and reassure her, she caught sight of Laz. The old man was standing at the base of the fallen bookcase, staring into the hole in the wall.

Beau had started forward, evidently planning to pick up the bookcase and stand it upright, but Darryl stopped him.

"I'll need to check out that hole," he said quietly. "Let's just get everyone into another room and I'll deal with the mess."

There became a bit of a clog at the doorway, as those inside the parlor tried to leave while Zoë, Emily, and Kelly all showed up with expressions of concern on their faces.

Sam stood and ushered Ana toward her mother. Zoë came to the rescue with the magic words, "Who wants hot chocolate?"

In the rush toward the kitchen, Sam hung back to help Beau and Darryl with the cleanup. Laz lingered for some reason.

"I'm sure the offer of hot chocolate can be extended to include a nip of something stronger," Sam told him. "Ask Zoë. She usually has a well-stocked liquor cabinet."

Laz edged away from the bookcase, but didn't leave the room.

Sam turned her attention toward Darryl who had pulled a flashlight from his back pocket. Of course he did—the man always seemed prepared for anything. He shone the light at the gaping hole in the wall and moved closer, stepping over the fallen bookcase. From the corner of her eye, Sam noticed that Laz had picked up something book-sized and tucked it inside his cardigan.

"Well, I'll be damned," Darryl muttered.

The hole was no mere accident. The space, approximately four feet high and three feet wide, revealed a set of stairs leading down into the dark. A doorway, hidden all this time.

"You didn't know this was here?" she asked.

Darryl shook his head in bewilderment. "We've lived in this house twenty years. It came with all the built-ins. I never had reason to remove any of this shelving before."

"Some of the bolts must have given way," Beau said. "I wonder what made it come loose."

"Don't know, but I'll get a couple of my guys to come and secure it. Not sure when … we're pressing to get this remodel done before the homeowner comes at Christmas."

"I'll help you," Beau offered. "Shouldn't take the two of us more than half a day."

"Aren't you going to check out the stairs?" Sam asked, practically bouncing on the balls of her feet. "You gotta find out if the house has a secret basement or something."

"No time like the present," Darryl said, bending to step through the hole. On the other side, he was able to stand up straight. He shined his light around the space. "Stairs seem sturdy enough."

He walked down, carefully taking one step at a time. Sam and Beau hovered at the hole, staring after him.

"Huh. This is it. Just a concrete space, maybe six by eight. It's not really a room at all."

Okay, Sam thought. Why would someone create a tiny space like that and go to the trouble of building stairs leading to it, then hide it all behind a built-in bookcase?

Darryl's voice came up from the hollow. "Ohhh … Interesting."

"What? What?" Sam couldn't contain herself.

"A door." He illuminated a black rectangle to his left. A large, rusted hasp held it closed, and hanging from the loop in the hasp was probably the most old-fashioned padlock Sam had ever seen.

"This thing's gotta be an antique," Darryl said, examining the padlock. "I'll check with Zoë, but I'm ninety-nine percent sure we've never come across a key for anything like this."

"I'll ask her," Sam offered. She could also get some boxes to pack up the books and other items that had fallen.

Zoë came up with four good-sized cartons but had no clue about an antique padlock or the key that would fit it.

4

Beau had always started his mornings early to begin his ranch chores, and retirement from the sheriff's department made no difference. He was up at four-thirty the next morning, and Sam followed suit.

"I need to check in at the shop and make sure Julio and Becky have everything under control," Sam told him, handing over his coffee in his favorite huge mug. "If all's well there, I plan to get over to Zoë's and figure out what's in that hidden room. She couldn't stop talking about it last night before we left."

"You'll probably see me there. Darryl was already gathering tools to start the job, but he needs to wait until the guests have left for their day's activities. I'll tend to the horses and get a couple things out of the way before I head over."

"Weird, wasn't it, how that staircase and door were hidden down there?"

"Somebody built it to hide something. The bookcase was attached with some old hinges, like there was supposed to be some kind of mechanism that would cause it to swing open and reveal the space."

"Seriously?"

He gave a shrug. "The piece wasn't merely bolted to the wall. And if the previous owners wanted to wall off the basement forever, why didn't they close off the opening with drywall?"

Sam could feel her excitement building. There was definitely a mystery here. What was behind the locked door?

* * *

Zoë was loading the dishwasher when Sam arrived at the B&B a little after ten, carrying two more boxes of pastries.

"We've got the place to ourselves for a few hours— well, except for the guys. I heard some hammering and a few good-sized clunks a while ago."

"And the guests?"

"Off to tour the pueblo. Elaine still can't conceive of 'an apartment building made of mud' that's been standing—and occupied—for more than nine hundred years. She had to see it for herself. Joe and Nina thought it would be a great learning experience for the kids, to visit another culture, not to mention resting their muscles after yesterday's skiing."

"Mind if I go check on the guys? I can't wait to find out what's in that room in the basement."

"Go for it. I'll be along as soon as I wipe down these counters and get a washer load of towels started."

Sam walked into the parlor where she heard low male murmurs from the hole in the wall. An extension cord snaked its way through the opening and down the stairs, and she saw that Darryl had hung an automotive droplight from a ceiling beam. The antique padlock lay on the floor beside a crowbar and small sledge hammer.

"Hey guys. So, what's in there?"

"Come on down and see. It's a little crowded, but you're welcome to take a look."

Beau reached out a hand to help her down the narrow stairs. Darryl stepped aside and gestured toward the door, which now stood open into a dark space. He grabbed the droplight and aimed it into the space, revealing what was no more than a small closet. On the floor of it there were two cardboard boxes tied closed with string, topped with a good inch of dust.

"That's it?"

"We haven't opened the boxes yet. They could be filled with gold bars or something really cool." The gleam in Darryl's eye told her he was teasing.

Beau started up the steps. "I'm guessing Zoë won't appreciate us at all if we carry those into her parlor without making some attempt at leaving the dust down here. I'll see what she wants to do."

"I heard that," came Zoë's voice. "Let me get the little vacuum cleaner. It sounds like using a dust cloth will only make the mess worse."

She was back in less than two minutes with a battery operated Dustbuster. Darryl made quick work of sucking up the worst of the dirt and handing each box over to Beau, who carried them up and handed them off to Sam.

"Look at this—the string is practically falling apart and the cardboard is almost brittle. Even the packaging must be more than fifty years old." She didn't need to cut the strings—they merely unraveled—and when she opened the flaps on the first box, her nose began to tickle and she let out two giant sneezes.

"You do it," she said to Zoë. "These are your property."

Zoë peered inside. "Photos." She dug into it and lifted out several frames. "Looks like a collection of old pictures. Look at the clothes. I'd say 1930s, '40s, maybe?"

Darryl was already into the second box. "Papers. Letters and documents."

"Oh my gosh, you guys. This could be part of the history of this house," Sam said. "I mean, surely it was the homeowner who stashed everything down in that closet. Maybe they just meant to store them safely, but forgot about them when they moved away."

Zoë had come across a large envelope and unfastened the clasp. She withdrew a dozen or more unframed photos. "Oh wow. These are pictures of this house. The exterior, other than the plants and trees, doesn't look all that much different."

She sat cross-legged on the floor and began to flip through them, passing them around.

"Here's one taken in this room," Sam observed. "The leaded glass on the front window is the same." She looked up, getting oriented. "The photographer must have been standing in the doorway over there. Look at the old-fashioned decorations! There were no bookcases against the west wall back then." And no hole in the wall.

"I wonder when these were taken," Zoë mused. "Knowing that would give us a time frame for when the basement was put in."

Darryl dropped an envelope back into the box. "I doubt the basement was added as an afterthought. That's not easy to do, with an existing house. It was probably here all along, but for some reason someone decided to add this hidden entrance. I'm going to see if we have any plans for this place. I don't want to seal it off until we know more." He got up and left the room.

Zoë's eyes followed him. "He'll be out in his workshop, I'll bet. It was a garage when we bought the place, but at some point in history it could have been a carriage house or ... who knows?"

Beau disconnected the droplight, stacked some boxed-up books in front of the opening, and bade the ladies goodbye, pleading ranch chores at home.

A glimmer of a reflection flashed across the room from the front window. A vehicle had pulled into the parking area. It stopped and doors began to slam.

"Oh my gosh, the Friedmans are back," Zoë exclaimed. "How long have we been at this?"

Sam glanced at the clock on the mantle. "It's after two o'clock."

"Sheesh. I could study these pictures all day but I need to finish laundry. And this room is a mess. We'll need to close it off and just use the living room for everyone to congregate. Maybe I can set them up with a movie and some hot chocolate."

"Don't stress over it. They only signed up for rooms and breakfast. They'll find ways to entertain themselves." Then Sam had an idea. "Would it be okay if I took these boxes over to Emily at the library? It would get them out of your way temporarily, and maybe Emily can find out more about the history of the house for you. That's what her grandfather did, after all, spent his lifetime studying the history of Taos and the surrounding area. His material formed the basis of the library."

"Great idea. And Scott! Your son-in-law is a historian

too—see what he might know about all this."

"Okay. No promises on how soon Scott can get to any of it—I never know about his writing schedule and book deadlines. But I imagine Emily would love to delve into this right away."

They stood, a little creakily, and stretched their muscles before refilling the old cartons and picking them up. Heading toward the back door to set everything in Sam's truck, they discovered the kitchen was full of chatty guests.

5

"It was so cool," said Adam, the fourteen-year-old who, so far, had barely uttered a dozen words in Sam's presence. "The pueblo buildings had snow on them, and the guide told us how they treat the adobe every year to keep it strong."

"Mudding it," Zoë offered.

"Right. And then we got some bread that a woman was just taking out of the …"

"Horno."

"Right. That little dome-shaped oven. It was *so* good."

"The Indians weren't even wearing any feathers or anything," muttered David, the older boy.

"The Tewa normally don't," Zoë said, "other than at some of the ceremonial festivities. But you probably saw some of them with long braids?"

Leah piped up. "I want to grow my hair that long, Mom. So I can have a braid all the way down my back."

Nina smiled. "We'll see about that. For now, let's change

out of our outdoor clothes and just chill for a while." She hustled the three kids toward the front of the house and Sam excused herself to get back to work.

"What's in the boxes?" Laz asked as Sam carried one past him.

"Old pictures of this house. I'm going to have a historian take a look at them."

"Hm. How old are they? You know, I stayed at this house once when I was a lot younger. I might recognize something."

"You did?" Elaine exclaimed from her perch at the counter. "When was this? Was your family with you?"

Laz turned toward his cousin and gave her a look before turning away and heading toward his bedroom.

"Strange thing to say," Sam commented as she put the first box in the truck and turned to take the second box from Zoë. "I wonder why Laz brought up something like that now. And why he didn't mention it a lot earlier in the visit?"

Zoë gave her a wink. "I'll see what I can learn."

Sam drove first to Sweet's Sweets to check on her crew. Assured that the orders were under control, she promised to be there early in the morning to help with a particularly tricky wedding design. Meanwhile, she was itching to get to Emily and the library to learn more about the secrets the B&B was hiding.

* * *

Her daughter's car sat in one of the parking spaces in front of the small Morton Library, the private library founded by Emily Plankhurst's grandfather, after a lifetime of collecting historical material from Taos and the surrounding area. Although anyone could access the materials, the small library was mostly frequented by serious historians and researchers. Emily had inherited it when her grandfather died, and she'd admitted to feeling in over her head at times. But then, she'd been assisted more than once by the ghost of her grandmother who, it seemed, continued to hang around the place.

Sam picked up the first of the heavy boxes and headed for the door. Hey, if the ghost of Valerie wanted to chime in and help with this mystery, all the better.

"What's all this?" Emily asked, peering into the first box as Sam set the second one in place.

"Surprises from behind the wall in Zoë's parlor."

"All I saw was a hole behind where the bookcase used to be," Kelly said. "So these were piled up in there?"

Sam explained about the closet-sized space behind the door with the antique padlock, and told them about this morning's discoveries. "Darryl is looking for floorplans that might show how extensive the basement once was. Zoë thought you might have some way to gather historical information about their house, based on these items or maybe things you already have here in the library."

Emily's eyes lit up. "Sounds like fun."

"Do you think it's a coincidence that the bookcase fell now, right when this particular family is staying there?" Kelly asked.

"Why—do you?"

"Okay, so I don't *know* ... but that night, after the crash and we all rushed in there ... Well, before I headed home, I decided to use the powder room at Zoë's, and as I was coming out of there I saw Laz walking toward the guest rooms. He had his back to me as he headed down the hall, but I saw him pull something out from under his sweater. It appeared about the size of a book, but yet it wasn't quite that. I don't really know how to describe it but—"

A small chime went off, signaling that the front door had opened.

"David! What are you doing here?" Sam's comment slipped out before she realized how rude it sounded.

"I ... I just stopped by." The teen's eyes went to Emily and a deep blush rose up his neck. "I brought you a little present."

He held out a Sweet's Sweets bakery bag, and by the scent Sam identified one of her shop's apple cinnamon muffins.

David turned toward Sam. "See, actually, I went to the bakery first because Zoë talks about it so much, and I wanted to see where you bake all those excellent pastries you've been bringing us each morning."

Uh-huh, right.

"And the lady at the counter said you weren't there at the moment, that you'd come here, and she gave me directions to walk over, since it's only a couple of blocks, and—"

Sam couldn't help but laugh. The made-up excuse, the rambling over-explanation, and the look on his face, the way his eyes glowed. This sixteen-year-old had a major crush on Emily. She should have noticed it the night of the dinner, how he'd maneuvered his way into sitting next to the young librarian. Oh, was Emily going to get some teasing over this! At twenty-eight, she could hardly be considered a cougar, but still ...

Emily accepted the muffin with good grace.

Kelly cleared her throat and said she ought to be getting home. "I left Scott and Ana doing some kind of science experiment in the kitchen, and I'd better make sure nothing has blown up." She stuck her arms in her jacket and slung her purse strap over her shoulder.

Emily picked up one of the boxes, moving away from the desk and heading toward the large library table with it. David jumped to service by grabbing the second box. She thanked him but when his back was turned, she gave Sam a pleading look that said *save me*.

"So, David, did you walk all the way over here from the B&B?" Sam asked.

"Yeah, it's not that far. In New York we walk all over the place, so I'm used to it." He straightened a little, trying to make his narrow frame seem more athletic.

"Oh, that's great. Well, it's going to be getting darker and colder in another half hour or so. Can I give you a ride back?"

He glanced toward Emily, evidently hoping she'd invite him to stay for … what? Coffee, drinks, more? She put on a faint smile and nodded toward Sam.

"That's a great idea, Sam. I need to close up now. I've got to be … on a date. Yes, a date, pretty soon." She gently began herding them toward the door.

On the ride back to Zoë's David fairly bubbled with questions about Emily. Sam kept everything neutral and tried to make up a generic enough story about whoever Emily was supposed to be dating. David's family would only be here four more days, and then he could go back to wowing the girls at school.

6

Sam's phone rang a little after eight p.m., just as she'd finished brushing her teeth. She rushed into the bedroom and saw that it was Zoë.

"Hey, hope I didn't get you out of bed."

"We may be of the early-to-bed crowd, but not quite this early," Sam said with a chuckle.

"I'm retreating to my bedroom for a little alone time," Zoë told her. "As much as I love having guests, I'm used to a night or two between groups. Anyway, I thought I'd share an interesting tidbit. While Emily is going through the old documents we found, I've been studying the photos of the house as it used to be. Without a magnifying glass, I didn't realize a lot of the old decorations were Jewish in origin. Elaine pointed that out as we were passing the pictures around this evening. One menorah, in particular, looked like an antique."

"So maybe a previous owner was Jewish? You know … I found it *really* interesting that Laz let it slip that he's been there before. He saw one of the photos of the parlor and said something like 'just like I remembered it.' Isn't that odd? When Elaine asked for details, he kind of backed off and muttered something about being very young."

"He stayed here a long time ago?"

"Well, that's the idea I got. He left the room right away, as if he didn't want to talk about it. He definitely didn't like my questioning him. I'd love to know more about the house and its history, but he just clammed up."

"Maybe those aren't happy memories for him, for some reason … I voiced that same thought to Elaine and Nina, but why would Laz have booked this trip and specifically chosen our B&B if that were the case?"

"And neither of them had any idea?" Sam moved toward the dresser, depositing her earrings in the carved wooden box where she kept such things.

"Not at all. And, get this, the ladies told me they still haven't figured out the whole relationship. Laz claims his mother was Elaine's great aunt, but she doesn't recall any of the names he's dropped, and Nina says she can't find the connection through the entries in her mother's old address book."

"So, Laz might not be who he says he is?"

"I asked that very thing. Elaine isn't quite willing to go so far as to call him a liar, maybe just some old-age confusion with the names. And maybe it's also that she doesn't want to rock the boat—he's paid for their whole trip, after all."

Sam heard another voice in the background.

"Darryl has some other news," Zoë said. She apparently put her phone on speaker, as his voice now came through.

"I found house plans, Sam. They show that we have a full basement. I swear, I've never found a clue about that. There's an outside entrance, one of those angular door things you can lift up, but I've been down there and it only led to a root cellar. Maybe ten-by-ten. Nothing the size of the entire house. I suppose I could shovel the snow off and give it another look."

"Do you think it's worth the effort?" Sam asked, applying night cream to her face.

"Probably not. And most certainly not until spring. You're right. I'll put it on the to-do list my lovely wife likes me to keep."

She could almost hear Zoë give him a gentle punch to the arm.

"Ouch! Anyway, I'm going to look around that space at the bottom of the stairs a little closer tomorrow. It's beyond me why someone would go to the trouble to wall off most of the basement if they were only going to put in a set of stairs and a storage closet. There's more to this—I just don't know what."

On that note, they ended the call, leaving Sam with his final words in her head. *There's more to this* ... That pretty well described everything that had happened in the past few days, didn't it? She realized she'd been unconsciously stroking the surface of the carved box. Now its dark wood began to warm up and gleam a golden color.

If only the box could let her see the past or the future. But that wasn't the way the magical artifact worked. She would have to save this topic for morning.

* * *

Sam's wakeful night brought no answers, although her kitchen cupboards were now amazingly neat and clean. She'd made Beau a huge breakfast, fed the dogs, and headed to her daughter's home, the beautifully restored Victorian that had, only a few years ago, been home to another of Sam's business ventures. Kelly greeted her at the back door, whispering that they should stay quiet. Scott was in the midst of their daughter's math lesson, up in his turret room office.

"That's fine," Sam said. "Emily called me this morning and I suggested she meet us here. I wanted to see if ... *the book* ... might offer answers to something Darryl told me last night."

They tiptoed past the turret and up to the third-floor attic, where Kelly and Sam often consulted. Kelly unlocked the door and started the small gas heating stove to warm the space. Eliza, the calico cat, had followed along and now curled up on the window seat where a warm patch of sunshine fell.

"There's Em now," Kelly said, looking down to the driveway below. "I'll go let her in."

Sam pulled the carved box from her backpack purse and used it to warm her hands. Kelly owned one too, the twin to this. The two boxes complemented each other's powers. She opened the leatherbound book that sat on the large refectory table, but the rune-like writing remained unreadable. So far.

She moved the book and box to a lower shelf as Kelly and Emily came into the attic. Her question about Darryl's floorplan could wait.

Emily was carrying a file full of pages and a small book that looked like a diary. She set them on the table and quickly shed her jacket.

"Did you know that there were prisoner of war camps in New Mexico in the 1940s?" she asked.

Sam felt her own expression mirror Kelly's—incredulity.

"A large one near Santa Fe housed Japanese soldiers, several others in the southern part of the state held captured Germans."

"But—"

"How does this relate to the documents you found at Zoë and Darryl's place? Glad you asked." Emily held up the diary. "This little journal was kept by a woman named Neumann, who writes of her family being terrified of this one German commandant—Wilhelm Gerhardt. The family had apparently escaped Nazi Germany. The account of how they crawled under layers of barbed wire and walked for days through dense forest with gunfire all around, is enough to make your hair stand up. They made it to friendly territory and were able to come to America where they met up with relatives in … yes, Taos. A quick search of the property records shows that the present-day B&B was owned by a Newman family from the late 1930s and well into the 1980s. Neumann was often Anglicized to Newman."

"But the German?"

"Commandant Gerhardt was taken prisoner in 1943 and brought to one of the internment camps here. There was an escape."

Emily was right. Sam felt the hair on her arms prickle as the tale unfolded of the high-ranking German who had escaped the prison camp, caught a train that ran within two miles of the camp, and was never found by authorities. But Gerhardt had a personal vendetta against the Neumann family, who had documented his crimes and, once safe in New Mexico, had turned the information over to the US military. Their information was partially what had led to his arrest in Germany, and they had good reason to believe he knew that. They fully believed he would come after the group who had escaped, as well as the extended family who had been living in America for several decades.

"Mrs. Neumann writes of their fear, their efforts to disguise the fact they were Jewish, including changing the spelling of their name and … hiding all their beloved family treasures so they could not be found." Emily paged through the folder. "Apparently, they continued to fear

Gerhardt even after the war was over, because they knew he would recognize certain members of their family."

Kelly let out a long breath. "Which explains why they created the hidden space in the basement and why all the pictures and decorations were removed from the house. But—"

"But where are all the treasures?" Sam asked. "We only found photos and documents."

But she already knew the answer. Darryl knew the house once had a full basement. They needed to get beyond the walled up sections. She picked up her phone and called Zoë.

"Don't let anyone go farther into the basement. Not yet. We need to do some more research. I have a feeling there's a lot more to the story of your current guests."

7

Calling out to Scott that they were leaving, Kelly, Sam, and Emily headed over to the B&B. The rental car was not in the parking area.

"Where's everyone?" Sam asked as they walked into Zoë's kitchen.

"The younger group are skiing again, making the most of their last few days here."

"What about Elaine and Laz?"

"Joe planned to drop them off at the Plaza to browse the art galleries. They'll catch the shuttle back."

"We'd better work quickly," Emily said, heading toward the parlor.

Zoë seemed a little perplexed but followed along with

the others. They stepped into the parlor, where shuffling and scraping sounds emanated from the gaping hole in the wall.

"Darryl—company!" Zoë called out. "He's been down there since breakfast. I have no idea why."

Boots clomped on the wooden stairs and Darryl's shaggy head appeared at the opening. "Sam—good. There's another mystery down here."

With her heart racing a little, she ducked through the hole and followed him down. He'd rigged the bright light again, but at first she didn't understand what he was pointing at. The plain black-painted wall to the left of the steps appeared to be nothing more than a dead end.

He ran his hands up and down, outlining a barely visible rectangle. "It's a door. No lock, no hinges. But it's definitely hollow behind here." He pounded on it with his fist to demonstrate.

The other three women stood at various levels on the staircase behind them. Zoë actually gasped at the sound that reverberated back.

"This could explain where the rest of the basement space is," he said. "Now if I could just figure out how to open it."

"Maybe it opens from the other side?" Kelly suggested. "That could be why we can't see the hinges from here."

"Could be." He stared at the thin crack that outlined the door.

"Beau discovered hinges on the bookcase, meaning it was designed to swing outward, probably once a hidden catch was released," Sam said. "I wouldn't be surprised if this door also has some kind of hidden latching mechanism. Rather than having to go through the outdoor cellar entrance and tear out some shelving, wouldn't it make more sense if the family installed this for quick entry and exit? It could have been some early version of a panic room or something."

"Ah, that makes sense," Kelly said. "They could dash down here, close the bookcase, then get behind this door. Even if someone discovered the entry behind the bookcase, all they would see would be the blank walls and the other door with the old padlock."

"So, how do we get into it?" Zoë asked.

Darryl was still feeling around the edges, touching and pressing to see if a hidden latch would release. Nothing happened.

Sam looked up at Emily. "You're awfully quiet ... and you've read a lot of the family documents. Any ideas?"

Emily rubbed the tip of her nose and sneezed. "Sorry—dust. Hmm ... I might have an idea. I need to grab that diary I was showing you earlier."

She edged past Kelly and left, but returned in less than five minutes.

"Okay, there was something. It made no sense when I first read it, before I knew about this whole basement thing. Let's see ..."

She sat on the parlor sofa and began to page through the book. Kelly and Zoë left the cramped quarters of the narrow stairs and sat on either side of her, but Sam and Darryl continued to poke around, looking for a hidden latch of some kind. Emily ran her index finger down the handwritten pages, looking for the clue. A dozen pages into the narrative she stopped.

"Okay, I don't know if this means anything at all. It comes at a point when the family is living in this house, but there are no references to their having done any remodeling or work on the basement so it might not be significant."

"Just tell us!" Sam was itching to know.

"Okay, this is word for word. *Twist the lamp. The tiny sound reveals all.*"

"What?" Zoë leaned over Emily's shoulder and read it for herself. "Well, you're right. It makes no sense. The writer is talking about what a harsh winter it's been, and then suddenly this reference to a lamp. Weird."

"I know, right? That's why it stuck in my head. Those few words make no sense in the context of what else is going on in their lives."

Sam asked her to repeat the wording, then she picked up Darryl's droplight by the handle and aimed it around the space. "Lamp ... lamp ... where are you, lamp?"

Darryl crept around her and opened the first door they'd found, the one that revealed the small storage space. "Maybe in here?"

Sam illuminated the now-empty closet. Unless ... She aimed the light upward. The ceiling of the little cupboard was probably eight feet high, and with the black painted walls the space seemed to vanish upward into nothingness. But the droplight revealed something, cleverly concealed out of sight.

"Guys, this could be it," she called out.

High on the lefthand wall, she spotted a small fixture, something that looked like a miner's headlamp from the early 1900s, but it was mounted flush to the wall. She reached for it and gave a twist. At first there was resistance from years of dust and corrosion, but then it moved. Just a fraction of an inch.

The women had crowded around the head of the

staircase again and she felt Darryl pressing in behind her, trying for a look.

"Wait, what was the second part of the quote?"

"The tiny sound reveals all," Emily answered.

"Okay, we need to be absolutely quiet," Sam said. She gave the lamp a firmer turn.

Behind her, from the nearly invisible door, came a small *snick!* and that was it.

"Check it, Darryl. Did the door open?"

He stepped back to it and felt the edges. "I don't think so. Try twisting the lamp a little farther."

Sam held her breath, praying that the old mechanism wouldn't break off in her hand. Slowly and firmly, she continued the turning motion. As the top of the lamp reached a forty-five degree angle to its original position, a mechanical whir sounded.

"It's coming, it's coming," Darryl called out.

Sam took her hand away from the lamp. The whirring sound continued, as the door operated on some kind of automatic opener she had activated. It swung away from them, into a chamber.

"It's blacker than a witch's hat in there," Darryl said, reaching to take the droplight from Sam.

By the time the opening was large enough to step through he'd aimed the light inside, revealing a huge space. The rest of the basement.

"Holy crap!" They both said it at once.

"What? What?" Kelly headed down the stairs. Zoë and Emily were quickly on her heels.

The light glittered off several golden objects, among them the menorah that Emily had pointed out in two of the old photos. Sam stared in wonder, trying to take in the rare items, the beautiful furniture pieces, the rolled-up carpets, and framed artwork. All the missing decorative items seemed to be here.

The treasure was found, but the mystery remained. Why had the Newman family stashed their valuables down here and not returned for them?

Zoë picked up the golden menorah. "This is simply amazing. It looks like a museum quality piece."

Sam joined her. "Well, I wouldn't flash it around until you learn more, but it would be worth showing to Joe. With his museum expertise I bet he'd have some idea of its value, or he'd know where to find out."

Zoë let out a long breath. "I suppose all of this is ours, since it came with the house, but I don't know … a lot of these pieces surely have value. Before we start picking through it, I'd better take an inventory."

"I'd be happy to help with researching the history of any items you want me to check out," Emily offered.

"Thanks, that will help a lot," Darryl said. The normally unflappable building contractor seemed a little stunned at the find.

"We'll address the rest of this once our guests have left," Zoë said. "Meanwhile, we need to close up the room and not say anything to anyone."

"I know," Sam said with a grin, "not even the bakery crew."

They all filed out. Sam went back to the lamp, gave a twist in the opposite direction, and the mechanism slowly operated to close the black door. Zoë climbed the stairs first, the gold menorah in hand, with Emily, Kelly, and Sam behind. Darryl rehung the droplight, switched it off, and followed.

One by one they emerged into the parlor, blinking at the bright light from the front window. The door to the hall stood open and there stood Laz, a rifle in his hands.

8

"Not so fast," Laz commanded. "Set the menorah on the floor and back over to the couch there." He waved the rifle back and forth to show that he meant all of them.

A hundred thoughts went through Sam's head. *How had he carried a rifle on an airplane? What happened to an entire morning of browsing the galleries with Elaine? Where was Elaine?*

Darryl took a step forward, a gentlemanly (and probably foolish) move to shield the women. "Laz, you don't want to do this. Put the gun down."

How much experience did a New Yorker have with guns? Did he even know how to use the thing?

"That menorah belongs to me," Laz said, his lip curling. "I thank you for finding it, but I'm taking it now."

Zoë had ignored his order to set it on the floor, but placed it on an end table instead. He would have to walk right up to her in order to get it. Sam cringed at the thought of what he might do if he were truly desperate.

"Laz," she said, forcing her voice to be firm but gentle. "Laz, what do you want with the menorah? How does it belong to you?"

"This family—these Newmans—they took what rightfully belonged to my father."

"The Newman family who owned this house?"

"Escapees, all of them. My father—"

"Was he a Newman? Your name is Nieman ..."

"Ha! Not hardly. We're proud Germans. My father was Wilhelm Gerhardt, part of an elite corps who sought to take what the Jews should never have owned, to return Germany's wealth to the proper Aryans."

Holy crap, the guy was a Nazi nutcase?

"My father tracked the Neumann family out of Germany, knew they somehow got to America. Knew they gave bogus testimony that put him away in a prison camp. But his Aryan luck held and he was sent to a camp in America, in the very part of the Southwest where his quarry had settled. He discovered that the names Neumann, Nieman, and Newman had become almost interchangeable, and the Neumanns from Germany came to live with their Newman cousins here. He brought me to this house when I was a lad. He had a plan to come back and raid the treasures, to take back what was his."

"He escaped a prison camp south of here, didn't he?" Emily asked.

"Escaped the incompetent American military and managed not to be found for another fifty years. He married my mother and even she never knew exactly where he'd come from. He only told me the story on his deathbed. And that's when I knew I had to come back here, to find the treasure and return it to its rightful place."

"Which is probably in Israel or in a museum," came a voice from behind Laz.

He spun, just in time for Elaine to clock him upside the head with a heavy ceramic vase. The rifle swung wildly and Sam caught herself ducking and praying it wouldn't go off.

Laz stumbled but didn't go down. Darryl rushed forward and grabbed the rifle by the barrel, wrenching it from their captor's hands. His eyes went steely as he turned the gun on Laz and backed him into a corner. The old man cowered, rubbing the spot where the whack on the head would surely raise a knot.

"Call the police," Darryl instructed.

Kelly was first with a cell phone out of her jeans pocket.

* * *

They watched Taos Police lead Laz out the front door in handcuffs before everyone sort of collapsed on the sofas in the living room. Darryl had presented his registration documents—the rifle was his—so the police didn't confiscate it. Apparently, Laz didn't know enough about guns to realize it had not been loaded. It was the reason Darryl had been so fearless in approaching the desperate man and disarming him.

Elaine, bless her heart, was a quivering mass once all the hubbub was over. She said Laz had been jittery all morning and she wasn't enjoying any peace at the art galleries, so that's why they'd come back early. She knew something was up with him, but she wasn't sure what until she saw him standing in the parlor doorway with the rifle.

"You acted quickly and decisively, and I don't even care about the broken vase," Zoë said. "It was put to good use."

"I'm just glad he didn't try that stunt with the rest of my family around. If he'd threatened my kids ... well, I would have found something a lot more deadly than a vase to bring him down." She gave a nervous little laugh.

Zoë offered coffee and they all retreated to the kitchen. While she ground the beans and started the coffee maker, Sam found a partial box of rugelach and set it on the counter.

Emily filled in the blanks in the story for those who

hadn't already heard it. She'd immediately remembered the name Wilhelm Gerhardt as the escaped German POW, the only one who got away, and she'd done some further research the previous evening and knew he had a wife and son. They'd been living in New York for the past forty years.

"But who would have ever guessed that Laz Nieman was really Gerhardt's son?" Elaine said. "Of course, I wasn't fooled about his connection to our family. The whole roundabout relationship to my mother's side. Ha. I doubted that from the start." She looked a little embarrassed as she stirred sugar into her coffee. "I guess I got lured by the all-expense-paid trip. And aside from what happened just now, it's been a lot of fun. Let's just don't tell the kids, okay?"

9

Zoë called Sam at the bakery three days later. She sounded exhausted.

"We went through Laz's bedroom and found something interesting. Among his papers was a description of our home's layout and a reference to the bookcase in the parlor. So that explains why he was poking around there a couple days after they arrived. His messing around may very well be why the bookcase collapsed. Under the bed he'd stashed a box, about six-by-nine and a couple inches deep."

The box Kelly had seen Laz take from under his sweater.

"It held an inventory list of the valuables from the

house, including the golden menorah. Which, by the way, Joe looked at it and sent photos of it to his colleagues at the museum. They want to see it for verification, but if it's the real deal—and Joe says he thinks it is—they're willing to offer a pretty huge amount of money."

"Wow."

"We'll see. Darryl and I haven't had much chance to really talk, but there's so much stuff in the collection. We may sell some of it, keep some as mementos, and just donate the rest. The menorah would make a nice donation to the museum, don't you think?"

"It would be an amazing thing to do," Sam agreed.

"Of course, none of that can happen until we see what happens with Laz. Right now, he's only charged with intent to assault with a deadly weapon and that might not even hold up in court. If he decides to push his claim to all the treasures in this house, we may have a long battle on our hands."

"But surely …"

"Yeah, I don't think there's a court in the world that would award stolen Jewish artifacts to the family of an escaped Nazi. If anything, it'll go the other way and everything will get shipped to Neumann family descendants. Oh, it's so convoluted—I'm not making any plans whatsoever for any of that stuff. It's been where it is for a long time. It can stay there a while longer."

"Agreed. You sound like you could use a rest."

"Thank goodness Hanukkah came a bit earlier this year. I have a full week off before the Christmas crowd arrives." Sam heard Zoë's sigh over the line. "They were a fun group, once the drama was over. Elaine is quite the performer, I have to say. By the time the kids got back from skiing she was so composed, you'd never guess what had gone on with the gun and the police. She organized games and activities for the little ones, and they sat around the next two evenings, just watching movies on TV and having a good time together."

Sam supposed that was the whole point of holidays with family. She piped an outline around a snowman cookie and added it to the tray for the bakery display case.

Author's Note

There really were prisoner of war camps in New Mexico during WWII, although none in very close proximity to Taos. I visited one of these quite a few years ago while researching a different book, at Fort Stanton near Capitan, New Mexico. It was a somewhat eerie feeling to walk through the fort's cemetery and see the grave markers with German names and to think of those who died while in captivity so far from their homeland.

More recently, I learned that there was actually an escape from another of these POW camps in our state, a man who caught a train to another state where he married and lived under a different name for more than forty years before admitting to his wife and to the FBI who he really was. The story was reported in the Albuquerque news, and apparently this escapee was never charged with a crime because he escaped after the war was technically over. He felt that life in the US would be better than what he would face in East Germany after the war, so he simply stayed.

All of this served as inspiration for my story here, but no more than that. None of the fictional characters are meant to portray any real person, living or dead. It's all fiction. I share these tidbits of fact because people always ask us writers where we get our ideas.

About the Author

Connie Shelton is the author of the *USA Today* bestselling Charlie Parker and Samantha Sweet mysteries and her newest—The Heist Ladies. She's known for a light touch when it comes to sex and violence in her stories, but is much more lavish with food and chocolate. Nearly 2 million copies of her books have been sold and downloaded, in more than 110 countries worldwide. She and her husband and two dogs live in northern New Mexico. Visit her website at connieshelton.com and get her free mystery newsletter.

Contact by email: connie@connieshelton.com

Follow Connie Shelton on Twitter, Pinterest and Facebook

Get another Connie Shelton book—FREE! Visit her website to find out how

The Samantha Sweet Series

Sweet Masterpiece

Sweet's Sweets

Sweet Holidays

Sweet Hearts

Bitter Sweet

Sweets Galore

Sweets Begorra

Sweet Payback

Sweet Somethings

Sweets Forgotten

Spooky Sweet

Sticky Sweet

Sweet Magic

Deadly Sweet Dreams

The Ghost of Christmas Sweet

Spellbound Sweets – a Halloween novella

The Woodcarver's Secret

The Heist Ladies Series

Diamonds Aren't Forever
The Trophy Wife Exchange
Movie Mogul Mama
Homeless in Heaven
Show Me the Money

Children's Books

Daisy and Maisie and the Great Lizard Hunt
Daisy and Maisie and the Lost Kitten

Praise for Connie Shelton's previous mysteries:

"The best yet!! Not only was *Sweet Magic* fantastic, it left me dying to see where life is headed for Samantha and her family! Heart-gripping, fast-paced, and amazing." – J.J. 5-stars, online review

"LOVE, LOVE these books!" —5 stars, online review

"Fantastic! Impossible to put down!" – 5 stars, Amazon reader

"Shelton again has done a superb job in bringing New Mexico to life." —*Albuquerque Journal*

"Connie Shelton gets better with every book she writes." —*The Midwest Book Review*

The Christmas Fairy
A Libby Madsen Cozy Mystery Novella

By Jennifer J. Morgan

~ ~ ~

1

Christmas in Arizona is always interesting. Will it be cold enough to feel like winter and the holidays? Will we get the infrequent photo capture of snow on the saguaro cactus? You just never know. Many years, temperatures will be in the sixties and lots of sunshine. Sometimes, however, it will cloud over and we could have freezing temperatures overnight. That's what we're getting this year.

I got out of my car and crossed the parking lot, wrapping my jacket around me just a little tighter as the wind caught it. I was actually shivering! As I approached the large tan adobe-style building with tall glass front windows, I also glanced up at the dark clouds moving in. *Rain is coming, and maybe the forecast is right? Light dusting of snow by morning.*

I opened the front door to find the work crew still putting the finishing touches on our new spa. My name is Libby Madsen. My business partner, Alexis Johnson, and I have had the dream of opening a day spa for many years. We're both licensed massage therapists and met about ten years ago at trade school and became fast friends. Ever since, our full focus has been on building a business together. Our version of 'day spa' is meant to be not only a place for massage, but overall relaxation therapies. Alexis is also a meditation teacher so we have created a space where she can hold her sessions and events, too. Someday we hope to incorporate a physical therapy unit to complement our current offerings. But, one step at a time; we are still figuring out how to afford our first phase.

"Good morning!" I called out to no one in particular as I made my way through the front door.

Somewhere from the depths of the building I heard, "Libby!"

Ahhh, Alexis beat me here. I ventured back through another set of doors toward the office at the back of the building. Before the contractors fired up their power tools, the place felt cold, empty, dusty, and lifeless. However, I could easily imagine a day soon where I would walk through these large open spaces filled with warm colors, furnishings, and, most importantly, clients.

"Hey, you!" I greeted, as I swooped in and set my bag down on the floor in the far corner. There were stacks of varying sizes of wood and hardware strewn out all over the floor. Alexis is the shining example of woman empowerment. Here she was in the midst of building a desk, and yet, her creamy mocha complexion glowed as though she was a woman of leisure, kicking back and eating bon-bons. Not a hair out of place and, of course, dressed stylishly in her deep blue flowing tunic which covered a black turtle-neck long-sleeved shirt and yoga pants. Who puts makeup on while construction is going on? My friend, Alexis, that's who! Perfect natural shades with a peachy glow. Angelic. "Wow, great progress on the desk construction!"

"You know, it's kind of therapeutic actually. But, I'm very happy we're not building *all* the furniture!" She smiled and hopped right up, came over and enveloped me into a graciously warm hug. We stood there for a long moment savoring the embrace. Alexis *always* greets everyone with amazing warmth and love—it's just who she is. I've learned to relax, accept, and appreciate every time I receive one of her greetings. "Welcome to another beautiful day at the spa, my friend," she whispered, squeezed my shoulders, then released me.

"Looks like they are making great progress out there. Should be done any day, right?" I asked, looking around just outside the office door.

"That's what they tell me," she replied, with an edge to her voice that indicated she didn't fully believe it.

I knelt down on the floor and looked over the instructions that were laid out near the wooden pieces closest to me. I'm fairly handy as long as I have instructions, but forget it if I'm expected to engineer something from scratch. Not my strength at all.

"It's really coming together though, isn't it? I mean, six months ago, we saw this shell of a building and it was all still a dream. Now, we have the inside rooms constructed, and we're so close to furnishing, decorating, and finishing it all out." Goosebumps appeared on my arm. *Dreams do come true!*

"I know! So exciting, isn't it?" Alexis all but squeaked in her excitement. "Hey, do you see a piece labeled 'G' or 'H'? Maybe right under those..." she pointed to a stack of wooden desk parts.

"Yep, got 'em. Here let me hold that ... there."

We worked together for the next hour, in sync following

the directions and both lost in our own thoughts. Sounds of drills and hammering were coming from all points throughout the building. It would be good when it was nice and quiet in the building. I could imagine it, but right now it was still very much a noisy construction zone.

"You know, Christmas is right around the corner," Alexis piped up. "I really am not ready ... I swear we've been so concentrated on the business, I nearly forgot I have a three-year old who is bouncing off the ceiling over Santa's arrival soon. What kind of Mom am I?"

"I'm sure Joshua doesn't know your attention is elsewhere. You are so good at being present where you are and especially with him," I smiled.

"Aww, I hope that's the case. I still have shopping and wrapping to do and feel like it'll never get done in time. It always does though, so I'm not going to worry."

"No worrying. You know it doesn't do any good," I laughed.

"Hey, what's your favorite Christmas memories with your mom when you were a kid?" she asked.

I had to think about that one. "You know, I think I loved how both my parents really got into the spirit of the holidays. From Thanksgiving on, our home was decorated to the hilt. They put Clark Griswold to shame!" I giggled remembering the lights my dad would string up all over our property and how *bright* it was at night.

"That sounds fun! Well, you know very well ... my family is part Hindu and part Christian. My parents raised us kids as Christian, but my maternal grandparents were Hindu. Mom tried to keep some of the Hindu traditions going, but after her parents died, it's almost as though she chose not to remember anymore." Alexis sat back for a moment, lost in her memories. "We did have a Christmas tree, but I don't recall a lot of decorations. Pretty simple stuff. I remember she was always trying to get us kids to *not* focus on the commercialized aspects of the holiday. Instead, she would teach the biblical and religious origins. As kids, I don't think we really appreciated that, but I do now."

"Oh man, talk about commercialization of a holiday—inside my childhood home, we had garland on stair banisters, huge Thomas Kincade-like village scenes, gingerbread houses, snowmen, and Santa scenes throughout the house—every surface was *filled* with some type of decoration. I remember it felt like a winter wonderland. I loved it!" I reminisced in wonder.

"I loved baking with my mom!" she said excitedly, but then suddenly looked sad. "I do miss her dearly." I reached out for her hand and squeezed. I knew how she felt; I missed my dad terribly, too.

"I really enjoyed baking as a kid, too. Ok, maybe it wasn't so much the baking, but definitely decorating cookies ... and then *eating them*! Hey, maybe you, Joshua and I should plan a day before Christmas where we bake some goodies?"

"I'd love that! And I know Joshua will be game. He doesn't even remember his grandmother since he was just born when she died." I saw her choke back her sadness again.

"How do you honor your Hindu religion at the holidays?" I asked.

"I make sure to share stories of our ancestors back in India. Joshua loves hearing all about the festivals filled with scrumptious food and celebratory dancing. They celebrate something called Pancha Ganapati. I honestly don't remember a whole lot about that tradition, but I know it's held in December—nothing to do with Christmas, mind you. I know my mom tried to educate us, but as kids, we just really loved the Christian holiday more. Grandma probably rolls in her grave seeing how Americanized we truly are!"

"Sad she also passed before Joshua could meet her," I said.

My friend had a wistful look on her face, but didn't say a word.

After tightening a few more screws, we both stood, one on each side, and lifted the desk into place.

"Perfect!" We stood by admiring our handiwork.

My eyes widened and I got as excited as a kid on Christmas morning ... "Hey! We've been talking about having a grand opening party for the spa. What about throwing a holiday-themed party?"

I saw my friends' shoulders slump forward. Poor woman, she can't carry any more weight of the holidays than she already is.

I continued, sweeping my arms wide, side to side, and venturing into each room as she followed me around. "Don't worry, I'll handle it all! Christmas trees here ... and here ..." I ran from one side of the room to the next. "And maybe over there, too. Garland, and tons of lights! Imagine this place just *lit up*! We could have several appetizer stations—like, over there ... and there. Drink stations in several places. With everything spread out, it disperses the people too." I just kept running from one corner to the next, illustrating my vision for the perfect grand opening holiday party.

Finally, Alexis cut in. "Um, Libby? Christmas is literally three weeks from now. The spa is due to open by end of *this week*. How on earth would we be ready for a party? I'm barely ready for the holidays at home."

"I know, I know. But, they have party planners that can take care of it all…" I proceeded to remind her how the painting, flooring, and furniture delivery was all due to be done within the next two days. The contractors will be gone and then we'd just have to decorate for the party. "We'll get caterers for food and drink. I'd take care of it all—leave it to me."

"We do still have a little money left in our start up budget. I can't imagine you'd find a party planner on this short notice, but hey—" she hesitated, still looked a bit forlorn, but then broke into her huge effervescent smile and said, "go for it!!"

2

Looking out my living room window, I was admiring some bunnies that were romping around in my desert landscape when she arrived. As soon as I saw Jordan climb out of her Mazda, with her enormous pregnant belly, my heart just sank. It's not that my sister and I aren't close. We used to be much closer, but she can be difficult. I love her—I do. She just tries to run everyone's life and there are many days I wonder how she manages her own.

At 39, she's slightly older than me, married her husband at twenty-one. She has three kids with Pat; eight-year-old identical twin daughters, Apple and Annie (I kid you not), and then five-year-old son, Chase, along with the newest bun in the oven. To me, the whole large family just seems like soooo much work. However, she clearly loves being a mother and, mostly, she makes it look easy. It shows; her kids are great—very well-behaved. The stunning part is that she does all this on her own now.

"Good morning, Libby. Sorry I'm running a bit late. Morning sickness is still kickin' my behind. And, I don't even know why they call it morning sickness—it's *any time of day* sickness, if you ask me!"

"No worries, I was at the spa all day and just got home myself. How far along are you now?" I asked as I led the way inside the house.

"Two more weeks this wee one should arrive." She patted her belly. "Oh hey, how is that hobby coming along? You haven't been around in a while so I figured it must be consuming all your time." *Here we go. She always has to make a remark about my profession. Hobby?*

"Yes, yes … the business is coming right along. You really should come by the spa later this week; construction should be all finished in just a few days. Oh, and I'll make sure you guys get an invitation to our grand opening party, too. We're doing a holiday-themed soiree!" I got excited again about the plans. I'd sure rather be doing that right now than wondering what other ripe comments my sister has for me.

"A holiday party for the grand opening … will you be able to pull that off in time? Cutting it a bit close, aren't you, Libs?" she grunted mid-squat onto the sofa. "I don't know how I'll ever get up again."

"I'm hoping to find a party planner that can help me get it done in time," I said, suddenly lacking confidence.

"I wish I wasn't about ready to pop—that's right up my alley, and I'd love to help. No way I can do it now though."

"Oh, I wouldn't even think of it. You have your hands full for sure." Even as I said it, I could feel the defensive energy she gave off.

"What do you mean? I've handled way more than this, you know!" *Sheesh, as though it was some competition!*

"Can I get you some water? Tea?" Trying to diffuse the situation, I walked into the kitchen and started the kettle for myself. Chamomile should do it.

"I'll have some of that," Jordan said in a quieter tone. "Seriously, Libby, I may be able to help you with the party planning. No, not me personally, but someone that Pat knows. Actually, I think he's a friend of another friend—not sure." She was already texting.

"Well, that would be a great start ... I feel better having a known reference. Thanks!"

I poured hot water over the tea bags and brought us each a mug. After setting them down on the wooden coffee table situated between the two brown suede sofas, I took a seat opposite my sister. *Why is she even here?*

"Oh, that was quick. Just got a text back. His name is Scott ... company is Arizona Parties. Here, I'm texting you the number so you can easily add it to your contacts."

"Thanks! So, where are the kids today? I thought you'd bring them with you?" I asked.

"Oh, thankfully Chase was able to stay and play with the neighbor kid. Apple and Annie, I dropped them off for piano lessons. Tomorrow is dance for those two. Pat works so much these days that he's rarely around for the kids—so much for co-parenting." She seemed a little sad.

"Um, Jordan, I'm a little confused about your visit

today. Did you need something?" I carefully broached the subject. The look on her face immediately told me I wasn't careful enough.

"What? You mean, I can't just come visit my sister without 'needing something'?"

"C'mon, you know I didn't mean it like that. You are welcome here anytime and I love that you came to visit. I guess I'm sensing there is more that you've not said yet, though?"

"Well, yeah. I need a favor." She hemmed and hawed, then continued, "I'm a little concerned when this one…" she paused to rub her bulbous belly, "makes its way into the world, I'll be alone. Pat is being called out of town on a project and the timing couldn't be worse." Her eyes cast downward and probably for the first time in her life, she appeared vulnerable.

My face lit up. *Maybe this is the beginning of a 'new' Jordan? Vulnerable and relatable?* "Of course, I'll be there for you, Jordan! Don't even think twice about that. I have no idea what's involved, but I can hold your hand and be there for my big sis."

"Thank you, Libby! It's been an awfully difficult year—first Pat leaving, then the pregnancy. I can't believe how hard it's been. Then, I remembered you and there's no one I'd rather have by my side than my sister." She smiled a wide showing of her perfectly white teeth. She picked up her mug, taking a sip of tea. In her sweetest little drawl as she rested her teacup on her belly, she added, "Besides, you have nothing else going on. I mean, other than your little *hobby*."

And, she was back … good ol' Jordan.

After we finished our tea and catching up a bit, she headed home. I immediately got on the phone with Arizona Parties before it got much later. I really needed to get the party planning started. *Nothing else going on—who does she think she is?! Just because I don't have a thousand kids, doesn't mean I'm not busy!*

"May I speak to Scott, please?" I asked the nice lady who answered the phone. Then, I cringed and pulled the phone away from my ear when she slammed it against a hard surface. I heard her yell, *SCOTT!*

Customer service today just isn't what it used to be.

"This is Scott." A man who sounded youthful picked up the phone. "How may I help you?"

"Hi Scott. Pat White referred me to your company. My name is Libby Madsen. I'm the owner of a day spa and we're having our grand opening on December 15th. We'd like to have this decorated as a Christmas themed holiday party ... I know it's short notice, but I'm really hoping…"

"Sure, no problem, Libby. I'll need to see the place where the party will be held and then we can talk over the specifics. I'm sure you'll need catering and such, so we can discuss that when we meet. How about tomorrow morning? 10 a.m.?" he asked.

"Excellent …10 a.m. it is!" I gave him the address in East Mesa and hung up.

* * *

As soon as I saw the man walk up to the front door, I immediately judged that he must be one of our contractors. A painter, maybe? He was a large man with a lot of dark brown hair—facial and, well, just *everywhere*. He wore a blue plaid button down short sleeved shirt and worn-out blue jeans.

"Libby?" he asked. Once I acknowledged, he thrust forward his hand, "Hi, I'm Scott with Arizona Parties." *Oh, not the picture I had in my head from the voice on the phone.*

"Hi Scott! I'm thrilled you were available so quickly. I figured it's the busy season, and I know I've waited to the last minute. Actually, we didn't even think of this until…" I paused, realizing I was rambling on, "oh, never mind that. Thank you for coming. Come on in and I'll show you around."

"Wow, this is big." He examined the space in the now-finished front reception area, and the unfinished larger rooms just through two sets of glass doors. "How many people you expectin'?"

"Not exactly sure, but I'd estimate about 150, but could be on upward to 200?" I explained what I envisioned for the party—spreading out various food and drink stations. I pointed out where I'd like several highly decorated Christmas trees, lighted garland, and fairy lights everywhere—hanging from the ceiling, outlining doorways, accenting cabinetry … the whole ten yards.

Continuing to look around, he just kept nodding his head in agreement.

"What do you think? Is this even possible to do in the timeframe we have?"

"When will these laborers be out of here?" he asked.

"By the end of the week."

"Sure, we have time. But, this isn't a 'cheap' job. You're looking at a few grand just for the food and beverages. Then, you have the labor and decorations on top of that."

"Ok, just give me a number and I'll review it with my

business partner. Can you have that to us this afternoon?"
I asked.

"Sure, not a problem. I require 75% up front and the
balance upon completion."

I showed him out and as he was walking away, Alexis
pulled up and parked in front of the building.

"Who was that? One of the painters—are they done
yet?" Alexis had her hands full, but managed to open the
hatch on the back of her Lexus. I helped carry a couple of
the boxes.

"Actually, he was with Arizona Parties ... someone Pat
knows."

"Interesting. Guess I would have expected a woman to
be the planner you were meeting with. How sexist is that
of me!?" She laughed as we walked through the front door.
Ironic that neither of us saw him as a party planner, but
more as one of the laborers.

I followed her to the office in the back of the building.
She set down the bags onto her new desk. I stacked the
boxes in the corner on the floor.

Alexis came over gave me a giant hug. "Care for some
tea?" she asked.

"Sure. You brought the kettle?"

"Yep, right here," she said as she opened one of the
boxes and pulled out our red electric tea kettle. "And,
in this one..." she wrangled open a smaller box, "is the
assortment of tea!" She glowed, very pleased with herself.

Once we both had some nice warm Ashwagandha tea,
and caught up on the status of our construction project,
we both sat down at our desks. I pulled my laptop from
my backpack and started researching more party planning
companies. I have no idea what parties cost ... this is not

in my wheel-house, however, I figure if we get at least three quotes, we should be able to ascertain a reasonable average and hire the best fit. Even though Pat's 'friend of a friend' was referred to us, I wasn't convinced that Arizona Parties was the exact right fit for the job. He didn't even make his own suggestions for the layout of the party … I essentially just planned it! Ok, maybe not catering and all, but shouldn't he have sold me on a fantastic party idea?

"Oh! I didn't…" Alexis stopped and started giggling. "I'm sorry, I didn't mean to startle you!"

I literally jumped up off my seat with eyes wide opened, "Jeez! You scared me" I started laughing too.

"Sorry, I just remembered that I wanted to show you something we received—the address label identified it being for 'Alexis and Libby—,' but there's no information about who sent it. Let's open it and see if we can solve this mystery." She stood and walked over to the boxes in the corner. After using the box cutter to slice open the tape, she peeled back the cardboard flaps, pulled out copious amounts of packing materials, and then carefully lifted out a statue-like object.

I got up and walked over to her, accepting the first of two beautifully decorated, but hefty bronzed statues she handed over. I was mesmerized by what looked to be a human, with an elephant head, sitting on a giant lotus flower. The object stood about five inches tall and maybe three inches wide. His belly was large, he had four hands, each holding something. I couldn't make out exactly what was in each hand, but I found it interesting how I was discovering all kinds of fun bits: colorful decorative crown, a shy mouse at his feet, intricate details throughout—simply beautiful!

Alexis broke my concentration on this fascinating object. "If I remember correctly, these appear to be relics from ancient India history. I haven't been great at memorizing facts such as these from my heritage. Even though I study meditation, I'm so bad at remembering Indian historical details."

I continued to turn him over and over, analyzing every element of this weighty artifact. "I cannot believe how intricate the artwork is and how *beautiful* this strange being is."

Alexis kneeled down and pulled the second statue from its box. She unwrapped a gorgeous tall figure about the same size as the one I was already holding; a woman wearing a flowing robe and delicate-looking strands of mala beads around her neck. This beautiful creature was standing in a large lotus flower that appeared to be filled with gold coins. She also had four hands, each holding something. It looked like she held flowers and coins. The colors she wore were dynamic: red, bronze, blue, and gold ... the lotus flower was a pink-purple blend.

"They look really old. Where did these come from? Is there a card in that box?" I said, still in awe, examining the relics.

"No. Nothing." She tore through the rest of the packaging while she looked for any clue. "The shipping label indicates San Francisco. I don't know anyone from there, do you?"

"Nope. But, what do you say we display these at the front reception desk?"

We walked toward the front desk. I held elephant man and she had the woman statue. Our front reception desk was a very long Corian countertop which was centered in and ran nearly the length of the room. It was the first thing you came to when you walked through the door. On either end of the long counter were waist-height swinging doors which allowed clients to the other side of the counter and to the doors to each locker room—women's to the left and men's to the right. Behind the reception desk, there was an additional employee entrance. Those frosted glass doors that led directly into what would be the Serenity Room when completed.

"What about right here for the elephant dude?" I asked as I pointed to a space on the counter which is seen front and center when you walk through the front doors. Alexis agreed, laughing at my description of the statue.

She placed the tall statue right next to the cash register which sat just below the countertop on the reception desk.

"Beautiful! I still would love to know where these came from." I stood back in admiration of our newest and mysterious décor.

I wonder who we have to thank for them, though?

3

A couple days later, I was finishing my cup of coffee and an English muffin at my kitchen table. Strewn all over the table were the notes I'd compiled from various different party planning companies I had already spoken to, and a huge stack of invitations I had printed out and stuck address labels to their envelopes.

The phone rang.

"Libs, construction is running a few days behind

schedule. The foreman explained there was an electrical issue in one of the massage therapy rooms, but they should have it fixed in a day or so. The flooring for the serenity room is also late; they hope it will arrive tomorrow and then it will take another day or two to install," Alexis explained.

"If it isn't one thing, it's another, huh?" I told her. "We *need* that serenity room completely finished in order to decorate for the party—it is the 'grand ballroom' for this event." My frustration was clear.

"I know. Maybe we shouldn't be pushing to do this right now? We can do the grand opening at any time. Maybe after the holidays would be best?"

Sadly, and looking around at all the work I'd already done for this party, I said, "I know it might not seem the best timing, but I really think we can have a smashing success with it. A party like this could make our grand opening extremely memorable—clients coming back for repeat business for years to come."

"Well, let's just remember that what's meant to be, will be. We can't force it. Speaking of which, did you even find a planner who is available?"

"Arizona Parties appear to be the only place in town available this month. The quote came in at $5500 and we have to put 75% down to book them."

"Yikes! *That* guy?" Alexis' skepticism was loud and clear.

"Yep. But, I'm sure he's just the one who quotes. There's probably a whole team of people behind the scenes actually planning."

"I didn't get the best vibes from him," she stated emphatically.

We finished our conversation and I went back to

searching for party planning companies. After becoming so frustrated, I called Scott with Arizona Parties and booked him to plan our grand opening. We agreed to meet at the spa to finalize and he would collect the check for the down payment, so I gathered up the invitations and headed out. First stop, post office.

* * *

Later that afternoon, I felt so accomplished after mailing invitations and hiring the party planner, I decided to head out on a hike. I live in a subdivision in Northeast Mesa that backs up to an expanse of state land with many hiking trails. In December, my favorite time to hike is late afternoon and today was perfect weather, so I tied up my hiking shoes and headed out the front door.

By the time I wound my way through the neighborhood heading toward the trails, the sun was low in the sky and hidden by a thin cloud layer. It was a spectacular continuous changing spectrum of color. First, yellow-orange, then brilliant red, and finally fading out to a lighter pink-orange. It reminded me of fancy cocktails with the colored layers that you'd drink while sitting at the beach.

Mesmerized by the sounds of the quail, the distant singing of the coyotes, and the diminishing afternoon light, I started thinking back about the interactions with Scott and Alexis' comments regarding him. I didn't see it, he seemed like a nice guy. True, he didn't look like a designer or planner type but I certainly didn't get bad vibes from him. Interesting. From there, I sorted out my mental 'to-do' list for tomorrow. Massage client, Sage's home, at 9 a.m. Hopefully, meet the flooring contractors at the spa by

1 p.m.—*the carpet better arrive*! There's something else I'm not remembering...

After several miles, I wound my way back through the neighborhood headed for home when my phone rang.

"Hi Alexis," I answered, just as it dawned on me the other task on the 'to-do' list was ... baking cookies with the Johnson family!

"Hey girl, did I catch you at a bad time?"

"Nope, just finishing my nature walk and heading home. What's up?" I realized I had really picked up the pace. I was winded answering that question.

"Flooring has arrived! And the electrician will be there tomorrow. What time are you planning to be at the spa?"

"I'll get there around noon, I have a session with Sage at nine."

"Perfect! I need to get Christmas shopping done in the morning and before our cookie decorating so I'm leaving the flooring guys for you."

"Yep, no problem. By the way, the deposit is paid to Arizona Parties and they'll start day after tomorrow." The silence made me think we lost connection. "Alexis, are you there?"

"Uh, yeah. So, you went with *Arizona Parties*? I thought we'd talk about it first." She was clearly not happy with me.

"Sorry. Yes, I just made the decision. There are literally *no other* companies available to do it on this short notice."

Again, huge long pause before I heard anything on the other end of the line.

"I'll see you later. Six, right?" she asked curtly.

"Yep, see you at six!" I tried in the most perky voice I

could muster up.

What's wrong with Alexis? She's normally so chill and we are partners, after all. I can make decisions, too… sheesh!

After a fitful night's sleep, worrying if I just blew it with my best friend and business partner, I went about my day checking off the task list, up until the moment I knocked on the Johnson's front door that evening.

From the outside, their house appeared modest, middle-income neighborhood, and very typical for the desert Southwest. It was a light gray stucco two-story structure, with dark gray trim and pillars outside the tall front patio and walkway. Their desert landscape had beautiful lighting all around, casting the shadows of the medium-sized palms and various drought-resistant shrubbery.

The door opened. "Aunt Libby!!!" Joshua thrust himself into my arms as I moved forward. No, I'm not technically his aunt, but he is my godson and that is what he calls me. I love it.

Jeff Johnson, Alexis' husband, who we call JJ, was standing just behind Joshua to greet me, also with a giant hug and kiss. His large stature makes it a natural bear hug, fully enveloped into his folding arms, my face squished against his chest.

Once he released me, I saw his light complexion, a bit flushed, as he stood back and said laughing, "Are you ready for the great Christmas cookie bake-off? Come in, come in …"

Clearly, JJ and Joshua were unaware of any tension between me and Alexis. Maybe it had passed and she truly wasn't as upset as I interpreted from the phone call last night? Praying this was true, I rounded the corner into their enormous kitchen. She was already mixing dough and had flour all down the front of her apron, and all over her face were smears of the white powder which stood out against her dark skin tone.

"Hey Libby." Alexis didn't make eye contact, but turned around to get milk out of the refrigerator.

JJ caught the snub. Looking at me, his eyebrows tightened, questioning. Usually, she would have hugged and made sure to transfer some of that flour onto me.

I pressed on trying to lighten the mood and ignored the undertones in the room. "I hear there's a great bake-off happening? Well, I'm here to beat this little guy!" I picked up my three-year-old surrogate nephew and twirled him around while he was laughing and squealing. We carried on for a few minutes before I approached my friend.

"How can I help?" I asked Alexis, and strapped on an apron I found draped over one of the breakfast bar chairs.

"Why don't you and Joshua take this dough I've mixed and make a bunch of one-inch round balls?" She directed, setting us up in seats at the kitchen table. "Once they are on the cooking sheet, press your thumb in the middle like this." She demonstrated and Joshua's face lit up as though he was going to enjoy sticking his fingers in the dough. "First, go wash your hands, little man!" She chuckled at her toddler.

JJ poured me some wine and delivered Joshua a glass of milk as we all sat around and relaxed into baking and decorating for the evening. Alexis was not her normal bubbly self. She was clearly still upset at me, but it didn't ruin the evening.

After the decorating was done, JJ, Joshua and I put our

best decorated cookie on a plate to be judged. Alexis studied each cookie carefully, making funny faces as though she were a serious judge, but mostly to just get Joshua laughing hysterically. When she made her final decision, she pulled out a small plastic trophy.

"… And the winner of this year's Johnson Family Christmas Cookie Bake-off is …" we all drum-rolled on the kitchen table, "JOSHUA!!!" His face beamed and he took his trophy, then proceeded to dance all over the house showing it off.

"Wow, you're going to have a hard time getting this one to sleep tonight." I laughed, watching him bounce around with so much energy. After all the cookies and dough that we kept sneaking when mom turned her back, yep, he's going to be wound up for awhile. "Well, it's late and I should get home."

As they walked me toward the front door, my friend said she'd walk me to my car. Outside, I turned to her, "Alexis, I'm sorry I didn't consult with you first on the party planner."

"Libby, it's ok. Yes, I was upset because as business partners, we need to make decisions together. I felt left out. However, I realize my reaction is not fair. I told you to 'go for it' when *we* decided to do the party. So, I'm sorry." She hugged me and we continued walking toward the driveway.

"It is overwhelming, isn't it?" I asked.

She looked at me questioningly.

"The holidays—with shopping, baking, decorating, and maintaining 'home life' too. Our spa construction is delayed. Now a party. I get it. It's a lot and I'm sorry to have added to your stress."

"Hey, the good news, is that we've got the carpeting in.

The party planners can decorate the main room now ... and the wood flooring in the rest of the building goes in tomorrow. And, you are right, a holiday party is just what we need to kick everything off!"

"It'll be beautiful. Oh, and to update you, all the invitations went out, I've posted all over social media about our grand opening, and a huge banner will arrive tomorrow announcing it as well."

"Thank you for all your work on this, Libby!"

We said our goodbyes and I felt so relieved that we'd cleared the air. Now, I just had to be at the spa early in the morning to meet the next set of contractors and the party planners.

* * *

The next day, after the flooring contractors were nearly done laying all the honey-oak laminate wood flooring late in the afternoon, I tried again for the fifth time reaching someone at Arizona Parties—no answer. No voice messaging service to leave a message. They were supposed to be here at eight this morning.

I went online to look up where their business was located so I could drive over there before 5 p.m. I found the website, but no contact information. No address. Only the phone number I had been trying. I called the phone number *again*. No answer. No voice mail set up.

From a deep abyss, the nausea was bubbling. My palms were sweaty. My heart racing as though I'd just finished an ultra-marathon. My mind numb, but also buzzing. I was still justifying why Scott had not called when they were late this morning. Excuses were swirling around in my brain as to why I couldn't reach anyone on the phone. Scott Smith was a very common name; it was going to take hours to call each listing for that name.

I fell into the nearest chair, bent over with my head between my knees, breathing deeply and trying my best not to throw up all over our beautiful new wood flooring.

4

Without any idea how I managed to get myself home, I was still absolutely distraught. *How could I be soooo stupid?* Continuing to beat myself up, I dreaded the call to Alexis. No, first, I will move mountains to find Scott before admitting to my partner that we lost four thousand dollars and have no planners for a party scheduled for a week from now.

Wait, did he cash the check? I ran to the kitchen table and set up my laptop. *If he didn't cash it, I could cancel the check. Problem solved.* It seemed to take an eternity for the computer to boot up and then for the website to load. I punched in my username and password and waited.

Shit! The funds had already cleared our business checking account. *Why? Why didn't I even ask to pay by credit card?*

I spent the next hour, all the way up until closing time for most businesses, calling the Better Business Bureau, Arizona Commerce Commission, and then my former brother in-law's cell phone.

As soon as he answered, I spat out, "Pat, that party planner … Scott. I need to know where he lives. Please…"

"Libby?" he sounded very confused. "Who are you talking about?"

"Scott! That guy you referred for our grand opening party!" I was nearly yelling at this point. I was desperate.

"Um, I don't know a 'Scott'… or at least, I don't know anything about referring anyone to you, Libby. Are you okay?"

"No, I'm not! Sorry to bother you, Pat." I hung up and dialed Jordan's number next.

"Libby…?"

"Who's that guy you referred me to? Scott, Scott Smith. He took my money, hasn't showed up to do the job, and now I can't reach him on the number you gave me!"

"Uh, well," she paused for an interminable amount of time.

"Jordan! What is going on? Who is this person and how do I get hold of him?" I yelled.

"Libs, I think I made a mistake. I'm on my way over now." She hung up.

The second she pulled in my driveway, I bounded out of the house and dragged her pregnant-self inside.

"Jordan—I'm in deep with Alexis now." My face was flushed, I was harried, and mad. I didn't even recognize the voice coming from my own body.

"Uh, I … I, need to tell you something, Libby." She was definitely a more diminutive version of herself. I'm not sure I recognized either of us in this moment. We seemed to have reversed sisterly roles here. "I, well…" she hesitated again.

"Spit. It. Out. Jordan!"

"Ok. So, I made the mistake of saying that Scott was one of Pat's friends'... friends." She hesitated, quietly continuing. Her eyes sheepishly looked up at mine. "There's someone else." And, her face fell toward the floor once again.

"What do you mean 'there's someone else'?" I had long since lost patience and now I was just confused and I wanted to slap the heck out of my sister.

"I, uh..." she slowly lifted her eyes again, "met someone at the gym. Um, before this..." she stared at her big belly.

I felt like I was just slugged in the gut. *What? Perfect home-maker, housewife extraordinaire, and mom-of-the-year ... cheated?*

"Who is Scott?" I calmly asked, as I sat down in my living room chair.

She just started to cry. Huge crocodile tears poured down her face and her shoulders bounced up and down as she sobbed. I gave her a few minutes. I forced every cell in my body to not react—either by killing her, or wrapping her up in a hug. I just let her cry.

Eventually, she started again ...

"I, uh," she wiped her nose, then continued, "I met Chester at the gym. You have to understand that Pat and I haven't been good for years." She saw my look of confusion. "I know, we're good at faking it."

"After Chase was born, we hit a rough patch in our marriage. I thought we were working things out when I learned he cheated on me with a twenty-something at work. He promised it was nothing—just a fling, and it was already over. We continued therapy, trying to fix it ... we even had a few good moments about a year ago. Or, exactly nine months ago," again her eyes cast downward.

I took her hand in mine. "Does Mom know?"

She wiped more tears, blew her nose, and started again. "No one knew exactly what was going on in our household. I was too embarrassed." She started to sob again. I moved closer and wrapped my arms around her. "Right before I was going to share the pregnancy results, Pat confided that he had met 'his soulmate'. He couldn't continue on in our 'sham of a marriage'."

I let her pour out all the pent-up emotion. When she was done, I asked if this was too much for her or if she'd share more about Chester. "Who is *Chester?*"

She grabbed a new tissue, blew her nose real hard, then continued again. "I met Chester Whitmore more than a year ago now. You see, I needed someone to talk to—outside the family. He listened to me during workouts; we ran on treadmills next to each other. That turned into outdoor exercise: walking, hiking, and sometimes we'd take a yoga class together."

My perfect sister was having an affair!

She must have read the look on my face because she quickly inserted emphatically, "I never had an affair with Chester! He's married. The only thing he was to me was my gym and workout friend and confidant, but it *never* went further than that." She looked wistful, then added quietly, "I won't lie. There were moments when I think I wished I had *someone* that cared about me romantically. I was incredibly lonely and constantly worried about Pat divorcing me. The three small kids…" Tears started flowing down her face again. She grimaced and rubbed her belly.

"Of course, of course." I just nodded and comforted. I couldn't imagine going through all this and I was heartbroken that she hadn't reached out to me while it was all happening. However, I could understand. She had built up this *perfect* wife and mom existence—no one could know differently. In fact, I was stunned she was confessing it all now.

"So, Jordan, who is Scott then?" We had gotten so wrapped around the axle about her failed marriage that I nearly forgot about the current problem at hand.

"Oh, well … it was Chester that recommended Scott. But, I couldn't possibly tell you that so I said it was someone Pat knew through a friend."

Suddenly, she bent over, groaning. She twisted over to her right side on the sofa, then slid down to the floor on all fours. "Aaaagggghhh…" The most insane demonic sound came from deep within her throat. I seemed to instinctively know what this meant because I reached for my pocket, pulled out my cell phone, and dialed 911.

"Libby, the baby. Don't leave me alone," she was sobbing still, and writhing in pain, but her voice was just a whisper. "Please."

The ambulance arrived and the EMTs checked all her vitals and determined there was still time to get her to the hospital. *Thank God!*

I followed the ambulance in my vehicle and struggled with whether I should call Pat. I decided to wait and ask her that question once she was settled in the hospital. The rest of the drive I spent ruminating over the day's events. The great news was that the construction work was now all done. The electrician finished. The flooring was in and was as beautiful as we had envisioned. Some of the furnishings—massage tables, cabinets, front reception chairs—were being delivered in the morning. The horrible news was that the party was scheduled for two days from now, people had RSVP'd and were excited about it, and now we had to solve the mystery of the missing party planner. We had no planner, food, drink, or money left. And I hadn't told Alexis anything about this yet.

And now, my sister is having her baby.

My stomach churned.

5

It was a very long night. Despite having delivered three other babies, Jordan's current one was holding on and not wanting to make an appearance into this world. After nearly twelve hours of labor, in the wee hours of dawn on December 14, little Ryan White made his debut. He was 7 lbs., 7oz., with full rosy cheeks and looked perfect in every way. Jordan was exhausted, but she did well. Pat did end up flying in and made it just minutes before the delivery. I decided to escape and let them have some time alone. *I don't even want to get in the middle of this debacle.*

On my way home, I tried calling Scott again. No answer. No voice mail.

I called JJ. He was a Mesa police officer so I figured I would get his advice on how to go about filing charges for fraud. What else could I do when this man had my money and was nowhere to be found? We had a nice long chat and until I could get more information, I really couldn't do much. For now, I'd have to grovel for a while with Alexis and figure out how we'll throw a decent party *in just a few days' time.* I headed toward the spa.

I walked in to see that our furniture had been delivered. The reception desk, behind the long counter, was complete now with an oak file cabinet that fit just under the Corian counter, a couple ergonomic chairs, and a stunning, large white shelving unit that extended from floor to just below the crown-molded ceiling and was approximately ten feet in length along the wall.

I looked around and saw the waiting area chairs had been delivered. Four slightly oversized and cushy upholstered chairs lined the glass wall the length of the building. Each was a different bold color: peacock blue, mustard yellow, bright coral, and sunflower yellow-orange. It was certainly bright and cheerful now, exactly what we were going for in the lobby area. The rest of the spa, behind the frosted glass doors, would be furnished in mauve and gray tones, and the walls painted in corresponding earth tones to invite calmness and peace.

Alexis popped through the frosted glass doors at that moment. She smiled and gave me a hug once she walked around the front counter.

"I'm off to pick up our logo decals for the doors," she announced as she headed through the front door. Turning back, she said, "I can't wait to see what the party décor looks like ... this is getting exciting!"

I just smiled. I found my feet rooted in place near the front door, just staring as she blew out of here and then drove away. *I have to tell her. JJ knows so this isn't good if she hears about it from him first.*

As I pivoted around toward the doors at the end of the counter, there in the bright coral colored chair was a very small woman. Girl? Woman? It was hard to tell. Let's just say she had very tiny features.

"Hello! I'm so sorry, I never saw you sitting there!" I said as I walked toward her and held out my hand. She touched my hand, a simple feather-light touch, and gave a quick snap of a nod. "I'm afraid I was so caught up in seeing our new furniture in place, I really wasn't paying attention."

All of sudden, she bounced up and flitted off—around me, to the left of the counter, she quickly moved through the swinging door that led to another door—into the women's locker room. It took me a second. *Wait, who is this? Where did she come from? Surely, Alexis would have introduced a new client? Or, did she pop in while Alexis had the door open—I mean, this tiny person is half Lexi's size, I suppose it's possible.* After a second or two and hundreds of questions running through my brain, I realized I should go find her. Our business is not open yet for the public.

I ran toward the locker room, pushed through the door, and stood there for a moment listening. *What if she was just using the restroom? Perhaps I should give her a moment.*

"Excuse me, miss? Are you in here?" I called out. No answer. No indication of movement or anyone occupying any of the stalls so I proceeded out the next set of doors and into our relaxation room.

"Ah, there you are!" I saw that she was making her way about the room, her face moving up and down, looking around with inquisitive looks. "Is there something I can help you with? My name is Libby … I'm one of the owners. Are you looking to become a client of ours?"

She smiled graciously, giggled a bit, and then skipped her way through the next set of doors that led to our massage rooms, office, and laundry facilities. She was *fast;* here one moment, gone the next. I followed, and it was then that I realized there were still contractors working in the therapy rooms. I would have thought Alexis would mention they were still here. Maybe this girl belongs to one of them?

The tiny being literally floated from room to room. *Am I seeing this right? She's so light on her feet ... is she flying? Nah, she's just really quick.*

I popped my head into the space where our contractor was working.

"Pete? Is this your daughter perhaps—running around?" I pointed outside the doorway. He got up off the floor where he was securing the floorboard.

"I don't have a daughter." He looked out the door anyway. His head turned right, then swiveled left, and then he looked back at me and shrugged, "I haven't seen anyone but Alexis in here today. Oh, and my helper, Danny, he's in the next room."

I looked around and didn't see the pixie-like girl, so I walked into the next therapy room and asked Danny. Nope, he hadn't seen anyone. This was very strange.

I found my little friend again in the laundry room.

"Miss, can I help you? We are not open for business yet." I remained friendly, but certainly used a more professional and firm tone.

In the tiniest, and syrup-sweet, sing-song voice, she said, "Nooo, but I can help *you*." Her finger pointed, she reached out and touched the center of my forehead lightly. She giggled again, her smile was almost luminescent. She held eye contact and I was captivated, unable to look away. I realized then that she had on the cutest little outfit. It was a soft pink leotard covered in a sparkling tulle skirt and she had a similar sparkly, pink rhinestone-encrusted top that flared out from her shoulders along her arms, almost like ... *wings?*

I was still admiring the miniature features of this beautiful outfit, thinking how brave this girl was to wear it out in public. Maybe she was on her way to dance class? *Isn't there a dance school near here?* Right then, Danny came out and approached us. When I briefly took my eyes off her and looked to him, she disappeared in a flash.

"Did you find who you were looking for?" he asked.

"Yes! That girl," I pointed toward the doors that led out front. "... She just walk ... er, floa ... uh, didn't you just see...she was right here talking to me?"

Danny looked around the room, then back at me. With his head tilted and clear confusion on his face, he said, "No ma'am, I haven't seen any girl around here today. Just Pete, Alexis, and ... well, you."

I realized in that moment that the very long night at the hospital coupled with all the stress of trying to get the grand opening party off the ground had taken its toll on me. I was exhausted. And, I still had to tell Alexis everything ... *and, figure out how to get a party together tout de suite!* At this point, I didn't even care if it was extravagant. We ... I ... have to come up with something that impresses and draws in new clients. People are expecting a grand opening party.

Panic was definitely setting in.

6

As soon as she arrived home, Alexis opened the mailbox, pulled out a pile of letters, advertisements, and catalogs, and then headed inside the house. Joshua was calmly playing a game on the laptop on the living room coffee table. JJ had just called to say he was running late.

Slicing open an envelope that appeared to have come from India, Alexis sat down to read.

Dearest Alexis,

I hope by now you and Libby have received my gift. I'm so proud of you two lovely ladies for following your hearts and realizing your dreams ... well aware of all the blood, sweat, and tears you've put into your business, and will continue to do, over so many years. You should be proud and know that whatever obstacles you encounter, you are now protected. Your dreams will continue to bring prosperity.

I want to tell you a story that only a few of our family members know. After I pass, you will be the only remaining family to carry on our legacy. Your mother never seemed interested in the spiritual history, but from what you've told me, it sounds like you are.

Hundreds of years ago, in my ancestor's very small town out in the countryside near Bangalore, my great grandmother and her very best friend found an old homestead made up of several buildings. This place must have been several hundred years old at that time, and it was abandoned.

They were always curious young ones and they explored the countryside endlessly for years upon years as they grew into young women. Once they found this particular place, though, they spent months turning up every stone and searching every crevice of the decrepit structures. They made up stories and played 'house'. I hear they concocted stories that one day they'd grow up and this is where their descendants would live for thousands of years to come ... they'd fix it up lavishly and it would be the new ancestral homestead.

It never happened. My great grandmother passed the knowledge of the homestead to future generations as she aged, but only a few actually showed interest.

Until I came along…

Many decades later, my best friend and I listened to the stories from my grandmother and decided we needed to explore and discover this place we'd heard of so many times over the years. We found it, and just like my grandmother and great grandmother, we had lofty dreams of somehow making this our descendant's home for centuries to come. These years were literally the best time of my life. It was like something kept drawing us back—we loved it there.

One day, just when we thought we'd found every room and closet in the dwellings, we came upon a door that we apparently had never opened before. It wasn't easy to open. It looked like many had tried. And, many failed. We found objects like a metal rod and some sticks to try and pry it open. After days of going back there and wrestling with this, we persevered and finally got it to open.

When I looked through the door, there was an ancient stone staircase leading into the depths of the earth. A secret staircase. We were so excited and immediately ran down, not even concerned about what dangers may face us.

Long story short, we were in grave danger, and we should have been more concerned than we were as adventurous young souls. I don't want to go into the scary parts of that story, that's not the point of my letter; we survived and that's all that is important. What I want to pass down to you, that I don't think your mother ever wanted me to, is the spirit behind the gifts I sent. You see, there are those in our family who see these gifts in a different light than I.

We found the ancient artifacts that day after venturing down the secret staircase. No one before us had made it that far, to open the door … but we found them. With the spirit of the deities, we not only survived our adventures, but my friend and I became very prosperous, in many aspects, throughout the rest of our lives. My belief is that we were the only two who were meant to discover the secret staircase. We were the ones chosen to find the relics. From that moment, the spirits were always with us to guide and protect us.

Let me introduce you to them—

Ganesha—the one who is part elephant and part man. He sets and blocks obstacles. He will protect you by blocking obstacles that will get in your way to prosperity. He's tricky though … he'll also set up obstacles for you, if they are necessary to keep you on the correct path. Whenever you have a new home—or new business—he is good to keep nearest the front door.

Lakshmi—she's beautiful, isn't she? I'm sure you've seen her with her long flowing beautiful robe and holding flowers and coins. This is the deity who will bring you luck and prosperity. Treat her with respect and give her the dignity she deserves by placing her in a prominent spot where cash flows.

Alexis, I see in you the great spirit of peace. From your description of the friendship you have with Libby, I see adventures far and wide. I hope you two take great care with these ancient relics. Keep them in your family … and yes, that means with the friends who have become family as well.

I love you dear child,

Namaste,

Grandma Kohli

She's alive? Alexis folded the letter and put it back in its envelope and then set it carefully in the top drawer of her desk. She grabbed a tissue from the box and wiped tears from her eyes. She'd only had the opportunity to see her grandmother on a few occasions in her homeland of India, at the homestead about which she wrote, but she felt immensely close to her. For years, they wrote to each other frequently and she always felt her grandmother understood her in ways that no one else did. *Who wrote this?*

My grandmother passed away five years ago.

"Mommy!" Joshua called out. "I wanna cookie."

"Not until we get some lunch in your belly, little man." She scooped him up and hugged him, then set him down in the kitchen and they proceeded to make peanut butter and jelly sandwiches together.

"Are we going to see Aunt Libby today?" he asked sweetly, as he proceeded to smear peanut butter across the slice of bread, over his whole hand, and onto the kitchen counter.

Alexis grabbed a wet paper towel and started wiping his hands before it was on his face and in his hair. "Probably not today, but the party is coming up. If you are a really good boy, and get a good night's sleep tonight, and take your nap tomorrow afternoon, then Dad said he'll bring you to the party for a little bit. Won't that be fun?" she asked excitedly.

He jumped down from the chair, yelling "Party! Party!" and running all over the place.

"Get back over here and let's gobble these up."

"Eat! Eat! Eat!" he chanted as he danced another circle and came back to his chair.

7

I had just left the spa after my strange encounter with our wee bejeweled visitor. The contractors were completely finished with the job now—what a relief! I paid them and still had to figure out how to pull off a party in about twenty-four hours, with no sleep.

First, I needed to talk to JJ.

"Hi JJ!" I greeted when he answered.

"Libby—to what do I owe the pleasure?" One of my oldest friends, he's always been a kind gentleman. I introduced him to Alexis about five years ago and they've been inseparable since.

"Have you mentioned to Lexi about Scott going missing?" I asked.

"Who? Oh, no, totally forgot actually."

"Good! Please don't tell her. I will talk to her first." I wasn't going to mention that my sister's labor interrupted me, but then I remembered they knew each other well. "Oh! Jordan had the baby early this morning!"

"Jordan had her baby?! What did she have? Another girl?" he sounded so excited.

"No, another boy … Ryan. Listen, I just remembered I didn't tell Alexis either … so please let me break that news to her first?"

"Sure, not a problem. See you tomorrow at the party. Wait, is there still going to be a party, Libby?"

"Of course, I'm going to pull this off one way or another." I sighed, said goodbye, and hung up.

Now, to the party store. I had already loaded my small SUV with all the Christmas decorations I had at home, and still had some room for a few bags of goodies. *What are we going to do for food and drink? One thing at a time, Libby.*

* * *

After loading up with plastic plates, silver plastic utensils, napkins in various holidays prints, I called it a day. Well, for shopping anyway.

I pulled up to the hospital and saw Pat pulling out of the parking lot in his red Subaru Outback. My heart sank as I remembered what Jordan unloaded on me last night. *I wished they could have worked it out.*

I decided to stop in the gift shop to quickly pick up a bouquet of flowers and then I was on my way up the elevator. As I approached her door, I stopped and took a really deep breath.

"Hi, new mommy!" I said as pleasantly as I could, walking in the door and setting the flowers down on the bedside table.

She looked up from her bundle who was nursing and smiled. "Good morning ... oh look, it's already afternoon? Good afternoon, Libby!" she laughed.

"How are you two doing?" I asked.

"Well, this one is a joy ... he's been so quiet and I actually got a little sleep. Looks like they're going to let us out this evening. You just missed Pat, he's going home to get me some clean clothes and a change for our bitty Ryan here, too. He'll be back soon." For a moment, I forgot they weren't living together as man and wife anymore. This all seemed so normal.

"Oh, he's gorgeous, Jordan." I admired the baby for a few moments. "I can't stay long; I've got a party to put on tomorrow night and I'm nowhere near ready." I said while watching baby Ryan's tiny fist close around my index finger.

"I'm very sorry, Libby. I had no idea what a flake Scott would turn out to be." She lifted Ryan away from her bosom, covered up, and turned his small body over, setting him face down across her stretched-out legs, gently tapping his back until we heard a little burp.

"Do you want to hold him?" she asked me.

"Really? Isn't he too *new*?" My pulse started racing, not sure what to do.

"No. Here…" she gracefully handed him over all swaddled in his blanket.

Once I was sure I wasn't going to drop this precious bundle, I just kissed the top of his head and cuddled. He made cute baby noises and drifted off to sleep. I could watch him all day, but I really needed to go. I motioned silently that I was handing him back to her.

"Thank you," I whispered and kissed her forehead. "I hope you recover shortly. Enjoy your sweet boy this afternoon. Will Pat be taking you home later?" She indicated yes. We said our goodbyes and I left.

* * *

On my way out of the hospital, I called JJ again.

"Scott Smith," he spoke deliberately, as he typed the name into the computer. "Hmmm. You aren't the only person looking for him apparently. Arizona Parties? Is that the name of the company?"

"Yep, that's it."

"Yeah, he's already a wanted man. Looks like three other cases of fraud have been filed against him. Can you come down and file a complaint?"

"Ugh! JJ, I have so much to do for the party now that he skipped out. Can it wait a few days?"

"Sure, it's up to you. In the meantime, I'm going to follow up to see if there's any progress on his whereabouts."

"Thank you, JJ … really appreciate any help you can give."

Now, back to the spa for decorating.

As I headed north on Dobson Rd., toward Loop 202, my eyes started to feel weighty, my arms were heavy and weak as they hung from the steering wheel. I was beyond exhausted. After another fifteen minutes of shaking my head to keep awake, I glanced quickly at the clock, it was just after three. I'm going to have to confess to Alexis that we don't have party planners. I need help.

I turned off the Loop 202, onto Power Rd., made a right-hand turn and proceeded toward my house. *Just a short nap, that's all I need.*

Mine was the first car at the light at Thomas Rd., waiting for it to turn green. I turned to my right and saw there was a man in a silver Chevy truck. He looked straight ahead so I could only see his profile, but I swear it was … *Scott Smith.*

I honked, just as the light turned green. He turned to face me, his eyes opened wide and he sped off heading south. It took me a second to realize what just happened and then I went speeding off as well.

He swerved from lane to lane avoiding slower traffic.

I followed, but more cautiously, several cars distance behind him. Carefully, I punched the button to activate my car's communication system and verbally commanded to call JJ.

"Hi Libby!" he answered cheerfully.

"JJ—Scott … I'm following him!" I yelled out.

"Libby, be careful! Where are you?" he asked.

"Heading south on Power, just passed … um," I looked around for signs. "University!"

"Ok, I'm close, but not on duty—just left the precinct." I could hear his vehicle accelerating now too. "Libby, please keep a safe distance. Don't get into an accident trying to catch up with this guy."

"Where are you, JJ?"

"Just approaching Power at Southern ... what vehicle is he in?"

"Silver Chevy pickup."

"See him ... I'll follow. You pull over and retreat. Don't hang up yet."

"Ok, I'm going to pull over into the Target parking lot," I said.

"Looks like that's where he's turning in ..."

"I see you both!" The line went dead.

Just then, JJ swerved his Tahoe right in front of the silver truck, nearly getting hit. Tires screeched and smoke billowed. I pulled over into a parking spot where I could see the action, but not near enough for either of the men to see me directly.

I began to dial 911 on my phone, but just as I started with the '9', I saw several Mesa Police vehicles fast approaching the parking lot and surrounding JJ and Scott's vehicles. There were a few tense moments, but then I could see one officer lead a handcuffed Scott over to his cruiser. That's when I decided to get out of my car.

"JJ!" I yelled. He snapped his head to the right and caught my eye, held his index finger up at the police officer talking to him. Then he waved me over.

"As I was saying, this lady," he pointed to me, "hired that man ..." he pointed to the cruiser where Scott was now sitting, "for a job and he didn't deliver. He still has her money." I gave a little half wave to the officer as I approached, hearing what JJ was telling him.

"Hi, Officer ... McLaughlin," I acknowledged, looking at the moderately overweight, older gentleman with the thin white hair and noticed his name tag. "I haven't filed an official report yet, but I saw that man," pointing to Scott, "who stole from me. I'd just like my money back, that's all."

"And, Tim, as you will learn here, there are several other fraud complaints filed against him," JJ added.

"Yep, we'll take it from here." He then turned to me, "Ma'am, please make sure you get that police report filed at your earliest convenience." With that, he turned away from us and joined the other officers.

"Well, that was good timing, wasn't it?" JJ asked.

It was now after 5 p.m. Even though my adrenaline had shot up during this pursuit, I was beyond weary. My hands shook as I reached out to hug my friend.

"Thank you, JJ. I'm so exhausted, I can't see straight." I sighed. "I haven't told Alexis about this snafu yet. I was at the hospital all last night, finished with the flooring laborers this morning, and managed to get a few party supplies and my Christmas decorations from home." I pointed over to my vehicle which was crammed to the roof with stuff, to illustrate I wasn't kidding. "But, I don't have any more energy right now. I truly hope it can all be done tomorrow." I let my breath out, my head fell, and I felt … defeated.

"Look, Libby … I'll talk to Alexis for you. She'll understand. How about all of us meet at the spa once you've rested? We can get this done!" God bless JJ and his endless optimism. I could only wish to have as great a man as he is someday.

"I'm going home now. I'll call you when I wake up and yes, I know one way or another, we'll get it all done. Thank you, JJ."

"Be safe, Libby!" he called after me as I walked over to my car and climbed in.

8

I opened my eyes and realized the daylight that shone through the edges of the blinds was super bright. *What time is it?* I rubbed my eyes, looked at the clock, and then shot out of bed.

It was 8 a.m. and I'd just slept more than twelve hours straight.

Today is the grand opening!

On what should have been the happiest day, I was suddenly in a panic.

I have so much to do!

I headed for the kitchen first and started the coffee pot. *Nothing happens before coffee.* Then I picked up my phone and hesitated for a second before dialing Alexis and JJ. *They have a three-year-old, of course they're awake.*

"Alexis?" I was hesitant as I spoke.

"Hey love, good morning!" she answered in her soothing and calm voice. "Are you ready to get busy decorating?"

"JJ filled you in on everything?"

"Yes, he did, honey ... no worries. Let's all pitch in together and we'll pull this off. I'm sure we can pick up some food trays at Costco, too. It doesn't have to be fancy, but we'll divide and conquer. We've got this!"

"Oh, Lexi! Thank you for not being upset with me. I really messed this one up." I was relieved.

"It happens. Give us about thirty minutes and then we'll meet you at the spa. Sound good?"

"Perfect!"

* * *

My arms were loaded with shopping bags, a box of Christmas ornaments, and I was trying to pull my keys from my purse. *I should have opened the doors first, then gone back to the car to unload.* Twisting the keys around in my right hand to find the right one and get it lined up with the keyhole, I finally heard the lock tumblers engage and unlock. Success!

Pulling the door slightly open, I shoved my left foot in the open space and finally managed to get my whole body through. The second I stepped into the lobby, I felt it.

I set my armload into the nearest chair.

My eyes started to well up as I looked around.

What? … Who?

It was stunning! Every inch of the lobby area looked like something out of a fairytale. I just started crying. It was *exactly* as I'd imagined.

Alexis, JJ, and Joshua showed up seconds after me. They walked through the door, suddenly stopped, and did as I had done. Their gazes were all over the place. There was so much to take in—huge, fully decorated Christmas trees in bright, bold, cheery colors placed at both ends of the lobby. Under the large trees, there were hundreds of small cloth bags in a variety of colors, cinched together closed at the top with red ribbon displaying tags inscribed with beautiful calligraphy, '*With Love,—Libby and Alexis.*'

There were three small tabletop trees placed equal distances along the length of the countertop, including lighted garland in bright bold colors. Looking up at the ceiling, there were literally thousands of fairy lights dangling from the ceiling, as well as hundreds of delicate white cut-out paper snowflakes.

"Uh, Libby … we said we'd help. You should have waited—wow, you've really outdone yourself!" JJ was still looking to the ceiling in amazement as he tried to get his words out of his head.

I was still taking in the sight of the stunning Christmas trees. "Guys … I, uh…I didn't do this."

We all stared at each other. Joshua was running from one end of the room to the other, "Party!! Party!! Party!!" he sung, dancing in circles.

Alexis broke the stare first, "Ok. Then who did?"

I just lifted my shoulders high, let them fall, and shook my head. "I really have no idea…"

Just then, we all seemed to have the same idea as our feet collectively moved and we walked through the frosted glass doors into the serenity room. Just inside the room, we were once again transfixed.

Looking up, thousands more fairy lights *everywhere*. Snowflakes—these looked like sparkling crystals, reflecting the spectrum of light throughout the room. The four corners of this room also had enormous trees, all exquisitely decorated in color themes … silver and mauve in the southeast and northwest corners of the room. The other two trees held deep maroon- and gold-colored ornaments sprinkled about perfectly. The rest of the spacious room had high-top cocktail tables, adorned in mauve and silver tablecloths with tinsel lighted centerpieces. There were two tables on each of the north and south ends of the room covered in black tablecloths, and each had various bottles of wine, liquor, and sparkling water.

As though we were all possessed, we moved as one through the next set of open frosted glass doors, into the next space. Here, we gazed over two long tables set up the length of the room, where multiple shiny silver chafing dishes were set up and ready for a feast. There was an envelope sticking out from one of the metal containers.

"Lexi, look." I opened the envelope and read the menu, "Roasted turkey medallions with a garlic herb butter rub, creamy mashed potatoes, classic gravy with fresh herbs, ciabatta stuffing with chicken sausage and cranberries, smoky maple brussels sprouts with lemon, and ginger cranberry sauce." Suddenly, I was famished reading the scrumptious menu. "It says they'll be here at five to set up." *Who?* was the big question in my mind. *How much is all this going to cost us?*

"Libby, over here…" Alexis called out. She found another envelope, at a similar spot on the next table. "Hors d'oeuvres? Listen to this … 'Bacon-wrapped scallops, mini brie and cranberry tartlets, prosciutto-wrapped asparagus,'" she read from the card. "Says they'll start serving guests appetizers as they arrive at 7 p.m."

Except for Joshua, who was running all around the tables, the rest of us were in the same trance, looking at each other as though we didn't know what to do next.

"Look, Mom! Santa Claus!" Joshua called out from the corner near the doors leading to the massage therapy rooms. There was a giant life-sized cut-out Santa positioned in what was clearly a photo-op area, with a Christmas tree standing prominently behind it.

We walked slowly around the room, taking in every single detail. Lighted garland around each doorway to the therapy rooms, our office, and the laundry room. Again, fairy lights all over. It was the most beautiful winter wonderland I'd ever seen.

"There's no way I could have ever pulled anything like this off," I said, staring at every detail.

Alexis' eyes were wide, she whispered, "Libby, how did someone get in the spa? If neither of us are responsible for this, *how* did someone else do it?"

I had no words. I just kept shaking my head.

JJ's sudden deep voice made us startle. "Well, I know for a fact that Scott is in jail … and that his party business has been shut down. He was stealing money from unsuspecting people. So, this isn't their doing."

None of us had an explanation.

9

I arrived around four that afternoon, already dressed in the only little black dress I own. I fancied it up a bit, draping a scarf over my shoulders. It was deep red, threaded with gold that sparkled and stood out nicely against the dark fabric. My outfit was complete with dark red heels I had been forced to buy as a bridesmaid some years ago. No, they weren't for the wedding, but instead they were required for a myriad of parties hosted during the entire wedding *weekend*. At least I was getting some use out of them again and they matched perfectly with my scarf.

Alexis floated into the room wearing a gorgeous apricot-colored princess line gown that accented her complexion perfectly. The layers of apricot tulle sparkled and she wore the deep V-neck style like the model this dress was made for. Her long neck complemented her new pixie-like hair style. She perfected the part of princess in this fairytale.

"Libby, you look magnificent!" she glided over, gave me a hug and a kiss, and proceeded to put her purse away in the locking desk drawer in our office.

"As do you, my friend. Can you believe this is the day? Our *grand opening*!" I smiled widely and thought my eyes were going to tear up again. I worked too hard to apply makeup for this evening, something I rarely do, so no crying for me.

"Libs, I have to share something with you." She turned and grabbed an envelope on the desk. Opening it, I could see that she was conflicted about something. "This letter. It's signed as coming from my grandmother." She handed it over so I could read.

"I thought she had passed?" I cautiously asked her after I had read the sweet writings.

"So did I. Why would my mom tell me that, if it weren't true?" I saw her eyes start to water.

"I liked the story she shared with you," I stated, trying to divert her attention. "And, now we know who sent the ancient relics to us!"

"Yes, it does solve that mystery, but I was sad to learn that since she mailed the letter, she really has passed away. I lost so many years with her! I don't understand." Her head dropped; her shoulders slumped.

"Hey," I said ever so gently, "I understand that feeling." I'd lost my dad when I was sixteen; my heart was breaking for her. "For tonight, however, I say we focus on her main message in the letter. She was so proud of you! She somehow knew of our plans to open this business and sent us good luck charms for its success." I rubbed her bare arm, and smiled. "Let's hold that gratitude, have the best grand opening any Mesa business has ever thrown, and do it all in honor of your grandmother. She'll be here with us tonight, I'm sure of it."

Tears were starting to trickle down her cheek. "You are right. Grandma would have loved this! She may not have understood all this," she swirled her arms around at all the lavish décor and laughed, "but she would have partied right along with us!" We hugged, then started busying ourselves with getting prepared for guests.

Within minutes, the caterers arrived. They brought in loads of food through the back door, eventually firing up the Sterno for each chafing dish, and expertly prepared everything. Alexis and I decided this was the perfect occasion to open up the two large rooms to be one. Just as some homeowners install wall-like folding glass patio doors, we had one installed inside to hold larger events.

"Wow, I love the space!" I said, admiring the lovely décor of the party space again.

"Perfect."

* * *

Our first guests arrived right at seven o'clock. Jordan, Pat, and baby Ryan who was tucked into his mom's over-the-shoulder sling, sound asleep.

"I didn't expect you'd be up to a party so soon after, I'm so surprised to see you guys!" I said, giving each a hug as though I was still in the dark on their big secret. "Where are the other kids?"

"We couldn't miss your big night, sis!" Jordan said with a big smile. "We aren't staying long, but we did have to make an appearance. The other rug rats are with our neighbor."

Pat shyly stated, "Hi Libby. Your place looks great." It was obvious Jordan told him that I knew, but for tonight, none of that mattered anyway.

"Thank you! Do look around, it's an open house, so check it all out … there are drinks over there," I pointed to the wall where the cocktail station was. "And, don't forget to grab an appetizer from one of the servers walking around—they look scrumptious!" He smiled and casually walked away.

"Jordan!" I called out before she followed her husband. Then in a quieter voice, I asked her, "Did you have anything to do with hiring a caterer, or decorators?"

She looked around the room. "This is stunningly beautiful, Libby. I don't know what you mean, though. I've been in the hospital. You didn't do this?"

"No! I, … er, we … no, we didn't do this," I said. "And, that man, Scott … he's been arrested. Apparently, I wasn't the only one he bailed on and ran off with the money."

"Oh no! Libby! I'm so sorry. I shouldn't have ever …" She hung her head, and I cut in.

"Don't worry about that. I just would really like to know how it did get done."

"Well, then, it had to be Alexis?" she asked.

I shook my head, then turned to see more guests arriving so I left my sister to trail after her husband. One by one, along with Alexis, we greeted our guests at the front door. Many we knew as existing clients, but there were many more who were new faces. We informed everyone about our raffle—many luxurious gifts, and the grand prize was a year's worth of free ninety-minute massages, one per month. People were signing up left and right.

"Hello. Welcome to the neighborhood!" A nice middle-aged woman with short, curly, red hair offered her hand and we shook. "I'm Michelle and this is my husband, Chester." Alexis shook their hands first, and began to talk to the husband. I shook Michelle's hand, still trying to catch bits and pieces of the conversation my friend was having, as I also half-listened to an issue this woman had with her hand. She asked if it was something massage might help with so we chatted a bit before they both moved on. I never got a chance to talk to Chester, but it *had* to be the same gym friend. *This could get interesting.*

As the night wore on, we filled the spa with conversation, laughter, and cheer. Our guests enjoyed drinks and appetizers; then, a bit later, filled themselves visiting the buffet line. At one point, between conversations, I sat back and watched everyone … Christmas music in the background, everyone was standing around at the cocktail tables eating, chatting, and seeming to be having a great time. I saw plenty of folks having fun taking pictures with the fake Santa and making new friends.

Just then, I swear I saw *her.*

A small lady, squeezed between a couple larger men, standing closer to our office. *Is that the tiny person who looked around here several days ago?*

I started making my way through the crowd, but was stopped several times and I lost sight of her. I looked around for Alexis because I really wanted her to meet this girl, if it was indeed the same person. Over the course of the evening, I would see her across the room, or quickly passing by me as I engaged with one of my clients. This happened numerous times, but she was always gone when I got around to where she had been. Once everyone was gone, I still hadn't talked to her or introduced her to Alexis.

"Wow, that was quite the party, wasn't it?" Alexis plopped down onto one of the chairs in the lobby and I sat down next to her.

"That's funny that our very first arrivals—well, not family, but actual *guests*—were the ones who won the year's worth of massage. I thought she was going to faint!" I laughed.

"He didn't look as happy," Alexis laughed too. "He was a tad weird, if you ask me."

"What was his name again?"

"Chester?"

"Yeah, yeah … I didn't get a chance to talk to him." I didn't mention anything to Alexis about his ties to my sister, which I had confirmed. She and Pat left fairly quickly after they arrived and I don't believe the two men were introduced. "Wait, what's that?" I pointed to the front desk where Lakshmi sat. Just under her was an envelope. Alexis stood up to grab it.

"Money?" she said inquisitively. Counting it, she said in almost a whisper, "Specifically, *four thousand dollars!*" Her wide eyes found mine.

Startling us, a man from the catering staff entered the lobby area. He was a thin, tall gentleman that I hadn't recalled seeing earlier. "If that'll be all this evening, ladies, we'll be on our way?"

I jumped up. Still realizing that I had no idea what company he worked for or anything about them, I held out my hand to shake his, and said, "Thank you, your staff did an amazing job tonight. Do you have the invoice? We need to pay you."

He released my hand and shook his head. "Not necessary. Everything was prepaid, including a very generous tip. Thank *you*!" he bowed slightly, and retreated to join the staff where they exited through the back door.

Alexis and I stared, perplexed, through the doorway for a minute or two, then turned our heads to look at one another, then turned back to the doorway again.

"Did you prepay them?" I asked her in a quiet voice.

"No."

"What is going on here?" I whispered.

* * *

We left the gorgeous decorations up until just after Christmas. The Sunday after, I got up particularly early and headed to the spa. Since all this was my grand vision, I didn't want to burden Alexis with the work of taking everything down. We never had figured out how the decorations were set up in the first place, or who to thank. Regardless, I take responsibility for the cleanup.

I entered the spa and nearly made it around the front counter before I noticed anything.

Everything was already back to normal. No more decorations. I looked up—no more fairy lights.

I pushed my way through the frosted glass doors to find the serenity room was cleared of all holiday décor. I ran farther, through the next door—in the center of the folding glass wall—to find it also cleaned with no trace of our winter wonderland.

A little flicker caught my eye; I whirled around.

My little tiny pink girl ...

"Wha...? Who ...?" I started walking toward her. "Wait!" I yelled out.

Alexis walked through the door, with a question in her eyes. "Wait for what, Libby? Who are you talking to?"

"You didn't see that girl who just passed by you?"

"Ah, a little too much holiday indulgence, Libs?" she laughed heartily, but wrapped me up in a hug.

As soon as I left her embrace, I ran to the lobby. "She ... little ..." I opened the front door that led outside to the parking lot and scanned the entire area.

"Libby, what are you doing here so early anyway? You took down all the decorations already?"

"NO! That's just it ... it was all put away when I got here!" I was still so shocked.

Alexis was standing behind the counter. She picked up another envelope, anchored by Lakshmi. "Wait, what's this, Libby?" She held it higher where I could see. "You think she left this? Whoever you saw..." she sliced open the envelope, pulled out a letter, and started reading.

My Dearest Alexis and Libby,

Just as I told you, Lakshmi and Ganesha will help you in ways you could never imagine. Blocking all obstacles, and bringing great fortune and prosperity to your business. Great job in knowing their perfect placement in the heart of your new world.

Dharma means 'purpose' and I see that your purpose is bringing your services to those in need. You two are Dharma Inspired.

Always looking out for you,

Grandma Kohli

Alexis had tears in her eyes. "Mystery solved. She's been here for us all along!" She picked up Ganesha and Lakshmi. "She and the rest of my ancestors, watching over us!"

We both knew then and there that *Dharma Inspired Day Spa* was bound to become a success in our new community.

Bonus Recipe!

Super Quick & Easy Cranberry Brie Tartlets

Ingredients:
2 containers of refrigerated crescent rolls (any brand)
8 ounces Brie cheese
1 cup of whole-berry cranberry sauce
½ cup chopped pecans (optional)

Directions:
Preheat oven to 375. Roll out the dough, pressing the perforated edges to seal. Cut into 24 pieces and press each into the ungreased mini-muffin cups. The dough should fill the entire cup (up the sides). Repeat with the second container of rolls.

Scoop approximately 1 round teaspoon of Brie and place into each cup; top with cranberry sauce and sprinkle with pecans.

Bake 10-15 minutes or until golden brown. Serve warm.

* * *

About the Author
Jennifer J. Morgan grew up in the desert Southwest where she always dreamed of becoming an author. Raised in New Mexico, and currently living in Arizona, she is a desert dweller through and through. Similar to her protagonist, Libby Madsen, she loves traveling and adventure. When she's not writing, Jennifer enjoys camping, hiking, and

traveling with her husband and two dogs. She is also an arts and crafts nut, always taking on a new project that sparks her creativity.

Fun fact: Most of her characters in the Libby Madsen Cozy Mystery are named after beloved pets that have blessed her life over fifty+ years. She is a HUGE animal lover (dogs, cats, birds...). Given the chance, she'd rescue them all (including a few goats, chickens, ducks, you name it...). Or, as she likes to say, *her animals have always rescued her.*

Her first novel, *Shadows in the Forest*, was a finalist in the American Fiction Awards competition.

Books in the Libby Madsen Cozy Mysteries series:
Shadows in the Forest
Spa Shadows
Shadowed Treasures
Shadow Retreats

Let's connect!
Website: www.jenniferjmorgan.com
Email: jennifer@jenniferjmorgan.com
Facebook: facebook.com/profile.
php?id=100076154359528
Twitter: twitter.com/JenniferJMorga3
BookBub: bookbub.com/profile/433830544
Goodreads: goodreads.com/user/show/148099219-
jennifer-morgan

Praise for Jennifer J. Morgan's Libby Madsen cozy mystery series:

"Readers know what a sucker I am for dogs, and the Libby Madsen mysteries are some of the best. I love, love, love Shadow and Libby and the adventures they get themselves into. Jennifer J. Morgan is destined to be one of the brightest new stars in the cozy mystery scene!" – Connie Shelton, *USA Today* bestselling author

"I'm hooked on this series. Completely adore Libby and Shadow (her companion black Lab pup--so adorable!). Without giving any spoilers at all, I couldn't put the book down once amateur sleuth, Libby Madsen, was on the search for a lost girl in the mountains. The suspense amid so many suspects, I never did figure out how it would all turn out. Overall, it's a clean read--appropriate for all ages." – lovereadingmysteries, 5 star online review

"This cozy mystery series has become one of my favorites! Libby Madsen, along with Shadow her dog... Alexis, her best friend/business partner, and her family ... and the gorgeous forest ranger, Greg! I love the friend group! And Jennifer doesn't disappoint in her second book of the series....I find myself turning pages just wanting to know what happens next. Hope the next title comes soon..." – 5 stars on Barnes & Noble

"After meeting Libby and Shadow, Greg, Alexis and JJ, and the other great characters in this series, I couldn't wait to get right into this second book. Excellent action, just as in the first one---a great overall whodunit!" – avidmysteryfan, 5 stars online review

Champagne Can Be Murder
A Charlie Parker Short Story

By Connie Shelton

~ ~ ~

1

Okay, I'll state it right out. The typical New Year's Eve celebration is not my thing. Dressing up, going to a crowded place with a bunch of people I don't know, waiting for an hour that arrives way past my normal bedtime—I don't do that. Yes, I'm probably the stodgiest thirty-something person you've ever met.

The champagne toast and kiss at midnight, well, that can be nice, but Drake and I have our own version. Our ideal New Year's Eve consists of a nice candlelight dinner at home—he usually grills a couple of filet mignons and I make a salad—then we get a fire going and sit with mugs of Drake's own special hot chocolate, and we talk. We share the high points of the past year, talk about our hopes for the new one, and at some point we tumble into bed and create some fireworks of our own.

And that was the plan this year, until he called from Double Eagle airport and asked if I would mind if we changed up the routine a little.

"Phil Schuster has invited us up to the Montaña Verde for the weekend, and I know we'd planned on doing our usual quiet celebration … but he is my biggest client."

Anyone who's lived in New Mexico any length of time has heard of the Montaña Verde Ranch. It's a huge, sprawling property up north, semi-mountainous acreage mixed with wide valleys of grassland where, literally, the buffalo roam. Not to mention the deer and the antelope, the wild turkeys, and a variety of other native wildlife. I can't recite the whole history of the property, but I do know that the term 'ranch house' does not do justice to the Spanish Colonial mansion that serves as ranch headquarters. Drake, having flown quite a few jobs for Schuster, has been there. I have not. And he knows I've been itching to see the place. So, of course, my answer was, oh yes!

There will be other New Year's Eves to spend by the fire at home.

"Pack my tux and your fanciest dress," he was saying. "If even half the guest list Phil rattled off actually shows up, prepare to be wowed. I'll be home in an hour and we should head right out so we can get there before dark."

I tucked the filets back into the fridge and called next door to be sure it was all right for our little spaniel, Freckles, to spend a night or two with Gram. That settled, I was staring into my closet when Drake walked in. And true to his word, we were back at Double Eagle, buckling into his JetRanger a little after noon. The flight would take slightly over an hour, and we had a beautiful day for it.

"So, tell me more about this soiree," I said once we'd cleared Albuquerque airspace and were out over open country.

"You know that new movie they've been filming near Pecos? I guess it wrapped up yesterday. It sounds like most of the cast and all the execs are included on the guest list for Phil's party."

I tried to remember what I'd heard on the news. I knew our hosts were a big media titan and his actress wife, Felicia Weis. And I seemed to recall she was in the film Drake mentioned, a Western adapted from somebody's bestselling novel. The young stars were this year's Hollywood power couple, and the director had some umpty-ump Oscars to his name. Felicia was playing the role of the town's boss lady—saloon keeper and gambling hall owner, or some such. What I know about current doings in the film world could not quite fill a teacup.

"We'll have time to settle into our room and relax a bit. The party starts around ten tonight, and I get the impression midnight is just the beginning for this crowd. Phil says everyone will party till dawn and then sleep it off for a day or so before jetting back to California."

I'm sure my expression conveyed my dismay. It's a known fact that I turn into a pumpkin, a mushy one, well before midnight.

"Don't worry. *My* plan is to try and get Phil-time this afternoon to talk business and line up a bunch of flight hours for the next few months at the ranch, then make enough of an appearance at the party to be sociable. We'll stay as long or short a time as you like. We get a decent night's sleep and fly back home before most of them have dragged themselves out of bed."

I nodded my complete agreement. "Do I at least get a tour of the ranch?"

"Why, yes, ma'am, you do. In fact, if you'll take note of that line of hills there to the north, that's one of the property boundaries. We'll be crossing over the southern boundary in another fifteen minutes or so."

He pointed out a distinctive peak at roughly our ten o'clock position. "The Montaña Verde property extends just to the foot of McDermott's Peak on the west. And I'm not entirely sure where the eastern boundary is. Doing some game counts in that area is part of the work I'm hoping to get, along with helping to round up some wayward steers from their herd. The last time I worked up here, Phil's ranch foreman told me they had nearly three hundred head that had wandered up into the forested part of the property."

Winter-brown grassland stretched out below, but it soon gave way to gentle foothills and then craggy red-rock bluffs dotted with juniper and dark green pines. Drake altered course slightly, keeping clear of the small regional airport where a couple of private jets sat parked on the tarmac.

I pointed downward at them. "Some of the guests?"

"Most likely. The ranch is only about ten miles away. I assume Phil is sending someone to pick up the new arrivals. It's a fairly long winding road from town out to his place."

And here we were, flying right in. I let myself enjoy a moment of snooty pride at arriving by helicopter. Thank goodness I'd thought to dress up my usual jeans and sweatshirt by switching to a cashmere sweater and adding suede boots.

Drake pointed out the road below us, a graveled trail that left the highway and wound its way alongside an arroyo and then into a mass of trees. I could see why the ten mile ride from the ranch into town easily took close to an hour.

We bypassed all that and approached the large Spanish Colonial hacienda. From the air, I spotted a circlet of smaller dwellings, some of them close to the size of our city house, and several outbuildings, including a huge barn with corral and a couple of maintenance sheds. On the east side of the main house stood a sprawling garage with five bays sized for cars and a taller one. An RV the size of a tour bus stood beside it.

"I usually land on that paved spot near the garages," Drake told me. He pulled a neat left-pedal turn and positioned the aircraft precisely the right distance from the RV.

I stretched and unfastened my harness as he let the turbine engine wind down. A man in jeans, plaid flannel shirt, and a sheepskin jacket came toward us, ducking his head as he passed under our spinning blades and approached the side door.

"Hey, Drake," he said when my husband opened the door and turned toward him. "Good to see you again. So glad you could make it."

"Phil, thanks." Drake turned to introduce me, and I realized this was the obscenely wealthy mogul I'd previously only seen in pictures where he was normally in a tuxedo, standing on a dais or a red carpet.

Schuster's graying hair was cut short, and his neatly trimmed goatee framed a smile that was more genuine in person than it came across on television.

"Charlie, good to meet you. Drake's talked a lot about you."

Really? Luckily, I didn't blurt it out. A handshake would be awkward across the width of the helicopter, so we exchanged nods and smiles.

"Once you're shut down, we can use Benny's little tow gizmo to pull your machine inside," Phil said, indicating the high garage door that was now rolling upward. "Then come on in the house. Maria's got some excellent cider that'll warm you up, and we'll get you settled."

He smiled again and turned back toward the mansion.

"Wow, privileged, huh," I said, staring into the well-lit opening of the garage.

"They treat you right here," Drake agreed. "Most jobs, I'd be putting covers over the engine cowling and hoping the ship didn't get battered around in the weather. A quick-moving storm front is coming through tonight. Wind and cold, not much snow. Hope that proves true." He gave a final tug to the rotor brake and locked it in place. "At least we don't need a runway to get airborne in the morning."

"I love you," I said, meeting his eyes.

"Love you more." He bent toward me and gave me a tender kiss. Then things took a turn for the busy, as a man approached. The guys quickly got the JetRanger inside the high ceilinged garage, we pulled our bags from the back seat, and a second man in a quasi uniform of black slacks and white shirt appeared to take charge of them, repeating Phil's invitation to come inside and warm up.

"You go ahead, hon," Drake told me.

I knew he had a checklist of post-flight tasks, so I followed the young guy who had our garment bag over one arm and my wheeled suitcase trailing behind. My down jacket was adequate for the twenty yard trip down a bricked path, but the young staffer wore only a suit jacket for warmth and I could tell he was already shivering. When he opened the wide carved front door to the mansion, I insisted he go ahead. He said he would deliver our bags to our room, and he vanished up a curved staircase to my left.

I stepped into a gracious foyer with a high ceiling and a Mexican tin pendant fixture that cast muted golden light over the Saltillo tile flooring. In one corner stood an eighteen foot Christmas tree, covered in handcrafted New Mexican ornaments and strings of traditional blue lights. An ornate table sat on the opposite side of the space, and a punch bowl of Mexican silver was being kept warm by votive candles. A silver tray of sandwiches waited nearby. The scent of apples and cinnamon filled the room.

"Mrs. Langston?" said a soft female voice.

"Just Charlie is fine." I'd never changed my last name from Parker, but I'm always happy to be associated with Drake's name in social settings. "You must be Maria?"

She wore a black dress with white collar and cuffs, and her soft voice and warm smile reminded me of a dark-haired version of my friend Linda Casper.

"Please, help yourself to refreshments and make yourself at home." She extended an arm to indicate a spacious living room through a wide, arched doorway.

"Thank you. I'll wait for my husband and then get something to eat, but I'd love to see the house right away. Can you give me a little tour?"

"I can handle that, Maria," said a male voice. I turned to see the same young man who'd taken our bags.

"I'm Bobby," he said. "Sorry, I didn't introduce myself earlier."

I chuckled. "You sort of had your hands full."

With a wave, he ushered me into the living room Maria had indicated. One end of the long rectangular space held a fireplace large enough that I could have stepped into it. At the other end, a grand piano sat tucked into a corner. Between them were several cozy groupings of couches and chairs, with a potted tree here and there. Next to the piano stood another tall Christmas tree, this one done up in a gold and silver theme.

Through an archway was the dining room. The long table was already set with an array of sparkling dinnerware and glasses.

"The fireplaces are mainly for mood, I think," Bobby said, pointing to another huge stone one in this room. "The house was built in the early 1920s, and they say it was really modern for the times, with a central heating system. These registers are in all the rooms."

I hadn't noticed the metal grillwork, but once he pointed it out I could see that behind the ornate three-foot-square decorative front there stood a cast iron radiator. Glancing back through the arched doorway, I spotted two of them in the living room as well.

"Through that door is the kitchen. Not that you'll have any need to go there. Any of these bell pulls throughout the house will get someone's attention and you can have coffee or drinks or snacks brought to your room."

We walked back into the living room, heading for a staircase near the piano, and I heard Drake's voice.

"We're in here," I called out to him, and he quickly joined us as we climbed to the second floor and started down a wide corridor.

"All the guest rooms are in this wing. You're in the turquoise suite," he told us, pausing to open the third door on the left. A brass placard had Turquoise engraved on it, in case all those doorways became too confusing.

The bedroom lived up to its name. Pale aqua walls matched the fabric of the duvet on the king-sized bed, and curtains of heavy silk were patterned in shades of the same aqua, a darker turquoise, and a vivid coral. Small touches— throw pillows, flowers in a Nambé vase, and a luxurious woolen throw—all mirrored the same color scheme. An ensuite bath with charmingly old fixtures followed suit. Our bags sat on a chest at the foot of the bed.

"There's a printed page … I don't know if you'd call it a program or something … It tells what time and where everything happens later. Mr. Schuster says you can just settle in and rest a little if you'd like, or you can feel free to explore the rest of the house. The private guest rooms all have these," he said, pointing to the brass nameplate, "just so no one will accidentally wander in on someone else."

"Great. Got it."

"Again, if you need anything, just pull on this." He stroked an old-fashioned embroidered strip which hung near the door. "And otherwise, we'll see everyone down in the living room this evening." He left, pulling our bedroom door closed behind him.

"Well, I don't know about you, but I'm itching to see more of the property. You know, poke into the corners."

"I could go for a little something to eat," he said, reminding me of the spread of sandwiches downstairs.

"We can manage both." I shed my down jacket and took a minute to hang our dressy outfits in the large armoire opposite the bed.

2

Instead of returning to the living room the same way we'd come, we took a left out of our room and strolled the long hallway, past other rooms named with colors on those little brass plaques. Nothing was simply red, blue, or green here—we passed doors announcing scarlet, cerulean, and forest. The hall turned to the left again, past a few more closed doors, and we came to the flight of stairs that deposited us back in the foyer where a dozen people all seemed to be talking at once.

Drake's eyes went immediately to the table with the food; mine scanned the gathering crowd. I spotted familiar faces—Kelly Fontaine and her husband Josh Tracker, the power couple who were the leads in the movie we'd heard about. Her cascade of dark brown curls fell over the collar of a sumptuously thick fur jacket (surely faux, in keeping with her well known beliefs about animals), and her jeans fit as though they'd been custom designed. His boyish grin, which had such an effect on women everywhere that it was probably a source of global warming, was aimed toward our hostess, their recent costar. Both of them turned toward the stairs as we descended, but as soon as they realized we were no one important, the smiles turned distant and they went back to whatever Felicia had been saying.

As far as I could tell, the rest of the crowd was entourage. Several carried tablets, on which they appeared to be studying schedules or whatever else underlings tended to on behalf of their powerhouse bosses. One guy who looked about twenty, with inch-long purple hair that stuck out at all angles, was munching a sandwich while thumbing madly at his phone screen. I noticed that Bobby was standing politely at the base of the stairs, a collection of designer luggage stacked around him. I nudged Drake and we moved aside so he could get past us. We descended into the fray.

Phil Schuster spotted us. He'd been around the other side of the huge Christmas tree and I hadn't noticed him.

He reached out and touched Drake's elbow.

"Want you to meet someone, Rory," he said to the fifty-something man who stood beside him. Phil's voice was pleasant enough but I sensed tension between the two. "This is the helicopter pilot I've been telling you about, the guy who does so much here at the ranch. He's a good man to know, get you some of those tricky camera angles you were talking about."

Drake turned to Rory Hammersmith, the director who was a household name, and extended his hand. My husband, in turn, introduced me and made a point of letting both men know that I am also a pilot and we frequently work together. Drake, however, is the star of the show whenever we arrive with the aircraft, and I'm used to standing quietly aside while he schmoozes the customers.

So it came as a complete surprise when Hammersmith reached out and placed an arm around my shoulders, pulling me close. His cologne smelled expensive and his breath revealed he'd already found a scotch or two.

"With pilots as pretty as this one, then hell yeah, we'll give your company a call," he said, more to the room at large than to Drake. To me, he turned and lowered his voice intimately. "You got a business card on you?"

I squirmed out of his grasp and gave Drake a *rescue-me* look. My ever-wonderful husband reached for his back pocket with the hand that would force the obnoxious director to step away from me in order to take the card. I edged my way toward Phil and asked if he would introduce me to his wife.

Felicia flashed her husband a lovely smile as we stepped toward her, the crowd parting as Phil walked through. He reminded her who Drake and I were.

"I see you met Rory," she said through her teeth, keeping the smile in place while her eyes flitted over the crowd. "Don't mind him. He's always like that. Just stay arm's length away and you'll be fine."

Really? Wasn't his type of behavior finally being outed in the news and was now considered unacceptable? I almost said something but remembered I was an outsider to this group. Evidently, Felicia came from that generation where women dodged grabby hands and didn't speak up.

Someone stepped up and whispered in Felicia's ear and she excused herself, saying she needed to check on something in the kitchen. Phil, similarly, had already been sidetracked by another actor whose face I knew but whose name I couldn't come up with at the moment. I edged my way over to the food table and filled a small plate for Drake.

He still seemed deep in conversation with Rory Hammersmith, so I circled and handed the plate over, making a vague excuse so I didn't need to stand there. A narrow door to the left of the stairs stood open, and I ducked inside.

The room was a small study with French doors at the far end. One wall was covered in a floor-to-ceiling mural, an elaborate trompe l'oeil depicting a life-sized window with a fountain beyond. An ornately carved desk sat angled in a corner, and there were two wingback chairs covered in an Indian blanket motif. A stained-glass lamp glowed from the desk and the small space exuded coziness, after the clamor of the foyer. I pushed the door halfway closed, determined to find a few minutes of quiet.

It seemed most of the guests were making their way upstairs, although new arrivals continued to come through the front door, and poor Bobby was running up and down the stairs non-stop. Suddenly, I really needed a breath of fresh air.

I made my way to the French doors and looked out into a little enclosed courtyard. Although the vines and plants were winter-dead now, I could tell this would be a secluded spot where a person could grab a book and sit at the outdoor table in the summer months. I debated stepping out there now, but a breeze rattled the doors and I knew I wouldn't last more than a minute outdoors without my coat.

"Ah, there you are," said a voice behind me.

I turned to see Rory Hammersmith stepping into the room.

"I was just leaving. You've got the room to yourself." I tried for glib, and I tucked myself on the other side of one of the wingbacks.

I'd just reached the door to the foyer when he made his move, reaching out toward my arm. I flung the door open wide and lucked out. A tall, barrel-chested man who'd been heading toward the stairs noticed the movement.

"Hammersmith. We need to talk." Tension flowed between them like electricity.

I went into ferret mode and slithered out, practically under the second man's arm. Drake was standing near the food table, looking as though he couldn't figure out what to do with his empty plate.

"I need to get outside for a while," I said.

3

So far, Drake had not gotten Phil's attention long enough to pin down more flight hours for our business.

But during our own exploratory scouting around the grounds earlier in the afternoon, he did manage to grab a productive half hour with the ranch manager, an old-timer named Wes McFarland. Wes was one of those men, rare these days, who grew up on a ranch in the same county where his father and grandfather had raised cattle. Hard work and long days were in his bloodline. He was respectful toward the Montaña Verde's current owner but in no way did he consider Schuster a real rancher. Wes was definitely the guy to talk to.

After the interesting tales of Wes's life and the history of the herds on the property, being seated among the Hollywood crowd during the long dinner was a letdown. There's only so much name-dropping and self-adulation a girl like me can handle. I stifled more than one yawn as Josh Tracker waxed prolific about his next movie role and Kelly talked about how she had to get pregnant within the next two months so she'd be back in shape for a shoot that would begin next November. I supposed it was a real concern, but I couldn't get my head into it.

The barrel-chested man I'd seen earlier in the library turned out to be a network executive named Bill Greenway. He was here to ramrod a new project through Schuster's media company, and, according to Drake who'd witnessed a little exchange between them, Phil wasn't exactly thrilled to have the man as a guest. My eyes kept switching between the two men, watching for undercurrents, but the person Greenway seemed to have issues with was Rory Hammersmith. Whatever they'd talked about in the library didn't appear to have been resolved. All in all, the dinner was an interesting one.

Now, we walked into a glittering wonderland of gold

and silver in the living room. Chairs and sofas had been pushed into different arrangements to leave space for fifty people to mingle and chat. A DJ had set up his rig on the mezzanine above and heavy-beat music vibrated the walls. The Christmas tree glowed golden, and an actual disco ball hung suspended from the Western wrought-iron chandelier in the center of the room. A dozen or so of the younger guests were dancing, eyes glazed and limbs fluid.

A sunroom provided overflow space. As if we hadn't just stuffed ourselves with a sumptuous meal, a long table filled with food sat along the far wall. Rory Hammersmith stood near one of the two bars, laughing way too loudly. A slightly pudgy young woman I'd pegged earlier as his assistant stood by, chatting with a skinny girl of about sixteen while keeping her eye on the boss.

"Poor Becca, she looks knackered," said one of two other personal assistants as they pushed past me, wearing the standard fitted black dresses and hair pulled back into neat chignons. In contrast, the glitterati wore the kind of designer outfits that caused people to ask "who are you wearing?" when they began a conversation.

Drake went to the bar to get a glass of wine for me, and I held my position near the doorway so I could feign an urgent need for the ladies room, just in case Hammersmith headed my way. Luckily for me, he'd directed his attention toward a pair of twenty-somethings who were either twins or copycats, the kind of girls who consulted to be sure they would be wearing nearly the same thing for every social occasion.

"Becca!" Rory's voice carried far too loudly.

He held out his empty plate and the tired-looking PA stepped over to retrieve it. Some words were exchanged and she crossed the room. Meanwhile, one of the 'twins' giggled at something he'd said, while the other shot him a murderous look.

I spotted Phil and Felicia at the top of the stairs. They must have come over from their suite in the other wing of the house, just in time to make an entrance. His tuxedo was perfectly tailored, his ever-graying hair in place, and his goatee freshly trimmed. Her gown was a shade of coral that must have been chosen by a color expert, it so perfectly set off her blond hair and light coloring. It fit her slender frame perfectly and was in much better taste than ninety percent of the others in the room—no cutouts or diaphanous panels to hint at body parts better left unseen in public. I had to admit, the room and the crowd could have easily fit into a seaside Malibu glamour pad rather than a remote ranch in New Mexico.

Drake and I wandered into the sunroom. The bartender was arranging a table full of champagne flutes and pulling bottles of the real French bubbly from huge iced tubs, and people lingered near the food table. As he began to pop the corks and fill glasses, I walked toward the wall of French doors and stared out into the darkness. The wind had picked up, leaking little bursts of cold around the glass, and I could see snow swirling frantically around some concrete tables and benches outside.

"So much for the forecast," I said, turning to my hubby.

"Yeah, the twenty percent chance of snow is now eighty percent," he said, consulting the app on his phone. "Still looks like it'll blow through by daybreak."

"Think we can quietly sneak away anytime soon?" I was completely bored with the personalities and my head was beginning to pound from the relentless music.

"Let's escape right after the toast at midnight." He sent me the smile that always makes my heart flutter.

I sneaked a glance at my watch and saw we had seventeen minutes to go.

"Anyone else here that you want to talk business with?" I asked. I know. We shouldn't be talking business at a party and on New Year's Eve. I simply had nothing else in common with this crowd.

He appeared to be considering the question when a loud shriek pierced the air. Both of our heads whipped around to look behind us. Near the food table, the group parted, several women held their hands to their faces. The men looked stunned. All stood frozen, staring at someone lying facedown on the floor.

Bless him, Drake was the only person to go into action. He set his drink down and rushed to the man's side, and I quickly followed. He rolled the body over. It was Rory Hammersmith.

4

The music wound down to a halt, as though the DJ had turned off the power without raising the needle off the record. Hammersmith's face was red and contorted and he didn't appear to be breathing.

"Oh my gosh, he looks like he was poisoned." I kept my voice low, thinking Drake might need the information, but Phil Schuster was at his side a moment later.

"Poisoned? Someone call for an ambulance," he shouted.

Drake shook his head, removing his fingers from the victim's pulse points. "Too late for that. We'd better get law enforcement out here." He already had his phone out of his pocket and was dialing 911.

There were gasps and quiet groans from the crowd as it sunk in that the famous director was dead. The word 'poisoned' ran through the crowd.

I turned to Phil. "We need to keep everyone close. The police will want to ask what we all saw."

Drake had stepped aside and kept his voice quiet. Now he motioned Phil and me over. "The sheriff's office took my call, but they say there's no way they can get out here anytime soon. The storm is worse than anyone predicted, and they've got their hands full with traffic incidents. I guess I-25 is a mess."

I could picture it—bad weather and drunk drivers are not a good combination. "So, what do we do?"

"I spoke to the sheriff himself," he said quietly. "He says he'll need a list of everyone at the party. Once we've got their names, they can go back to their rooms or whatever. The immediate area should be closed off, and all food and drink is off limits in case something was poisoned."

"My god," Phil said. "So we just have to leave a body lying right here in our sunroom?"

"We can at least cover him up, can't we?" I suggested.

Drake nodded. "I think that would be okay. Hon, can you find something to write with and start taking names? Phil, you should say something, try to reassure people. And for heaven's sake, don't let anyone snap pictures and post them anywhere."

"You're so right." Phil, for once, looked shaken. He took a deep breath and turned to gather his guests. How was he going to spin this?

I spotted an inventory sheet at the bar and asked for a pen, then positioned myself near the archway to the foyer. Drake had found a tablecloth and, mercifully, covered the body. He pulled two straight-backed chairs over to the staircase, blocking it as an exit. Anyone leaving the room would need to pass by me and give their name for the sheriff's list.

While Phil begged everyone's cooperation in not releasing the news on social media—a real feat if he could accomplish it—I began listing the names I already knew. Felicia, in a complete fluster, stepped over to me. I put her to work, telling me who was who.

"Can't we at least get *that* out of the room," she practically wailed, unable to take her eyes off the cloth-covered form on the floor.

"I'll ask. For now, help me focus on this list." I realized it was probably the first time in her life she'd had a party go bust. Well, there was not much to be done about that right now.

Within minutes I felt I had a complete list of the guests, so I made my way around to the staff and extras—the bartenders, DJ, and caterers. Hopefully that would satisfy the sheriff when he arrived. Drake and I ended up near the food table, and I helped him drape extra tablecloths over the food. Some of the guests were fairly wasted by now and we couldn't take the chance that anyone would ignore the warning about not picking up something.

"Was Hammersmith eating or drinking anything at the moment he collapsed?" I asked.

His assistant, Becca, was still standing nearby. She nodded silently and pointed to a broken glass and shattered plate near the body. I requested some plastic bags from Maria and gathered the items, tucking them under the body cover.

Phil stepped over, clearly thinking in terms of damage control. "*Why* did I invite that guy from the *Hollywood Reporter*? He's already been on the phone to his boss. It's no secret that I had my differences with Rory Hammersmith. They'll have me tried and convicted in the press."

Drake turned to him. "The news is bound to get out, and there's not a lot you can do about that. The sheriff may not get out here until morning. I suggest we find someplace to take the body, maybe one of the maintenance sheds? The cold will help preserve evidence, and the guests will be less stressed once he's out of their sight."

Felicia had drifted toward us and she took her husband's arm. "Maybe we can still serve the champagne?"

All three of us gave her a look.

"I'm afraid that moment has passed," Phil said gently.

Just then, the clock struck midnight.

5

"My wife is a partner in a private investigation firm," Drake told them. "I'd suggest you allow her to ask questions, try to establish what happened and who might have had an even stronger motive than you."

Phil looked at me. "Yes, excellent idea. You can prove I had nothing to do with this."

I sputtered a little. "I don't know … I'm not sure this is a good idea at all." I'd never stepped into a murder investigation before the police had been there. And what about the resentment that would come my way if local law enforcement believed I'd been meddling?

"People's memories are always fresher at the beginning," Drake said. "You've told me how frustrating it is to try and get answers after time has passed and they've forgotten details."

Phil and Felicia both jumped on the bandwagon. "Yes, yes, this is much better than having a dozen cops in uniform showing up and bullying our guests."

Phil turned to the crowd, most of whom were standing around in small groups, whispering madly to each other. "Attention, everyone. Charlie Parker, a private investigator from Albuquerque, has offered to take all your statements. Just tell her what you witnessed. She can even come around to your rooms so you aren't inconvenienced. Cooperating will get everyone out of here that much quicker."

Sheesh. There was so much wrong with that statement. I'm not licensed, I have no pull whatsoever with law enforcement, and I certainly couldn't clear the witnesses to leave. What was he thinking?

But all eyes were on me and I had to do something. "I'd like to speak with each of you privately, so I'd recommend that you go to your rooms and I'll come around. Anyone who would prefer to stay downstairs can, um ..." I turned toward Phil and quietly asked for use of the study. "Yes, that works. Come and meet me in the study, just off the main foyer. I'll be there in, let's say, ten minutes."

"Meanwhile," Phil announced, "the bars are still open, and I'd say this is as good a time as any to indulge in a little relaxer."

I turned to Drake. "Since I can't quite imagine questioning potential suspects in an evening gown, I'm running up to our room to change."

He handed me the key. "Good. I'll get a couple of the staff to help move the body out to one of the sheds and we'll lock the evidence safely away."

Precisely ten minutes later I arrived back in the small study, much more comfortable in my jeans and sweater, and rummaged the desk for a notebook and pen. The whole time I was upstairs, my mind had been whirring back over the scene at the time Rory collapsed, trying to remember who was nearby, thinking back over the conversations of the afternoon and coming up with the names of those who would become my main suspects.

A glance through the open doorway showed only three people waiting. Of course. Who among this bunch was going to willingly come in for questioning?

I called in the first, Maria, the household cook who had greeted us when we arrived. She edged her way into the room and I closed the door. Her face was puffy, eyes red, and her hands wouldn't stop moving.

"Miss Charlie, I am so afraid. People are saying I poisoned the important director. I know nothing—" Her voice broke and the tears began again.

I showed her to a wingback chair and picked up a box of tissues from the corner of the desk.

"Why do they think that?" I asked, once her sobs subsided. "Did you know him personally? Had he harmed you?"

"No! I never saw him before this day. I never spoke a word to him."

No motive as far as I could tell.

"And the food—I prepare some, but most was brought

by the caterer. So, how do these people think I poisoned this man?"

"Did someone specifically blame you, Maria? Or were they only commenting on the food that *might* have been the source of the poison?"

She blinked twice and shrugged. "Maybe only that."

"What about the catering staff? Were any of them talking about Mr. Hammersmith?"

"No, I heard nothing like that. Only the usual talk about getting the cold foods out at a certain time, the hot foods out at once, the type of thing kitchen people talk about."

I'd caught Trudy, head of UpClass Catering, and gotten names of all her people. I could talk to them later.

"They're packing now," Maria said. "Caterer. Picking up their dishes and pans, loading it in the vehicle."

"It's okay, I suppose. No one can leave. Mr. Schuster already called Wes McFarland and told him to block the driveway. The sheriff said the roads aren't safe anyway."

"Finish whatever you need to do in the kitchen, Maria, and then go to your room and try to rest. With this many people stranded here, there will be meals to prepare tomorrow. You might as well get a good night's sleep."

Her expression told me that was going to be impossible.

The other two witnesses waiting outside the study gave much the same story. One was a bartender who said he'd been so busy mixing drinks all evening that he'd barely looked up. "That many people in a room, and with the music pounding like it was, you tune it all out. Aside from getting a guest's drink order, I don't really pay any attention. The man who died—he did snag a bottle of champagne for himself. Kind of hinted at some romantic rendezvous, but I only saw him drinking it."

The other young man was a local from town, hired for the party to clear plates and carry dirty glassware to the kitchen. He seemed most worried about getting home. I told him I felt sure Wes would make arrangements. There had to be a bunkhouse or some kind of sleeping quarters for the ranch hands, and surely, they could fit in a few extras.

When he left, I spotted Hammersmith's assistant, Becca, heading for the stairs. I beckoned her over.

"I know this is a terrible time for you," I began. "Can I just have a minute or two?"

She followed me into the study, looking white as a marshmallow and thoroughly shaken. I eased into the questions, but she took a while to put her thoughts together.

"I was right there, beside him, like, a minute before. I thought he looked sleepy or maybe just drunk ... I don't know ... He always wanted me nearby so he could get my attention. I mean, that's what the normal day was like. But this being a party, he was all into the other guests. You know, most of them had been working together on the set every day for a couple months." She straightened her shoulders. "Anyway, he didn't seem to need me and I was thinking I might find a quiet spot for a few minutes."

"Was there anyone from the film with whom he'd had a fight or a grudge or anything like that?"

Something flickered across her face but it was gone in an instant. "Well, he and Josh got into it a couple of times, over some of the more difficult scenes in the script."

"Anyone else?"

She shrugged. Something told me there was more, but she just shook her head. I let her go. I could always find her later if I needed to.

I made notes about what each of the witnesses had

told me, then stepped back into the foyer. Since no one was waiting for me, I would have to seek them out. With more than fifty people to talk to, if I only spent ten minutes with each, it was going to be a very, very long night. I needed help.

I spotted Drake, still looking remarkably gorgeous in his tux, entering the dining room through the kitchen door.

"Everything going okay outside?" I asked.

He nodded. "How about in here?"

"Slow. No one wants to answer questions, so I'm faced with tracking them down." I pulled out a fresh yellow writing pad and handed it over. "So, consider yourself conscripted. These are the main questions we need to ask. If you'll visit with the staff and household help, I'll try to get the guests to talk. Just make a page for each person you talk to and jot down their answers. At least it will give the sheriff a starting point once he gets out here."

He glanced over the list. "This looks pretty basic. Where were you up to the time the victim collapsed? Did you have any interaction with Hammersmith before this? Do you know anyone here who disliked him?"

"I know. It seems kind of lame, doesn't it? I can't think what else to ask, unless something they reveal leads to more questions. Feel free to follow those threads."

With that, Drake turned back into the kitchen and I headed toward the living room where some of the Hollywood bunch sat in the upholstered chairs, which they'd gathered into small groupings again. Most held drinks. Few looked sad. Stunned, maybe, but not grief stricken.

I walked over and joined a group that included Josh Tracker and Kelly Fontaine, perching myself on the edge of a heavy cocktail table.

"I guess you know I need to ask all of you some questions." I tried my best to look apologetic while watching their reactions.

"Sure, fire away," Josh said, setting an I-don't-mind tone.

Okay, I might as well lead with my best ammo. "I understand you and Rory had some clashes on the set."

Kelly Fontaine piped up. "*Everyone* had clashes with Rory on the set, so don't start getting ideas about Josh wanting to kill him."

I sat back, holding up one hand in a stop motion. "Hey, no fingers are being pointed by me. Just trying to get a feel for anyone's motivation. The sheriff is going to come along and ask these things, so maybe we can shorten his visit by making some notes. That's all."

"Okay," Kelly said. "Just so you understand, Rory was not the type of director who offered his actors positive suggestions, who worked with you to get the scene just the way he wanted it. We were all supposed to be mind readers and get it right the first time."

"Yeah, budget was a big pressure on this one," said Freddy K. (Taking my original list, I'd learned his real name was Fredrick Kaye.) "We were reminded daily that we didn't have unlimited time. Running through a scene a few times before the camera rolled was not an option. Pissed us all off."

I took a deep breath, letting emotions settle. "So, help me out here because I don't know this stuff ... who was putting pressure on Rory to be this way? I mean, if budget was the issue, who was—?"

"Executive producer. That'd be Bill Greenway. With him, it's money, money, *money.*" Josh slapped the back of one hand against the palm of the other each time he repeated the word.

"Okay. So those two clashed a bit too?"

"Oh yeah, like *all* the time," Kelly said.

Looked like Greenway could move up my list.

"What about with Felicia? She's a Hollywood legend. Did Rory push her around too?"

Freddy lowered his voice. "Not quite as much. There would be Phil to answer to, if he did that."

So, Phil and Felicia were definitely on the list, too.

"Anyone else? Can you think of anything that's happened within the last day or two that would have been serious enough to kill for?"

All three shook their heads. Josh finally put it into words. "It was no one incident, just a build-up of tension. Everyone felt it. Would anyone act on it? I don't honestly know."

Both Kelly and Freddy nodded agreement. I thanked them for their candor and told them I might have a few follow-up questions at some point. By now, the living room had cleared out. It was after one a.m. and with the party a complete fizzle, I imagined most had retired to their rooms.

I wandered to the sunroom and stared out into the darkened patio, watching snow swirl frantically against the walls, creating drifts. Josh and Kelly's words came back to me. Their remarks reminded me of the atmosphere in the foyer as everyone arrived. Chilly. Kind of like the view out this window.

6

I took the main staircase up, noticing that the DJ had left his equipment stacked against the railing on the mezzanine, everything packed into cases. He was probably like everyone else here, couldn't wait to get out in the morning.

Maybe Drake would be tucked away already in our room and we could just snuggle in and put all this out of our minds. And maybe unicorns are real.

On my way to our own Turquoise, I passed rooms labeled Amber, Lapis, and Coral, and it was the fact that the door on the latter was standing slightly open that caught my attention. A male voice came from within and—yeah, I can't help myself—I paused and pressed my back to the wall, shamelessly eavesdropping.

"… an Oscar? That's what you're thinking?" Thirty seconds of silence. "Well, yeah, I suppose that's true. Posthumous nominations can really help build buzz for the picture. I did my best to keep costs down, but—" Another long pause. "Yeah, yeah, yeah. Well, give it some thought. We can figure out how to put some lipstick on this pig yet."

I heard a beep as he ended the phone call, so I waited a full minute and then tapped lightly on the door. Heavy footsteps, the door swung open, and Bill Greenway stood there, glaring.

"What? It's late." I tried not to let everyone else's opinion color mine, but I could easily see why Rory Hammersmith didn't like this man.

"I realize that, but the door was partially open and I saw the lights on. Figured you might spare a few minutes?"

He'd removed his tuxedo jacket and the tie, but otherwise was still dressed as he had been at the party. Clearly I'd not caught him ready to fall asleep. He knew who I was and why I was here, and he didn't have much choice but to usher me in.

"Ask away," he muttered, picking up a heavy looking crystal glass with a half-inch of amber liquid in it.

"Shall we sit down? I really will only take a minute." Without invitation, I headed toward a small round Queen Anne table with two chairs flanking it. I took my time opening my notebook and clicking my pen, ready for notes. I began with the standard questions.

"I'd walked out the front door for a smoke," Greenway said, "so I didn't see what the fuss was about until I came back in. Rory was lying on the floor and that pilot guy— oh, I guess that's your husband—was bending over him. Somebody said something about poisoning. Shocking."

So, Greenway wouldn't have had access to put something directly into Rory's food or drink. But, more horrific, would he have spiked an entire bowl of dip or something?

"I didn't figure there was anything I could actually *do*," he continued, "so I just stepped back and kind of watched the whole thing."

While making plans to get Rory nominated for an Oscar and capitalize on the tragedy? I studied my notes rather than let him see my face.

"I understand you and Rory clashed a few times on the set, these past couple of months. What was that about?"

"Clashed? Oh, not really. I had to keep costs down. The picture was already over budget. The actors were all hounding for more rehearsal time. Felicia, especially, was ragging on about her costumes. What is it with modern women that you put into a period costume? They want everything tailor made and of the best fabrics. This piece was set in the Old West. Clothes were basic and cheap."

"So all those subjects came up in conversations with

Rory, and the two of you disagreed?"

He shrugged it off. "At times."

"Can you think of anyone here, anyone at all, who had a motive for killing your director?"

He tipped the crystal glass up and drained it. "Nope. Not at all."

Closing ranks against the investigator. I could see that this is probably how it would go. This crowd would tattle certain things, but they'd been at the game long enough to know that it never went well when they talked to the press or the law.

I thanked him for the skimpy information (okay, not in those words), and got up to leave. At the door, I turned, putting on my Columbo face. "One more thing …"

He almost smiled.

"Mr. Hammersmith sort of … came on to me, when we first arrived. I got the feeling he maybe had that reputation. Was he like that with the cast or crew?"

"He liked 'em young, slim, and pretty, yes."

I got the feeling I was supposed to be flattered, but I didn't take the bait. I sent him a steady stare. "So …?"

"Kelly would totally be his type, but Josh is super protective. Rory knew he wouldn't get away with anything there. Felicia … well, she's out of his league in every way— married to Phil, a legend way before Rory came on the scene—and she's aged off of his radar, if you know what I mean."

Yeah—someone in her sixties wasn't qualified. I left and closed his door firmly behind me.

Two doors down, I opened the door to our own Turquoise room and stepped inside. Drake was back already, and he looked comfy in flannel pajama pants and a long-sleeved tee I'd given him for Christmas. His tablet of notes lay on the nightstand beside him.

"Any luck with the questions?" he asked, taking my hand and pulling me down beside him on the bed. I tossed my notebook down and snuggled in next to him.

"Some interesting revelations, but I can't say I have a firm suspect yet. You?"

"The household staff is mostly worried about keeping their jobs. A few seem terrified that the death of a powerful man will get pinned on them."

"Yeah, Maria was really scared when I talked with her. You don't think Phil would do that, would he? Fire someone or turn them over to the sheriff?"

"That seems extreme, unless there's strong evidence."

"And we don't even know the exact cause of death. An autopsy will have to be done to determine what the poison was—or maybe it was a drug, or the booze. Until they know that, it would be impossible to figure out who had access. Our little 'investigation' is really pretty lame, isn't it?"

He planted a kiss on top of my head. "It's not a waste of time, hon. Whoever killed him needs to know that it's being investigated, especially if it was one of these high-power types who might think that just because we're far from the city and dealing with a small county sheriff's department that no one's checking up. They need to know they won't get away with it."

"You're right."

"Okay, let's get some sleep. It's after three already. We're both exhausted, and I'm still hoping we can fly out of here at a reasonable hour in the morning. Well, later this morning."

While I brushed my teeth and washed my face, he filled me in on the weather situation.

According to the weather service, the leading edge of the cold front had moved through. A glance out the window confirmed that the snow was no longer swirling as it had been earlier.

"They say the roads still aren't great—there are drifts and icy patches—but you and I don't have to worry about that. We'll pull the ship out of the garage and be able to get airborne."

"Do you think the people with private jets will ask you to ferry them out to the county airport? We could get tied up with that."

"They can ask. I don't have enough fuel to run a shuttle service." He seemed to consider the logistics. "Well, we'll play it by ear."

7

I woke before dawn, less than three hours into my sleep, with a thought. I had asked Greenway about Rory's relationship with the cast and crew. He'd only answered about the main cast members. What about the crew? If an old lecher meant to hit on younger women, it would be crew members, those over whom he had some authority, who would feel the pressure to comply.

Once that thought entered my head, I couldn't fall back asleep. As pale gray light began to show around the curtains, I slipped out of bed. Picking up my jeans, sweater, and boots I padded to the bathroom where I splashed a little cold water on my face, brushed my teeth, and dressed. My notebook was on the nightstand and my down jacket lay draped over a chair, so I grabbed both of those.

Hoping Maria might have some coffee ready, I made my way along the corridor of closed doors. If I got lucky I might carry an insulated mug along and take a little walk outside.

Miraculously, in a way that never happens in ordinary homes, the foyer and living room were immaculate, with no sign of last night's party other than the cloth-draped table concealing the food. That was another surprise. If a staff member had something to hide, surely the table would have been cleared, evidence destroyed, apologies offered.

I followed my nose to the dining room, where a buffet held a huge coffee urn. At the other end of the long table, Maria was loading stainless steel trays that smelled like bacon and eggs into stands where they would stay warm by means of little Sterno cans. Phil Schuster stood at the coffee urn, turning toward me when I greeted Maria.

"Another early riser," he said with a smile.

"Yeah, afraid so." I draped my jacket over the back of a chair to free up my hands.

"Felicia's the queen of sleeping in, but I'm always up early. I do my best thinking then."

"I suppose I do, too. And, of course, I woke up thinking about everything last night. I talked to so many people I guess my head was full of conversation. I actually had you and your wife on my list to talk with today. Have you heard any word from the sheriff?"

"He's fairly sure he can get out here by mid-morning."

"I'm sure you'll be happy to have Mr. Hammersmith's

body taken to the medical investigator's office, and let the officials take over."

He set his full mug aside and picked up two sugar packets, giving a noncommittal nod.

"Several people last night mentioned problems between Rory and various cast members," I said, picking up a mug from the neat rows someone had laid out. "Was your wife one of them?"

Phil paused and turned. He faced me, leaning a hip against the table and crossing his legs at the ankles, the very picture of a relaxed and unconcerned man.

"Charlie, I like you and I literally trust Drake with my life when we fly together. But I'm afraid I can't say anything more about Rory Hammersmith or the events of last night."

He'd been talking to his lawyer, I'd bet money on it.

"Okay then."

He shook the two packets one more time, ripped them open, and dumped the sugar into his coffee. I filled my own mug and took a sip as he started to leave the room.

"I'd still like to speak with a few of the others, some of the personal assistants and crew members. Can you tell me where their rooms are?"

"Sure. Some were given rooms on the first floor, out beyond the kitchen." He raised his eyes toward the ceiling. "In the old days, I guess the servants of the guests would sleep in tiny rooms adjoining their employers, but the house was remodeled about thirty years ago, and a lot of those spaces were converted to bathrooms and closets. Rather than needing to shout out for the assistance of an underling, nowadays anyone is only a text message away." He chuckled, apparently finding humor in the story.

"Those who aren't here in the main house would have been given a room in one of the guest houses. Those all have a small living area and kitchenette, so they'll have coffee and rolls or something out there. Anyone in particular you're looking for?"

For a guy who refused to talk about the case he was still very interested.

"No, not really. I'll see where the questions lead me."

I finished my coffee and plucked two strips of bacon from the heating tray before donning my jacket, tucking my notebook into one of its roomy pockets, and walking out the front door.

One of the guest houses had smoke coming from the chimney so I headed toward that one first. My tap at the door brought a "come in." The two young women I'd tagged 'the twins' last night were sitting on a pair of overstuffed chairs, cell phones in hand. Now, wearing fuzzy robes, no makeup, and their hair down to their shoulders, they really didn't look much alike.

I introduced myself and reminded them that I was asking a few questions to save everyone from having to be questioned by the sheriff later. The responses were neutral and both pairs of eyes went back to their phone screens.

"I can leave quicker if we just cover a few basics," I said, walking over to stand where they couldn't possibly ignore me.

The guy with the spiky purple hair stepped out of a bedroom just then, curious about the newcomer. He agreed to talk with me, and even reached a toe out to nudge each of the girls. I learned that none of the three had actually been in the same room with Hammersmith when he collapsed. All three claimed to have been dancing. A look passed among them, some little vibe that told me they'd been under the influence of some designer drug and totally blissed out and very much unaware of their surroundings at the time.

"Were all of you out at the location for the filming last week?"

Nods all around. It turned out the two young women were PAs for Kelly Fontaine and John Tracker, so wherever the couple went, they went.

When I asked about possible sexual harassment or unwanted advances from the director, a universal bland look came over their faces. For the sake of keeping their jobs, they weren't admitting anything.

I caught movement from the corner of my eye and saw another bedroom door slowly closing.

"Who's staying in this one?" I asked purple-hair.

"Becca and her sister."

I'd spoken with her last night, one of the first I'd interviewed, and she'd been pretty shaken up. "Think it's okay if I peek in on her?" I whispered.

Purple-hair shrugged, why not.

I walked toward the bedroom door and tapped lightly. "Becca, it's Charlie." The latch hadn't caught, and the door swung inward. Becca stood in front of a large wooden wardrobe, and she visibly started when she heard my voice. She was dressed already, wearing black slacks, a green bulky sweater, and a long bright pink scarf.

"I hope this isn't a bad time. I just wanted to see how you're doing. Last night was rough."

She nodded, and tears pooled in her dark eyes.

"Becca? What is it?"

She shook her head.

"It's gotta be hard, seeing your boss die like tha—" The obvious answer finally hit me over the head. "Becca, was he making unwanted advances?"

A bitter laugh escaped her. "What, me? I'm twenty pounds over Rory's ideal."

"Becca …" I made my voice soft and gentle. "Sweetie, you'll have to talk with the sheriff when he comes. You can tell me, if you'd rather."

"No!" Her eyes darted about the room. "I mean, I can't talk about it. It's too upsetting. Can you just go now?"

"Okay, okay. No problem." I held up both hands and backed away. "You're right. You need some time alone."

I thanked the others, who all ignored me completely in favor of their phones, and stepped outside. Becca's reaction troubled me. I wanted to find Drake and talk this over, but I also felt the need to keep an eye on the guest house in case Becca had worked out a way to leave the ranch before the sheriff arrived.

I stepped to the other side of the house, to a spot where no one inside would be able to see me, and I phoned Drake.

"Hey, early bird. What's up?"

"Have you heard anything from the sheriff's office this morning?"

"Nothing more than I already mentioned. They'll try to get out here by mid-morning."

I looked at my watch and saw it was approaching nine.

"I think I have a strong suspect, but I have no evidence to prove anything." A plan was taking shape in my head. I went over the details with him.

"Sure, I can do that."

I waited ten minutes, hoping Becca would come out

and head for the big house on her own. She didn't. I went back to the front door of the guest house and walked in without knocking.

"Hey, everyone, I forgot to mention … Mr. Schuster has a fantastic looking breakfast set out in the dining room at the main house. He asked me to let everyone know to come over."

The twins looked at me as if I were out of my mind. Big breakfasts didn't go along with keeping one's weight at 112. Purple-hair perked up and said he just needed to put on some shoes. He did my job for me, tapping on Becca's door and ordering her to get a move on and come along with him. She answered something that sounded affirmative. I ducked out before she could see me and waited in my little hiding spot. Within a minute purple-hair came out and turned left toward the mansion. Where was Becca?

I went back inside, ignoring the twins and heading for Becca's room. A tap brought no response. Okay, I'd just heard her voice. I slowly opened the door. The room appeared empty, as did the adjoining bathroom. Huh. Unless she'd popped over into someone else's bedroom she had to be in here. She definitely had not left the house with her friend.

I'd last seen her standing in front of the big carved wardrobe. Maybe she was hiding in there. But wait— someone had mentioned Becca's sister, and I'd seen her talking with a teenage girl last night. Maybe the sister was hiding out. But why? She had no reason to think I would come back looking for her. Still … I opened the double doors and took a look. Empty.

Except for one thing … All the clothing was pushed

to one side except for a slip of bright pink fabric. It looked like the scarf she'd been wearing just now. So, why was it on the floor of the closet and why could I only see a six-inch square of it?

I bent down and gave the pink fabric a tug. It got longer and longer as it pulled out from beneath … a door? There was a door at the back of the wardrobe?

I took a step back and examined the thing. It sat flush against the wall, without even a hint of light passing behind it. The cabinet had been built right onto the wall. And so where was the scarf coming from?

Running my hands over the sides and back of the wardrobe's interior, I finally felt a small dimple, the size of a shirt button. And when I pressed it, the back of the cupboard slid aside, soundlessly, on a smooth track.

Beyond, a concrete platform, about two feet square, dropped away to a flight of stairs going downward. A secret staircase. A bare bulb lit the way, probably switched on by the same button that caused the hidden door to open.

Okay, suddenly I felt like Nancy Drew.

Where did this go? No matter. It seemed pretty obvious that Becca had fled this way. I pulled out my phone, in case I needed a flashlight, and started downward. Fourteen steps later I came out in a skinny corridor, lit by three more lightbulbs, evenly spaced. After about twenty feet, there was a bend, and an open door stood before me. I peered into the dark. Beyond the blackness I caught the faint glow of more light, similar to what I'd just come through.

With my phone's flashlight, I checked out the vast-feeling interior of the dark space and I think my mouth dropped open. I was standing in the doorway of an old-time speakeasy with wood-paneled walls, art deco chandeliers, and plush carpeting. In a room that must surely be forty or fifty feet square, there were three poker tables, a roulette wheel, and a craps table. At the far end was a bar with a brass rail along the bottom and leather-seated barstools. Dusty bottles of liquor lined glass shelves behind the bar, and if I'd put my imagination to it, I could have conjured a bartender and a crowd of flappers and mustached men in pinstripes.

I aimed my light at the other end of the room, where a raised platform would have hosted a jazz band. In fact, a small drum set still sat there. A string of tiny lights was suspended above the small parquet dance floor.

"Holy cow!" My whisper echoed through the room.

I wondered if Phil knew about this. How well had he explored the property when he bought it? I could have stayed and examined the details for another hour, but I remembered why I was here in the first place. Following Becca.

I saw no sign of her, so I wended my way between tables, heading toward that other faintly glowing light. It had to be where she'd gone, unless the place had some other hidden room or an exit. No, I was at least a dozen feet underground. There wouldn't be a simple door leading out.

The dim light revealed another skinny corridor and another flight of stairs, leading upward. And that's when I heard the faint scratching noise. I quickly switched off my phone light and followed the overhead bulbs, taking the stairs quietly. As I rounded the bend at the landing I could see Becca at the top, fiddling with a closed door, obviously trying to find out how to open it.

"Shit, crap, damn!" Her voice was shaky, almost crying.

"Becca," I called softly. "Becca, let me help you."

She spun, shock registering on her face. "What— How did you—?"

"Never mind. Let me help."

"You can't … No one can help now. I've screwed up so royally." The tears came in a flood now.

I kept taking one step at a time until I was four steps below her, close enough to converse but not so close that she could kick my teeth out if she should decide to.

"Why don't you tell me about it? What's the thing you screwed up so royally?" I held out her pink scarf. "He went after your little sister, didn't he?"

"Shelly came out for Christmas and visited the set. After the movie wrapped, we just wanted to go home, to spend New Year's Eve in Indiana with our folks, but then he wouldn't let me."

"Wouldn't *let* you? How's that?"

"Well, not *let* me, so much as he got all charming again and really pushed for me and Shelly to come with the whole crew and spend the weekend here. I knew he'd try something with her, and it's just so—ugh—creepy, him being as old as my dad and everything."

"So, what did you do …?"

"I didn't mean it. I swear. I only meant to give him enough of the pills that he'd pass out. You know, like drunk or something. He'd sleep it off and then it'd be morning and we'd get on the plane and leave …"

"You slipped him a sedative."

"Right. But I guess it was too much. I think I was angrier than I meant to be, you know."

This poor girl. I could only imagine her mindset. No, check that—I couldn't really imagine. Shelly falling under the power of such a man, especially in a culture where his behavior seemed semi-acceptable. The medication was probably something Hammersmith took anyway, and Becca thought she would just slip a little extra into his food or his glass, and he'd fall asleep early and just leave them blessedly alone.

But maybe she'd given too much. Or, quite likely, the amount of booze he'd consumed all day had reacted with it.

"Do you have to tell the sheriff, Charlie? I'm so scared."

"Let's get out of here, find Shelly, and then we'll talk about that." I turned to retrace my steps back the way we'd come, but all at once I heard a faint whirring noise.

The door at the top of the steps was sliding open.

"I don't know what I did but I must have touched something," Becca said.

We found ourselves in the study, the very room where I'd sat and questioned witnesses. The door to the stairs was part of the painted window on the wall mural. I stared at Becca and she stared at me, our eyes equally wide.

"What do we do?" she asked.

I had my hands on the painting, feeling for a button similar to the one in the guesthouse. When my fingertips found it, the window in the mural slid quietly back into place.

Out in the foyer, I could hear the voices of new arrivals. The sheriff and his men.

Becca began to crumple. "What should I do?"

My moral compass swung wildly before I answered. "If I were a lawyer, I'd advise you to not say anything. Let them draw their own conclusions."

8

The next hour was a flurry of activity as Hammersmith's body was loaded into a van, the sheriff talked quietly with Phil, and I handed over Drake's and my notes from the witnesses. I hadn't had a chance to add anything from Becca's and my final conversation, but that was okay. I did mention to the sheriff that I'd heard that Rory Hammersmith took some prescription medications and that he'd had quite a lot to drink that night, including an entire bottle of champagne he'd conned out of the bartender before midnight.

I didn't say anything to Phil about the secret staircases or the casino that surely dated back to the heyday of the property during Prohibition. It had nothing to do with the death, and he could discover that little hidden gem for himself.

It was a little before noon when we finally wheeled the helicopter out of its snug little nest and loaded our bags. While we packed, I'd asked Drake if we could give Becca and Shelly a lift to the airport, send them on their way to Indiana. He agreed, and we were soon airborne, happy to leave the Hollywood crowd behind.

By mid-afternoon we'd completed our mission, and were safely tucked in at home with our pup at our side well before dark. The steaks came out of the fridge, a warm fire glowed in the fireplace, we raised our glasses to each other, and then we proceeded with our own New Year's fireworks, just like always.

About the Author

Connie Shelton is the *USA Today* bestselling author of more than 40 novels and 3 non-fiction books. She has sold nearly 2 million copies in more than 110 countries worldwide. She taught writing for six years and was a contributor to *Chicken Soup for the Writer's Soul*. She and her husband live in New Mexico with their dogs. Visit her website at conniesshelton.com

Contact by email: connie@conniesshelton.com

Follow Connie Shelton on Twitter, Pinterest and Facebook

Get another Connie Shelton book—FREE! Scan the QR code to visit her website and find out how.

Praise for this *USA Today* **bestselling series:**

"Charlie is just what readers want." –*Booklist*

"A page turner!" - K. Coonce, 5 star review

"I always love Charlie's escapades. She keeps me glued to the story, unable to put it down. Love the mixture of humor and suspense. Can't wait for the next adventure!"
– Meg, 5 stars on Amazon

"Each book in the series just keeps getting better and better." – Vine Voice reviewer on Amazon

Books in the Charlie Parker Series